TRIAL

TRIAL

▲

PARNELL
HALL

THE MYSTERIOUS PRESS

Published by Warner Books

A Time Warner Company

Mysterious Press books are published by Warner Books, Inc.,
1271 Avenue of the Americas, New York, NY 10020.

 A Time Warner Company

The Mysterious Press name and logo are registered trademarks of Warner Books, Inc.

Printed in the United States of America

First printing: February 1996

10 9 8 7 6 5 4 3 2 1

Library of Congress Cataloging-in-Publication Data

Hall, Parnell.
    Trial / Parnell Hall.
      p. cm.
    ISBN 0-89296-570-3
    I. Title.
  PS3558.A37327T75   1996
813'.54—dc20   95-7565
                                                                  CIP

For Jim and Franny

TRIAL

"I didn't do it."

That was a surprise. The man was one of Richard Rosenberg's clients, and Richard Rosenberg's clients *always* did it. That's because Richard Rosenberg was one of New York City's top negligence lawyers, and the *it* that his clients always did was injure themselves, usually by tripping on a crack in the sidewalk and falling down. Which, in Richard Rosenberg's humble opinion, entitled them to sue the city of New York for a zillion dollars. So if Mr. Anson Carbinder hadn't done it, what was I doing there?

I frowned, and noticed for the first time that Anson Carbinder was not wearing a cast. Which was also a surprise. Richard Rosenberg's clients always wore casts. No injury, no case. Without a cast, it was hard to recognize the guy as a client. But he must be; otherwise, why would Richard have had the switchboard beep me and send me over?

I'd been beeped, called in, and either Wendy or Janet, one of Richard Rosenberg's two switchboard girls, who happened to have identical voices, had given me the case.

It occurred to me now, Wendy/Janet had not mentioned the client's injury. At the time, I hadn't thought anything of it. Aside from a voice, Wendy and Janet shared an uncanny inaccuracy, so leaving out an important bit of information was par for the course. With them, I figured if I could get the address or phone number right, I could at least *find* the client and get the rest of the information from him.

I know, I know. This is a long and rambling explanation. Particularly since all I'm leading up to, all I'm trying to explain, is that when Anson Carbinder told me he didn't do it, all I could think of to say was "Oh."

Which wasn't the right response.

He grimaced. "I know, I know," he said. "That's what they all say. But that's the fact. I swear. I didn't do it."

My turn to frown.

Anson Carbinder was a prosperous-looking man of about thirty, with bright red hair, thinning and receding from the ever-increasing forehead of a slightly pudgy face. His portly figure was disguised by a custom-tailored suit that probably cost more than the book value of my car. Granted it was ten years old—still, Toyotas hold up remarkably well.

But I digress.

Again.

To recap the conversation, so far it had gone, "I didn't do it." "Oh." "I know, I know. That's what they all say. But that's a fact. I swear. I didn't do it."

If I had been called upon to evaluate the situation at that moment, my best guess would have been that Anson Carbinder had been involved in a two-car accident and sustained a whiplash injury, which for some reason did not require a neck brace, and was attempting to establish the fact that the accident had not been his fault.

Remind me never to get a job as a prognosticator.

"So," I said, "what exactly is it that you didn't do?"

He frowned at me. "What are you, a comedian?"

"No, I—"

"This is a hell of a time for that."

"For what? I mean—"

"You want to make allowances for the fact I'm upset?"

"I can see you're upset."

"So don't kid around."

I put up my hands. "Whoa. Time out. Flag on the play."

He looked at me. "What?"

"This is one of those irritating situations where, if I read it in a book, I'd throw the damn thing across the room."

"What are you talking about?"

"We're talking at cross purposes." I shrugged my shoulders. "I have been told nothing. I have no idea why I'm here. I am not rude, just ignorant. Now, you wanna take offense, or you wanna fill me in?"

He looked at me in amazement. "You mean they didn't tell you?"

"Exactly. So please. *You* tell me. What is it you didn't do?"

He looked at me. Sighed. A huge sigh, that rippled the custom-tailored contours of the three-piece suit.

"Kill my wife."

I blinked.

Reality check.

"I beg your pardon?"

"I swear I didn't do it."

"I'm sure you didn't. Ah, Mr.? . . . "

"Carbinder."

"Yes. Mr. Carbinder. You'll pardon me, but did you just say you didn't kill your wife?"

"I swear to god. Now, look. Richard said you'd help me."

"Richard did?"

"Yes."

"You know Richard?"

"Of course I do."

"Then you didn't call in response to the ad?"

"Ad?"

"The TV ad. For Rosenberg and Stone."

"Are you kidding? I called Richard. He told me he'd send you."

"Me?"

"Yeah, you. At least, I assume it's you. What's your name again?"

"Stanley Hastings."

"Yeah. That's what he said. Hastings. He had to be in court, but he'd send the detective."

"Oh," I said. "That explains it."

"What?"

"Why I got no information. Richard's switchboard girls have the I.Q. of a turnip. If he had to be in court, the only message he'd trust them with would be to send me here."

Anson Carbinder put up his hands. "Fine. Great," he said. "I'm so glad you got that figured out. But, if you don't mind, I happen to have a small problem."

"I'm sorry. Of course you do. Please. Tell me about it."

"Okay." Carbinder took a breath. He held it a few moments, then exhaled noisily. It was like watching a deflating plastic blow-up toy. He looked at me helplessly. "I don't know where to begin."

"Start with when this happened."

"Last night."

"Can you be more precise?"

He gave me a look.

"Sorry," I said. "I'm just trying to understand. You say this happened last night. What time last night?"

"I don't know. I wasn't there. I just got home and there she was."

"What time did you get home?"

"I don't know. Around two."

"Two in the morning?"

"Yeah."

"You came home at 2:00 A.M. and found your wife dead?"

"That's right."

"How was she killed?"

"With a knife."

"A knife?"

"Yes."

"What kind of knife?"

"A kitchen knife."

"From *your* kitchen?"

"I think so."

"You're not sure?"

"No. I suppose it's from the kitchen. But I don't do the cooking. So . . ." he shrugged helplessly.

"Anyway, she'd been stabbed with the knife?"

"Yes."

"Was the knife in the body?"

He shuddered. "Body."

"I'm sorry," I said, "but I have to ask these questions."

"No. The knife was on the floor."

"And where was she?"

"On the bed."

"You came home, found your wife in bed stabbed to death and a knife lying there on the floor?"

"That's right."

"Next to the bed?"

"Yes."

"Did you see it at first?"

"I beg your pardon?"

"When you walked in—did you see the knife? Did you know she'd been stabbed?"

He shook his head. "No. The lights were out. I had no idea."

"You mean? . . ."

"Yeah. That's right. I took off my clothes, slipped into bed. And then . . ." He shuddered again. "It was awful. Like that scene in *The Godfather*. You know, with the horse's head?"

"Yeah."

"I felt something sticky. And . . . strange. I didn't know what happened. I sat up. I switched on the light." He shook his head. "Jesus Christ."

"Take it easy," I said. "But get a grip and tell me what you saw."

"Yeah, yeah," he said. "Easy to say. Well, there was blood everywhere. Everywhere. She'd been stabbed several times. And her throat had been slit from ear to ear."

I'd been steeling myself for it, but I shuddered nonetheless. "And what did you do?"

"I called the cops."

"Right away?"

"Yes, of course, right away. What else would I do?"

"I don't know. Like maybe try to see if she was still alive."

"There was no chance. No chance. I guess I did, really. But . . ." He shook his head. "There was nothing to be done."

"So you got blood on you?"

"Oh, sure."

"And the cops found you like that?"

He nodded. "That's it. That's it, exactly. They came, they saw me, blood on my hands."

"They arrested you?"

"That's debatable. They took me in for questioning. Then Richard showed up and they let me go."

I could imagine that. Next to money, there's nothing Richard Rosenberg loves more than bopping cops around. If the whole thing weren't so grisly, that thought might have amused me.

"You called Richard?"

"Absolutely. I'm no dope. I knew what it looked like. I needed a lawyer."

"You called Richard Rosenberg at two in the morning?"

"That's right."

"How did you get him?"

"I called him at home."

"You called him at home?"

"Sure. I wasn't going to spend the night in jail."

"You have his home number?"

"Of course."

Of course, indeed. I'd worked for Richard Rosenberg for years, he'd acted as my attorney several times, and *I* didn't have his home number. As a result of which *I* had once spent the night in jail.

But I wasn't about to point that out to Anson Carbinder. As the man said, he had his own problems.

"You called Richard at two in the morning, he came and got you out of jail?"

"Not jail. The police station."

"You weren't charged with anything?"

"No."

"You weren't arraigned? Taken before a judge?"

"No."

"Good for Richard."

Carbinder nodded. "Yeah. He was something else. Anyway, he sent me you." Carbinder looked at me somewhat dubiously. "I suppose there must be a reason."

I took a breath. "Did Richard tell you to cooperate with me fully?"

"Not specifically. He just said he couldn't be there, so he'd send someone to help."

"Fine. So those are my instructions. Since I wasn't given any other. I was sent here to help. So tell me everything I need to know."

"Like what?"

"Okay. Time of death. Do the cops know when she was killed?"

"If they do, they didn't let on."

"They didn't ask you where you were between the hours of such and such?"

"Oh, sure. They asked me where I was all night."

"Where were you?"

"At a poker game."

"A poker game?"

"Yeah."

"Until when?"

"Until then."

"When is then?"

"Two in the morning. I played until two in the morning, came home, and found her dead."

"When did the game start?"

"Huh?"

"The poker game. When did it start?"

"Oh. Early. Right after dinner. Eight o'clock."

"After dinner?"

"Yeah."

"You have dinner with your wife?"

"No."

"You didn't?"

"No."

"Who'd you have dinner with?"

"Actually, I ate alone."

"Oh?"

"I was working late. I had the game to go to. I just went out and grabbed a sandwich."

"Where?"

"What?"

"Where'd you eat?"

"Oh. It's a deli. Near the office."

"The office?"

"Yeah. I was working late. Like I say. I ran out, grabbed a sandwich, went to the game."

"So you never went home at all last night?"

"That's right."

"You call your wife?"

"Huh?"

"Speak to her on the phone?"

"Oh, sure. I called her, said I had to work late."

"How'd she like that?"

"Fine. She was going out to the movies."

"Oh?"

"Well, why not? I was playing poker. She knew I'd be late."

"How long you been married?"

"Seven years."

"You and your wife have a close relationship?"

"Of course."

"But yesterday you didn't see her at all? From the time you left for work in the morning—that's the last time you saw her alive?"

"That's right."

"And yesterday after work you went to a poker game, played till two in the morning?"

"That's right."

"How many people in the game?"

"Six."

"Including you?"

He thought a moment. "No. I made seven."

I nodded.

That was good news. At first I thought Richard had handed me a hot potato. Stuck me with a guy who in all likelihood had killed his wife. Evidently not. Not with six independent witnesses who could give the guy an alibi for the six-hour time span during which the woman surely must have been killed.

So this wasn't a particularly difficult or demanding job. It was, in fact, a rather routine and boring one, that of interviewing and taking witness statements from half-a-dozen poker players. Which, I was sure, was all Richard expected of me. I wouldn't even have to see the crime scene.

I winced at that rather unsettling thought.

And another thought occurred to me.

"Excuse me," I said.

He looked at me. "Yes?"

"Why are you here?"

"I beg your pardon?"

"I can understand the cops letting you go, with Richard putting the pressure on and all. But I'm surprised they released the crime scene so soon."

"Oh. They didn't."

"I beg your pardon."

"They didn't release it. It's still locked up."

"Wait a minute. The crime scene's your bedroom?"

"Right."

"The cops locked up your bedroom?"

"They sure did."

I frowned. "I don't understand. What's to stop us from walking right in?"

"I don't know. I suppose they have a guard."

"You suppose?"

"I imagine they do."

"You didn't look?"

"No. Why should I?"

I rubbed my forehead. "Well," I said. "Let's go take a look."

He frowned. "Now?"

"Yeah, now. Where's the bedroom?"

"The bedroom?"

"Yeah. Where's the bedroom. Let's go take a look."

He stared at me as if I were a lunatic. Then his face registered comprehension. "Oh," he said. "They didn't tell you."

"Tell me what?"

"You think this is my apartment, right?"

I blinked. "This isn't your apartment?"

"Of course not."

"Well," I said, "then whose apartment is it?"

As I said that, the front door clicked open, and a knockout of a young blonde walked in.

Which made it a brand-new ball game.

We were sitting in the living room of what I had assumed was Anson Carbinder's Park Avenue apartment. If, however, the apartment was actually the property of the young blonde who had just let herself in the front door, then I needed to revise my estimate of the whole situation.

Just in case there was any doubt as to that, the young lady in question squealed, "Anson!" raced across the room, and, as he rose to meet her, fell sobbing into his arms.

Okay.

I rose and awaited an introduction.

And wondered if Richard knew about this wrinkle.

When the young woman had sobbed herself out, which actually took several minutes, I said, "Excuse me, Mr. Carbinder."

He looked up from wiping the tears off her cheek. His glance was irritated, as if I'd interrupted a special moment.

"I'm sorry," I said, "but if I'm going to help you, you have to help me. I hate to appear nosy, but who's your friend?"

The blonde snuffled, looked over at me. The look was not kind. "Anson," she said. "Who's he?"

"He's a detective. My attorney sent him."

So. My attorney. Rather than Richard. Which would imply Blondie didn't know Richard. I wondered if I should count that as a point in his favor or one against.

Blondie didn't appear convinced. Her bloodshot eyes were wide. "A detective?" she said.

"That's right," I said. "My name's Stanley Hastings. I'm a private detective. I've been asked by Mr. Carbinder's attorney to look into the events surrounding the death of his wife. I know these are difficult times and you're obviously very upset, but I'd appreciate your help in this matter."

She blinked. "*My* help?"

"That's right."

"And how could *I* help?"

I had to bite my lip. It occurred to me, she could help best by getting hit by a truck. Just let the cops get one whiff of her, and Anson Carbinder was going to be charged with murder, attorney or no attorney.

It also occurred to me that, tactful or not, it was an idea I needed to get across.

"I need any information you have," I said. "I realize you may not have much. I've just begun, so I don't know what's what. I'd appreciate it if you'd cooperate and fill me in. Believe me, Mr. Carbinder needs your help."

Blondie looked as if she were going to start crying again. She turned to Carbinder, looked up at him. "Anson," she said.

Anson Carbinder put his arm around her shoulders protectively. "There's no call for this," he said. "She's obviously very upset. Anything you want to ask her, ask me."

"Fine," I said. "What's her name?"

"Connie Maynard."

"This is her apartment?"

"Yes, it is."

"How did you get in?"

"I beg your pardon?"

"If this is her apartment, how did you get in?"

"What's that go to do with it?"

I shook my head. "No good."

"Huh?"

"I thought you were going to answer questions for her. If you can't do any better than that, I'll have to ask her."

"Now, look here—"

"No, *you* look here. Your wife is dead. The cops tend to think you did it. Connie here, if she wasn't crying, would look like a million bucks. You havin' a key to her apartment, as far as the cops are concerned, would practically clinch the case. Now, how did you get in?"

"Connie let me in."

"When was that?"

"This morning."

"What time?"

"Around nine o'clock."

"This building has a doorman. He'll know when you went in. He'll know when she went out. I could ask him. So could the cops. What do you think he'll say?"

"Why do you say that?"

"Are you kidding? I was sitting right here when Connie came in the door. When she threw herself sobbing into your arms. Now, how do you think that looks? You think that looks like she let you in earlier this morning and the two of you had already discussed the murder of your wife?" Carbinder considered that. "So, can I assume you have a key?"

He scowled. "You can assume anything you like. But I don't like your insinuations."

"Maybe not, but mine don't matter. When the cops start insinuating, you'd better pay attention. Now, do you have a key?"

"I won't have when the cops pick me up."

I held up my hand, shook my head. "No, no. You're missing the point. Remember about the doorman? You're a murder suspect. The cops will be tracing your actions.

They'll know if Connie was here when you came in. If they can prove you have a key, it's bad. If they can prove you *got rid of* a key, it's ten times worse. Get the picture?"

Connie looked as if she were going to start bawling again. "Anson, make him stop."

"Damn it," he said. "See, you're getting her upset."

The thought, *yeah, well, I didn't kill my wife,* flashed to mind.

Which was disturbing on many levels. First was the hostility factor. Was my resentment of Anson Carbinder due to his attitude, his position, or the fact that he was playing around with a flashy blonde?

Second was the realization that I had all but convinced myself of his guilt.

"Very sorry, I'm sure," I said. "Look. I'm not a lawyer, I'm a detective. This isn't really my place. I make the suggestion because Richard isn't here. I'm saying to myself, What would Richard want? You want me to stop doing that, fine. At least I'll be able to tell Richard I made the attempt. For what it's worth, I advise discretion. What you do is entirely up to you."

I took a breath, exhaled. "Now, to the matter at hand. This is not your apartment. Where *is* your apartment?"

"It's not an apartment. It's a town house. On East Sixty-second. Between Park and Lex."

I tried not to raise my eyebrows. Connie's apartment was at Park Avenue and Sixty-fifth. The phrase, *just blocks away,* came to mind.

I did not voice it.

"You own a town house?"

"That's right."

"The whole building?"

"Of course."

"Anyone else live there?"

"No."

"Just the two of you?"

"That's right."

"No children?"

"No."

"No basement apartment? No maid, no super? No one else on the premises?"

"No."

So. No one to interview. That simplified that.

"Okay, let's talk about your alibi."

"What about it?"

"This poker game—where was it?"

"At Sammy's house."

"Uh-huh. Who's Sammy, and where's his house?"

"Sammy is Sam Kestin. He has a town house on Fifth Avenue."

"Where on Fifth Avenue?"

"Actually just off Fifth. On Sixtieth Street."

"I'll need his address. And the name and address of everyone else in the game."

"The names I have. The addresses I would have to look up."

"Where are they?"

"In my address book."

"Where's that?"

"At home."

My beeper went off, and when I called in, Wendy/Janet gave me an assignment to go to Harlem and interview a man who'd fallen on a city bus. There was no talking her out of it, either. Richard hadn't told her I was investigating a murder, and until she heard differently, I was on the clock. And there was no way she could hear differently with Richard in court, so if cases came in they were mine.

In a way, I was glad. I could handle a trip-and-fall on a city bus. That was about my speed.

The Anson Carbinder case was something else.

4

"I'm sorry I didn't think of it."

The person who was sorry was Richard. The thing he was sorry about was not telling Wendy/Janet to stop assigning me work when he'd called in from court during noon recess. But he hadn't thought of it, and so, after the trip-and-fall in Harlem, I'd done a hit-and-run in Brooklyn, a medical malpractice on Staten Island, and another trip-and-fall in Queens. As a result, I'd missed Richard's conference with his client later that afternoon and been lucky to catch him when he'd stopped by the office on his way home.

"No problem," I said. "I'm just telling you why I wasn't able to work on this."

"Damn."

"Hey, but no big deal. Your client isn't even charged."

"I consider that a mere formality."

"Oh?"

Richard shrugged. "Husband/wife thing. Cops always pick the husband. Here they got one with blood on his hands. Quite a bit, from what I hear."

"There was blood in the bed."

"Indeed there was."

"And he got into bed in the dark."

Richard grimaced. "Try selling that to a jury."

"Are you saying you couldn't do it?"

"Are you kidding me?" Richard got up from his desk. He was a small man but compensated for it with an incredible amount of nervous energy. Let him argue a point and he became immense. He swung into full spiel now. "Is it unusual that a man would get undressed and get into bed in the dark? I think not. We are talking about a man who had been married—how long?—seven years? He's out at a late-night poker game—returning when?—two in the morning? Do you think such a man really wants his wife to wake up and say, What are you doing? What time is it? Why are you so late? And . . . How much did you lose?" Richard shook his head. "No, I don't think we'll have any problems on that score. The problem is *The Godfather* bit."

"Huh?"

"In bed with the dead wife. Feeling the blood. Throwing the covers off. Just like the horse's head."

"That's just what Carbinder said. That it was like *The Godfather*."

"Of course he did," Richard said. "It was the first thing he thought of, first thing I thought of, first thing the jury's going to think."

"And that's bad?"

"It sure is. *The Godfather*'s a movie. You give people a scene from a movie and you know what they think? They think you made it up."

"Oh."

"But that's not your problem. That's my problem. Your problem is chasing down these poker players."

"It will be, once I get the list."

"Oh?"

"His address book was home. He couldn't go home because his apartment's a crime scene."

"He's home now."

"Oh?"

"The cops released it."

"Just like that?"

"It took a little prodding, but what the hell. They had their shot. They can't hold it forever."

"Right."

"So give the guy a call, get your list, track 'em down."

"Will do. Just tell the girls not to give me any work."

"No problem. Sorry about today."

"You going to be here tomorrow, or are you still in court?"

"I'll be here."

"Oh? What happened to the case?"

"They settled."

I was sure they had. Opposing counsel in Richard Rosenberg's cases usually settled as soon as they saw the effect he had on juries. Ordinarily, being deprived of battle would have pissed Richard off. Fortunately, he had this murder case.

"I see," I said. "Listen, Richard."

"Yes?"

"You've evidently known Anson Carbinder for some time."

"Not really. He's a member of my club."

"Oh?"

"My country club. I play golf with him."

"You play golf?"

Richard cocked his head. "Are you kidding? I happen to be a seven handicap."

That was a surprise. I knew nothing about Richard's personal life and had no idea he was athletic. "Uh-huh," I said.

"Why do you ask?"

"I was wondering how well you know him."

Richard frowned. "Why?"

"When you spoke to him today, was that at his house?"

"No. It hadn't been released yet."

"I'm wondering just where you saw him."

"I assume the same place you did."

"Would that be the apartment of a Ms. Connie Maynard?"

"What's your point?"

"I'm wondering if the police know of her existence."

"And why would you be wondering that?"

"Because it would seem to be a material point."

"To who? Stanley, this man is not accused of having a sweetheart on the side. He's accused of killing his wife. If you're saying this looks like a motive for the crime, I beg to differ. If the guy's banging the broad already, what's the problem? It's not like his wife's preventing him from doing it. So why knock her off?"

"Richard."

"No, no. I'm very upset that you would think that way. It's just the type of wrong thinking that makes a case like this so hard to try."

"Richard," I said, but he was off again.

"What we have here is your basic motiveless crime. Now, the cops might *like* to say this young girl's a motive, but it doesn't wash. Why does he kill his wife to get her when he's already got her? They'd have to have something else. Like his wife knew of the affair, was threatening him with divorce, and was in a position to take him to the cleaners if she did."

"You're saying that's not the case?"

"Don't be silly," Richard said. "And even if it *was* the case—even if that were true—the whole thing still makes no sense. I mean, assume the guy's lying. Assume Anson Carbinder *did* kill his wife. Well, what must have happened then? He goes out, plays poker till two in the morning, comes home, wakes up his wife, and cuts her throat.

"Then he calls the cops. They arrive, find his wife dead and him covered with blood. Of course the cops would never suspect a thing. It would be the perfect crime."

I smiled. "Hey, Richard."

"Yeah?"

"Save it for the jury."

5

Alice got right to the heart of the matter.

"Did he do it?"

"I don't think so."

Alice frowned. "Your judgment isn't that good."

"Thanks a lot."

"I mean in things like that. Of course your judgment's good. I just mean in matters of human nature."

It's sometimes hard to tell what Alice means, because what Alice says means whatever she wants it to mean. My wife, Alice, could anchor any debate team in the United States. She is without peer. Over the years I have learned that whatever her opinion is, I agree with it. Because, if I don't, it will not take her long to convince me that I should. So why bother?

Admittedly, that is an intellectual judgment and will not work on any emotional issue. Particularly with regard to sex, where often I will find myself arguing a lost cause.

But I had no wish to argue this.

"Alice, my opinion is the guy didn't do it. But I could very well be wrong."

"Why do you think he didn't do it?"

"It's too stupid."

"What do you mean?"

"That was Richard's argument. The guy calls the police, covered with blood, says, Someone killed my wife. If he's guilty, did he really think the cops wouldn't suspect him?"

"Same thing if he's innocent," Alice said.

"What do you mean, same thing?"

"Same situation. Why wouldn't he think the cops would suspect him?"

"Because he didn't do it. If you're innocent, you don't expect to be suspected."

"And if you're guilty, you do?"

"Of course."

"So you don't do it if you're guilty?"

"That's right."

"So," Alice said. "If he killed his wife, he wouldn't call the cops and tell 'em she was dead, because he'd think they'd suspect him?"

"That's right."

"But," Alice said, "he's an intelligent man and he knows that. So he says, If I call the cops, they'll think I did it. But if I *don't* call the cops, they'll *know* I did it. Because not calling the cops is an indication of guilt. So calling the cops has to be an indication of innocence, so that's what I'll do."

I blinked. Alice had taken the logic three hundred and sixty degrees back to what it originally was.

"Right," I said. "Calling is a sign of innocence. He called the cops, so he's probably innocent."

"No, no, no," Alice said. "You're missing the point. We're taking the premise that he's guilty. And saying, if he's guilty, would he call the cops? Or can we justify his calling the cops if he's guilty. Which, of course, we can. So, for all we know, the man is guilty."

See what I mean? Can't argue with her.

"Right," I said. "For all we know. Because we don't know anything yet. When we get the results of the autopsy, when we get the medical report, when they fix the time of death—then we should be able to prove he didn't do it."

"How?"

"He was playing poker most of the night. From eight until two. If she was killed in that time frame, he's off the hook."

"Otherwise, he's on it?"

"Not necessarily. He can't prove where he ate dinner. But with a little legwork, maybe I could."

"Uh-huh. Is that what you're supposed to do?"

"I don't know, because they don't know the time of death yet."

"Right," Alice said. "Well, is that it? Is that the case against him? The fact that he had the opportunity? As well as the means—the knife from his kitchen, right? That leaves only motive. Did the guy have any motive for her death?"

"Well . . ."

Alice pounced. "Well, what?"

"He's involved with a younger woman."

"Is he, now?"

"Yes, but it doesn't mean a thing."

"I'm not sure I like that attitude."

"You know what I mean."

"No, I don't. What do you mean?"

"I mean, why would he kill his wife?"

"Did you ever see *Double Indemnity*?"

"Who says she had insurance?"

"Doesn't she?"

"I have no idea."

Alice rolled her eyes. "Men."

"What does that mean?"

"How can you solve this case if you don't have the facts?"

I put up my hands. "Whoa. Slow down. Solve the case?

I'm not the cops. I'm not even the attorney. I'm just some dipshit P.I. hired to get the facts."

"And what *are* the facts?"

"I don't know."

"Nice job."

"I told you, Alice, I haven't even started. Today I took cases for Rosenberg and Stone."

"You start tomorrow?"

"That's right."

"And what are you going to do?"

"Check the alibis. Get a list of the guys he played poker with and run 'em down."

Alice looked at me. "This is for real? This is not a game?"

"Of course."

"Richard's really going to court?"

"Yes, he is."

"He's never been in court before."

"He's in court all the time."

"You know what I mean. Not like this. A murder case."

"No. Not like this."

"He's going to handle it himself? He's not going to bring in some criminal attorney?"

"Not on your life. The guy's living out a fantasy. He's happy as a clam."

"What about his client?"

"What about him?"

"I wonder if he's as happy with the situation. If he's in deep shit, and Richard's having fun."

"It's not like that."

"No?"

"The guy's a friend of Richard's. He knows him. He trusts him."

"That just makes it worse."

"Alice, I've known Richard a long time. When he says something, I can believe it."

"See? You too." Alice shook her head. "So, be that as it may, that's the situation. Richard's preparing for trial, and he's hired you to investigate?"

"That's right."

That's when Alice cut to the heart of the matter.

"How much is he going to pay?"

6.

Richard looked stricken.

"What did you say?"

"You heard me."

"I don't think I did."

"I want two hundred bucks a day plus expenses."

"My god, I did."

"Yes, you did."

"I don't think you understand the situation."

"I understand it just fine. You've taken on a murder case. You'd like me to investigate. I'm perfectly willing to. But my rate happens to be two hundred bucks a day plus expenses."

"Your rate is ten bucks an hour and thirty cents a mile. That's what we agreed on way back when."

"Exactly."

"What does that mean?"

"Way back when. That was a long time ago."

"So? Nothing's changed."

"Time's passing. There's inflation."

"What inflation? We're in a recession."

"Richard—"

"No, I can't believe you're doing this."

"I'm not doing anything. Everybody gets a raise."

"A raise? Do you know what you just asked for? Did you do the math? A hundred and fifty percent."

"That's not the point."

"Not the point?" Richard sprang from his chair, began pacing the room. "Ladies and gentlemen, the man says the amount of money is not the point. Next, he's going to tell you it's the principle of the thing." He waved his finger. "Do not be deceived by these tactics. What we have here is a case of unmitigated greed."

I shook my head. "Sorry, Richard. Not this time."

"Not *this* time? You mean you're going to ask *again?*"

"No, I mean I've asked before. To absolutely no avail."

Richard shook his head. "This is ridiculous. I have a murder case to deal with. And so do you. You should be out now, tracking down those witnesses. Instead, you're in here hassling me about money. And charging me for the time, I suppose."

"I'm not charging you for the time. I'm not on the clock. I haven't begun to investigate the murder yet. I don't plan on investigating it unless I'm hired to do so. If hired, I'll expect two hundred bucks a day plus expenses. Which is rather reasonable in this day and age. But perhaps you can find someone who'll do it for less."

Richard stopped, considered. He walked over to his desk, sat down, tipped back in his chair. He took a deep breath, exhaled slowly, the way the basketball coach had once taught me to relax before shooting a free throw.

"What you ask," Richard said, "is outlandish. It is unreasonable, outrageous, and out of the question. Still, I suppose you have a point. A murder investigation is a special case."

"No, Richard. Actually, *I* am a special case."

Richard's eyes narrowed. "And just what does that mean?"

"I've been working for you a long time. A raise is in

order. Not just because this is a murder investigation. I need a raise straight across the board."

Richard nearly gagged. "For *trip-and-falls?* You want two hundred bucks a day for *trip-and-falls?*"

"I want two hundred bucks a day to investigate. Whether it's a murder, a trip-and-fall, or what have you. The work is the same."

"Yeah. The same as ten bucks an hour. You come in here with I-need-more-money-because-it's-a-murder-case-and-it's-special. The minute I concede you might have a point, suddenly it isn't special at all and you're holding me up? I'm shocked. I'm wounded. I am cut to the quick."

"You're grossing millions a year."

"That's incompetent, irrelevant, and immaterial. What are you, on commission? You're a hired employee."

"Who needs a raise."

"Two hundred bucks a day base rate—you know what that comes to? That's twenty-five bucks an hour."

"I can do the math."

"Can you? Then do the math on this—I got six investigators besides you. What if all of them wanted two hundred bucks a day plus expenses?"

"You'd tell 'em they couldn't have it."

"And they'd say, But *he's* getting it. Do you know what resentment that would breed?"

"Bullshit, Richard. You gotta work before you get a raise. None of them have been here long enough to even ask for one. Someone complains, you say, No one gets a raise until they've been here two years. No danger of that. Aside from me, no one's even lasted one."

Richard looked at me for a long moment. Then he got up, took off his jacket, draped it over the back of his chair. He reached up, yanked the knot of his tie down a couple of inches, and unbuttoned the collar of his shirt. He was wearing suspenders, probably just in case he had to argue in

court. He looped his thumbs inside them, pushed them out
and back, as if stretching before the fight. Then, without
taking his eyes off me, he scooped up the phone and pushed
the button for the intercom.

"Hold my calls."

7

"Marvin Wainwright?"

"Yes."

"I'm Stanley Hastings. I'm investigating the Carbinder murder."

I was indeed. Richard Rosenberg, after a long and painful negotiation, had finally worked things out. What we'd agreed to was of course a compromise. For investigating the murder I was being paid two hundred bucks a day plus expenses. No compromise there. That was reasonable, and there I would not budge.

Where I lost out was the routine Rosenberg and Stone work. No matter how hard I argued, there was no way Richard Rosenberg was paying me two hundred bucks a day. After all, as he pointed out, the work was erratic— some days I might work as few as three or four hours, and there was no way he was paying two hundred bucks for that.

In other words, there was no way Richard would guarantee an eight-hour day. He'd pay a flat rate for actual time served, and that was it.

When Richard wouldn't budge, I tried for the equivalent—twenty-five bucks an hour and a dollar a mile. I didn't get it, but the twenty bucks an hour and seventy-five cents a mile I finally settled for was more than I'd expected. So, all in all, I was in a fairly good mood.

For someone discussing a homicide.

At two hundred bucks a day.

Marvin Wainwright, the young man I was discussing it with, was a junior vice-president of the firm of Gladrags, Foster and Vale. Since the company was a textile manufacturer, I assumed Gladrags was a trade name, but Mr. Wainwright informed me there actually was such a person.

He also informed me that two nights before he had indeed played poker with Anson Carbinder.

"How long have you known Mr. Carbinder?"

Marvin Wainwright was a pudgy man with horn-rimmed glasses. He took them off, frowned. "Why do you ask?"

"For the purpose of identification. If you never met the man before, how could you swear it was him?"

"I see."

"Or if you'd, say, played cards with him once or twice, but it was over a year ago—you see how that would be."

He jammed his glasses back on. "No. How would it be?"

"You could identify him, but it wouldn't count for much. As the ADA would point out."

"The ADA?"

"Assistant district attorney. The prosecutor. When he cross-examined you."

"Cross-examined?"

"Yes, of course. You'd have trouble, because he'd bear down on the identification. If you barely knew this guy, how could you swear it was the same man?"

"I see," Wainwright said. He did not look happy.

"But that is not the case, right? You've known him for years and you know him well."

"Yes, I do."

"Then there's nothing to worry about. Just tell your story, and don't let them rattle you."

"My story?"

"Poor choice of words. Just tell what happened."

"I see."

"So you might think of this as a dress rehearsal. You can tell me what you're going to tell them."

"Nothing much to tell. We had a poker game. Anson Carbinder was there."

"Where was the poker game?"

"At Sammy's"

"And Sammy is? . . ."

"Sam Kestin. The game was at his place."

"Where's that?"

"Fifth Avenue and Sixtieth Street."

"Is this a regular game?"

"Pretty regular. About once a month."

"Is it always at Sam Kestin's?"

"Usually. Sometimes it's at Phil's."

"And Phil is? . . ."

"Phil Janson. He's an actor. Has an apartment in the Village. Sometimes we play there."

"I see. And was he at the game that night?"

"Yes, he was."

"Who else was there?"

"Let me see. Me. Sammy. Phil. Anson, of course. Tim Hendricks. Ollie Pruett. And Barry Brown."

That checked with the list Carbinder'd given me.

I nodded. "Is that it?"

"That's it."

"No women?"

He smiled. "No women."

"Is that coincidence or policy?"

"That's just the way it is. A poker game's a chance to get away from the women. You know what I mean?"

"I suppose so. And what about Anson Carbinder?"

He frowned. "What about him?"

"What time did he get to the game, and what time did he leave?"

"Oh. The game started at eight. He got there around then."

"Everybody show up at once?"

"No, of course not."

"Well, when did you get there?"

"Around eight."

"And who was there then?"

"I beg your pardon?"

"When you got there, who was already there?"

"Is it important?"

"I mentioned the ADA. The prosecutor. If you go on the stand, this is the type of question he'll ask you. It would help if you were able to answer."

"I see."

"So, when you arrived at the game, who was already there?"

"Well, Sammy, of course."

"Because it was his apartment?"

"Right."

"Who else?"

"I think Phil was there."

"You think?"

"It's hard to remember. I didn't know it was going to be important."

"Of course. So what about Anson?"

"What about him?"

"Was he there when you got there?"

"No. He came later."

"Later?"

"Not later. But after I did. Everyone was there by eight-thirty. In what order they came, I can't tell you."

"But you personally got there around eight?"

"That's right."

"And Sammy and Phil were already there?"

"I think so."

"So Anson, Tim Hendricks, Ollie Pruett, and Barry Brown were not?"

"I didn't say that."

"I know you didn't. I'm saying it for you. Feel free to contradict me."

"I tell you, I don't really remember."

"That's fine, if that's really the case."

He frowned. "What do you mean?"

"It's better to say you don't remember than to take a guess and wind up contradicting yourself. Because the prosecutor will pounce on any inconsistency and try to build on it. See what I mean? If you say Phil was there when you got there, and then make a statement that implies he arrived later, the prosecutor will jump on that and try to make it appear you're lying. See?"

Wainwright grimaced. "I don't like this."

"I hate it myself. And I doubt if Anson Carbinder is too happy, either." I smiled. "Look, I'm not trying to hassle you, I'm just trying to help. I know you want to help Anson. His attorney needs to know what you're going to say when you get on the stand."

"Yes, of course."

"So, Anson arrived sometime between eight and eight-thirty. And what time did he leave?"

"The game broke up at two."

"He was still there?"

"Yes, of course."

"There's no *of course* about it. Guys get cleaned out, fed up, or just leave."

"That didn't happen."

"Everyone stayed till the end?"

"That's right."

"Including Anson?"

"Including Anson."

"Did he leave the game at any time during the course of the evening?"

"No, he did not."

"Not even for a short time?"

"Not at all."

"He didn't get up to go to the bathroom?"

"Don't be silly. Everyone gets up to go to the bathroom."

"Well, there you are. Did he ever go to the bathroom, take a long time coming back?"

"No."

"Are you sure?"

"Yes, I'm sure."

"And you've known Anson Carbinder for years, you'd recognize him anywhere, you couldn't possibly be mistaken, and you know he was at the poker game the whole night?"

"That's right." After a pause, Wainwright added, "I ought to. He beat me out of a big hand."

"Oh?"

Wainwright leaned back in his chair, shook his head. "Yeah. It was seven stud, high/low. We play two-buck limit, three bumps a round. That adds up. This was a big pot."

"And Anson won?"

"Sure did. He's sitting there with ace, two, three, four showing. Perfect low. We're playing straights and flushes swing. So if he's got a five, he can go both ways, take the whole pot. And I'm hoping he will, because I got a flush."

"Oh, yeah?"

"Yeah. So if he swings, I got the whole thing."

"Did he?"

"No. The son of a bitch has two aces and a four in the hole, and goes high with a full house."

"And you went high too?"

"Sure did. So did everybody else. He was the only low on board. Looked like he had it locked. And he's bumping like crazy, like he had a sure thing. So everybody goes high and he takes the whole pot."

"That's good."

He looked at me. "Why is that good?"

"Hey, I'm sorry you lost your money. I mean it's good you remember. Any specific incident like that is something you can throw at the prosecutor. He says, How can you be sure the guy was at the game? You say, Are you kidding? he beat me out of a big pot. The specific event lends much more weight than just insisting he was there."

Wainwright nodded judiciously. "I see."

"Anything else you remember about the game? Anything else that might help?"

"I don't really see how *this* helps?"

"Well," I said. "It's early yet."

He frowned. "What does that mean?"

"If the medical examiner puts the time of death around when you were losing that big hand, it'll help a lot."

8

Sam Kestin worked in a bank.

Don't get me wrong. The guy was no wage slave. This was not some poor teller, counting and recounting stacks of money all day long for people cashing checks. No, Sam Kestin wore a three-piece suit and sat in an alcove cordoned off from the rest of the bank by a velvet rope, behind a desk, to which I had no doubt the privileged few would be summoned, one at a time, to be told with an icy smile why the loan they had requested had not been approved.

Sorry. I'm a bigot. It's entirely possible Sam Kestin was a benevolent banker, engaged in the humanitarian work of dispensing wealth and wisdom to the upwardly mobile middle classes in an effort to help them better themselves.

But I doubt it.

"I'll try to make this brief," I said. "I realize you're busy."

There had been a half a dozen people waiting to see Mr. Kestin. Not wanting to wait with them, I had barged ahead with my ID.

Kestin waved it away. "I'm always busy. No need to rush. Sit down and tell me what you need."

Sam Kestin sat at his desk. He was a young man; indeed, he looked too young for his position. He was plump, with a pudgy baby face. It occurred to me, in terms of the poker game, that made three for three.

"Now, then," Kestin said, "this is about Anson?"

"That's right."

He shook his head. "Terrible business. Terrible. I knew Barbara, you know."

"Barbara?"

"His wife. Didn't you know her name?"

"I did, but I think you're the first person who referred to her. As Barbara, I mean."

"Yeah, well, I knew her. Known them for some time. We even had dinner."

"Are you married?"

"No. Why? Oh, you mean for a dinner date. No, I brought a girlfriend the times we went out."

I was sure he had. I was also sure she was half his size, sleek, svelte, every inch a knockout. Ah, the simple joys of prosperity.

"And you run a poker game," I said.

He frowned. "Well, I wouldn't say *run*. I play in a poker game. It's sometimes at my house."

"I didn't mean to imply you were Nathan Detroit. The fact is, two nights ago there was a poker game in your house."

"That's right."

"This was a regular game, though not necessarily at your house?"

He nodded. "Exactly."

"And Anson Carbinder is a regular at this game?"

"Yes, he is."

"And was he there at your house two nights ago?"

"Absolutely."

"Was he there for the whole game?"

"Absolutely."

"What time did he get there?"

"I don't know exactly. But sometime between eight and eight-thirty."

"Was he the first to arrive or the last?"

"He wasn't the first and he wasn't the last. Somewhere in the middle. I think Phil was first and I think Ollie Pruett was last. You remember those. First, because you're alone, so when the guy arrives it's just you and him. And the last because you're all there except him. And you're saying things like, Should we start, or should we wait for Ollie?"

"Right. And Anson Carbinder?"

"Arrived somewhere in between. If you want to guess, I'd say eight-fifteen. It might have been closer to eight. It might have been closer to eight-thirty. I just don't know. But sometime in that half hour."

"And when did he leave?"

"Two o'clock. When the game broke up."

"Are you sure of that?"

"Absolutely. He stayed till the last hand."

"Did everybody stay till then?"

"Oh, sure. Except for Tim Hendricks. He always quits early."

"Tim Hendricks?"

"Yeah. He cut out at midnight. Always does. You could set your watch by it."

"I see," I said. "So how many people played the last hand?"

He paused, thought. "Six."

"You sure?"

"Sure. There were seven in the game. Tim went home, that left six. Right. The last two hours there were just the six of us."

"And one of them was Anson Carbinder?"

"Yes, of course."

I frowned. "That's not what Marvin Wainwright said."

Sam Kestin's eyes widened. Then narrowed. "You mean Marv said Anson wasn't there?"

"No, no," I said. "I didn't mean that. But according to him everyone was there at the end. He didn't tell me anybody left."

"Oh, that," Kestin said. He smiled. "I'm not surprised. Marv's a nice guy, but he's the type of guy wouldn't notice if it was raining. You can't really go by what he remembers."

"That's a shame," I said, "because it just might matter."

"I know," he says. "But I wouldn't worry. There's enough of us who'll get it right."

"I know," I said. "But that's not the point."

"What is?"

"We're going to wind up with six separate recollections. The more they differ, the more the prosecutor will have to pick apart."

"I see," Kestin said. "But don't worry. I'll straighten Marv out."

I put up my hand. "I'd be careful there. Sure, you don't want glaring discrepancies. But if your stories dovetail too nicely, they sound rehearsed."

Kestin nodded. "I hear you. Anything else?"

"Not really. Unless Mr. Carbinder happened to leave the game at any point during the evening. I assume if he had, you'd have mentioned it."

"Yes, I would. But the fact is he didn't."

"Anything else you can remember that might be of help?"

"Like what?"

"You remember any of the specifics of the game—particularly with regard to Anson—that would help cement the idea he was there? Any particular hand, for instance?"

"Oh, sure," Kestin said. "There was one killer of a hand

Anson won, where he went high when it looked like he was going low."

"Would that be seven-card stud?"

"That's right. Seven stud, high/low. Anson looked like he had a low straight, turned out he had a full house. A lot of people got burned."

"Including you?"

"Especially me. I could have gone low with a nine. But I also had three eights. Anson's showing four to a wheel. That's ace, two, three, four, five. We call it a wheel, because it goes both ways if you're playing fifty-four low. Anyway, who's going to go low with a nine looking at a wheel? Particularly sitting with trips? So of course I go high and get burned."

"Along with everybody else?"

"Well, I think he'd bumped half of us out by then. But it was still a big pot."

"And everyone went high?"

"Sure did. And Anson took it all. I remember thinking, this was his lucky night." Kestin snorted. "Yeah. And look what he went home to."

"Right," I said. "And this hand—was that just before he went home?"

"Not just before. Maybe an hour or so."

"That would be around one o'clock?"

"That's a guess. But somewhere in that neighborhood."

"You have any idea if it was before or after one?"

"Not really. Around one's the best I can do."

"I'm sorry to push. But it might be important."

"Why? Oh, is that when it happened?"

"We don't know yet. That's why I say it *might* be important."

"Right. Well, you gotta understand. You're playing cards, there's no reason to remember when a particular hand took place. A big hand, you're concentrating on the cards, not looking at your watch."

"I understand. Can you think of anything else that might help."

"Not offhand. If I do, who should I call?"

I took out one of Richard Rosenberg's business cards, scribbled my name on the back. "The attorney's Richard Rosenberg, of the law firm of Rosenberg and Stone. I'm Stanley Hastings. You can reach me through this number."

We both stood up and he offered his hand, I guess out of habit. As I shook it, he said, "For what it's worth, I hope they catch the creep who did this."

"Me too."

"I feel terrible about this. I liked Barbara. I like Anson."

I guess I'm just a cynic.

I couldn't help wondering if he liked Connie Maynard.

9

"Anson won a big hand."

"Oh?"

"Yeah. Real big. It was a high/low hand and he won it all."

Ollie Pruett hadn't bothered with any of the amenities. I'd barely gotten in the door when he started telling me about Anson Carbinder's big hand.

Ollie Pruett was a fidgety little man. He was the first nonpudgy poker player, and the first one whose manner was decidedly nervous. I wondered if the two went hand in hand. At any rate, the man was certainly jumpy. I could imagine him in a poker game, agonizing over every bet.

Not that he needed to. Where Ollie Pruett matched the other poker players was in being affluent. So much so, he didn't seem to see the need to go to work on a mid-week afternoon. Of course, if you own your business, who's going to complain? Ollie owned his—a chain of camping-supply stores which I understood were doing well. At least well enough to let Ollie maintain a rather nice penthouse apartment on Central Park South.

And to stock it with birds. Ollie Pruett's living room boasted a spectacular view of Central Park, and upwards of fifty varieties of birds.

Exotic birds. Colorful birds. I know nothing about birds, but it occurred to me they must be valuable. It also occurred to me that some of the birds were tropical, and the living room was rather warm.

Most of the birds were in cages, but a few were flying around wild. I found this strangely disconcerting. "A big hand, you say?"

"Yes, yes, that's right," Pruett said. "Oh, I'm sorry. Please sit down."

I did, not without some trepidation—would sitting down make *me* seem a perch?

Ollie sat himself across from me on a chrome and leather chair, looking himself very much like a bird that at any moment might take flight. "Yes, that's right," he said. "Anson won a big hand."

"Oh?"

"Yes. It was a seven stud, high/low, and Anson won the whole pot."

"A big pot?"

"Real big."

"Tell me about it."

Ollie hesitated a moment. "You talk to the other guys?"

"Some of them."

"Didn't they tell you about the hand?"

"Sure. But I'd like to hear your version."

"Version?"

I smiled. "Everybody remembers things differently. No two people's recollections are going to be the same. It's interesting to compare and contrast."

"Is that what you're doing?"

"Sure. So tell me what you remember."

Ollie Pruett frowned, looked uncomfortable. "I don't like this."

"What do you mean?"

"It's like it's too important. You know. Like Anson's in trouble if I don't get it right."

"Not at all," I said. "There's no right or wrong. There's just what you happen to remember."

"Uh-huh," Pruett said. He still didn't look happy.

"So just tell me what you know."

"Well, it was a big hand, and I thought Anson was going to go high, but he went low."

"Oh?"

Pruett made a face. "I'm sorry. I mean the other way around. I thought he was going to go *low* and he went *high.*"

"Are you sure?"

"Oh, yes. He had four low cards showing. So everyone thought he was going low. But he went high and won the whole pot."

"Because everybody went high?"

"Right."

"Including you?"

"Sure."

"What did you have?"

"I'm sorry," Pruett said. "Do you want something? Coffee? A drink?"

I couldn't imagine eating in that apartment. There were bird droppings on the floor. I wondered if he noticed. "I'm fine," I said. "But about the hand."

"Oh. I had two pair. But Anson had a full house."

"Uh-huh. Did you stay in till the end?"

"Yeah," he said. When I said nothing, he added, "Well, you know how it is. You get sucked in, and then it's hard to fold."

"Right," I said. "A lot of other people stay in?"

"Yeah. A lot did."

"How many?"

He frowned. "I'm not sure. There were seven in the

game. I don't think they all stayed. But how many actually did? I'm really not sure."

"Sam Kestin?"

"Huh?"

"Did Sam Kestin stay?"

He squinted at me. "You talked to him already, right? Well, if he says he did, he did. I just don't remember."

"You remember when the hand was over?"

"What do you mean?"

"When Anson had a full house. Wasn't there talk about why didn't anybody go low?"

"Oh, sure."

"And *could* anyone have gone low?"

"Huh?"

"Anyone have a low hand? Anyone say, Damn, I should have gone low?"

"I think so. But I don't remember who."

"*You* weren't thinking of going low?"

"No. I didn't have a low. I had two pair."

"Right. Anyway, when Anson won the pot, you remember what time it was?"

He frowned. "No, I don't."

"Would you know if it was before or after midnight?"

"I really couldn't say."

"You have no idea at all?"

He shook his head. "That's how it is in these poker games. You lose all track of time."

"Uh-huh. But you know what time you got there?"

"Between eight and eight-thirty."

"And who was there then?"

"Let me see. Sammy. Phil. Marv, I think."

"What about Anson Carbinder?"

"He was there."

"When you arrived?"

"I think so. Either then, or right after. Everyone came more or less the same time."

"What time did you go home?"

"Two o'clock. The game broke up at two o'clock."

"Was Anson still there?"

"That's right. Anson was still there."

"He ever leave the game?"

"Huh?"

"Between the time he got there, between eight and eight-thirty, till the game broke up at two o'clock—did he ever leave the game? Did he ever leave the apartment? Did he go out for any reason?"

"No."

"You're sure of that?"

"Absolutely. That I would not have missed."

"Anyone else leave the game for any reason?"

"No. Oh, except Tim went home early."

"Tim?"

"Tim Hendricks. He leaves early."

"Uh-huh. But, aside from that, no one left the game all night long?"

"That's right."

"Including Anson Carbinder?"

"Including Anson Carbinder."

"Uh-huh," I said. "You remember anything else about the game? Anything at all that might be important?"

A parrot settled on Ollie Pruett's shoulder. It was a beautiful red and yellow and green.

He barely noticed. "No, I don't," he said.

"You've told me everything you know?"

"Yes, I have. That's it. Everything."

"You sure?"

"Yes, I'm sure," Ollie Pruett said.

But he did not look happy.

10

"So how's it going?"

"Okay, I guess. I'm really just getting started."

"Uh-huh," Richard said. "How many of the poker players did you talk to?"

"Three."

"Stories jibe?"

"Pretty much. A few discrepancies. As you'd expect."

"But nothing out of line?"

"No. Why, should there be?"

"There should not. But that doesn't mean it won't happen."

"Uh-huh. So what's up? Why'd you call me in?"

Wendy/Janet had beeped me as I was leaving Ollie Pruett's and when I'd called in she'd told me to report to the office. I'd assumed it was to meet with Anson Carbinder and was surprised to find he wasn't there.

Richard tilted back in his desk chair, cocked his head. "I thought we should map out our campaign."

"Campaign?"

"Yes. It looks like this may drag on a bit. I don't expect it to go away."

"Neither do I."

"So we need to take a long-range viewpoint. What is the

worst-case scenario? Anson Carbinder is charged with murder and goes to trial."

I said nothing. Richard might describe that as a worst-case scenario, but I happened to know there was nothing the man would love better. It would be the fulfillment of a lifelong dream.

"If that is the case," Richard said, "we have an incredible amount of preparation to do. The bit with the witnesses is fine, but it's really just scratching the surface. There's still an awful lot to be done."

"Why?"

Richard frowned. "What do you mean, why?"

"Just that. If the poker alibi checks out, how can there be a case?"

"No alibi is airtight. Everything is based on allegation and belief. These guys are friends of Anson. The prosecutor will make the argument that they would certainly lie to save him." Richard shrugged. "Now, the more the merrier. You give me six stories that check out, that's hard to break down. But, still, even the best testimony isn't rock solid."

"You're saying the prosecution will try to break down the alibi?"

"But of course."

"Then tell me something."

"What's that?"

"Why aren't I tripping over policemen?"

"Huh?"

"I talked to three of the poker players. None of them mentioned being questioned by the cops."

"Because they haven't been."

"Why not?"

"Because Anson was a good boy."

"Huh?"

"I told him to shut up and he did. Which is remarkable. Most clients don't. But I know Anson and he knows me.

And he knows that if I tell him something there's a reason. So he did it and more power to us."

I looked at Richard. "You're saying the cops don't know Anson was in a poker game?"

"That's right."

"Then they don't know he's got an alibi?"

"Right again."

"Wait a minute. You're telling me he's made no explanation whatsoever?"

"On the advice of his attorney, he's refused to comment."

"So, for all the cops know, he did it?"

"Of course."

"And he's out walking around?"

Richard bowed. "Thank you very much. I wish I could have videotaped that last exchange. What a great advertisement for a criminal attorney. *And he's out walking around?* Perfect. Priceless. And a great line-reading on your part. You couldn't stage it any better."

"Richard."

"Yes? What was your question? What do the cops know? Nothing, except Anson Carbinder called in and reported that his wife had been stabbed. By the time they got there he had also called me and I told him to shut up. Which he did, so they took him to jail. I got him out. And that's the whole story."

"You got him out without *telling* his story?"

"Absolutely. He's innocent until proven guilty. He has the right to remain silent."

"He *has* those rights, yes."

"True," Richard said. "We all *have* those rights. It's only when we start *exercising* them it gets sticky. But that's a fact. Anson hasn't talked, and he's out walking around."

"Why isn't he here?"

"Huh?"

"When you called me in, I thought it was because you wanted me to talk to him."

"No, no. I don't. For a lot of reasons."

"Oh?"

"For one thing, I don't want him to talk. Once you start talking, it gets to be a habit. He tells the story to you, it gets easier to tell it to somebody else. You see?"

"I suppose."

"And he doesn't *need* to talk to you. I'm his attorney, I'm perfectly capable of passing on anything you need to know."

"Are we on a need-to-know basis?"

"You joke," Richard said, "but there's some truth to that. Suppose he said he did it—would you want to know that?"

"What?"

"Say Anson confessed—would you like the responsibility of knowing he killed his wife?"

"Good god, are you saying he did?"

"Are you asking me to give you that responsibility?"

"No, I—"

"Then how can you ask me if he killed his wife?"

"Is that what you're saying?"

"Do you want to know?"

I blinked. Took a breath, blew it out again. "Richard, what are you doing to me?"

"I'm showing you the position you put yourself in. You're not an attorney. If you cover up a crime, you're guilty of criminal conspiracy."

"And you aren't?"

"I have professional privilege. A guy tells me he cut his wife up in little pieces and he kind of liked doing it, and I don't have to tell anyone at all. In fact, I could be disbarred if I did."

"Jesus, Richard."

"Now, you're such a schmuck I don't want to worry you, so I hasten to add that such is not the case. Anson

Carbinder happens to be innocent. Which is a bit of a nuisance, because it makes it that much harder to get him off." He put up his hand. "Yes, I'm speaking flippantly. But I'm also speaking truth. If the guy came in and said, You gotta help me, I killed my wife, his story would doubtless be so simple and straightforward it would be no problem to get around. But in this case, we don't know what happened."

"Do we have a time of death?"

Richard shrugged and grimaced. "That's the other thing. I got you out there running around, nailing down the alibi, we don't even know if it's going to do any good."

"You can't find out the time of death?"

"Communication is a two-way street. Which isn't really fair. My client has a constitutional right not to talk. Is that any reason for the cops to clam up on me?"

"Are you saying there's no point in me checking these alibis till we know if they're going to do any good?"

Richard shook his head. "No, no. They need to be checked. There's no question about that. There's just the question of priorities. Of what's important at the present time."

"What *is* important?"

"That's the hell of it. I don't know. I can't get the information. Which is why I pulled you in."

"Oh?"

"There's certain things we need to concentrate on. The biggie is the time of death."

"Isn't there such a thing as discovery?"

"Sure there is, if we go to trial. I can't wait for that. My client hasn't even been charged yet. Not that I want him charged. But until he is, what's my official status in the case? You see the problem?"

I did, but I wasn't sure what I was supposed to do about it. I exhaled. "Richard, what do you want me to do?"

"Like I said. The time of death, that's the main priority. I want you to work on that."

"Work on it? What the hell do you mean, work on it?"

"I need you to find out the time of death."

"How? I mean, pardon me, Richard, but how the hell am I supposed to do that?"

His eyes faltered.

It was momentary, but it was enough.

Suddenly, I knew.

"Who is it?" I said.

"Who is what?"

"Don't give me that, damn it. Who's the cop in charge?"

"Stanley—"

"Son of a bitch! I can't believe it didn't occur to me before."

"Stanley—"

"Don't Stanley me. Jesus Christ, I should have known the minute you gave me the goddamn raise."

"That wasn't why."

"Oh, no? Then tell me, who's the cop? Who's in charge of the Anson Carbinder case?"

Richard exhaled. He shrugged, and his smile was a shit-eating grin.

"Sergeant MacAullif."

11

"What's the big deal?"

Predictably, Alice's reaction was the exact opposite of what I'd expected. After years of marriage, she still keeps me off my guard. You'd think I'd learn. But, no, each time she does it, there I am, asleep at the switch, shocked as hell to discover she's crossed me up again.

I blinked. "What's the big deal? Weren't you listening? Didn't you hear what I just said?"

"Yes, of course. So?"

"Richard lied to me."

"How did he lie to you?"

"He didn't tell me MacAullif was on the case."

"That's not a lie."

"It was deliberate."

"It's still not a lie."

"I don't care if it was a lie, Alice. The fact is, he deceived me."

"And how is that a fact?"

"I told you. He lied about MacAullif."

"Lied?"

"Don't start that. I don't mean *lied*. I mean withheld the information."

"Withheld? What do you mean, withheld?"

"Exactly that. He withheld the fact."

"Did you *ask* him if MacAullif was on the case?"

"What?"

"Did you ask him?"

"Alice—"

"Come on. Did you ask him?"

"Of course not."

"What's of-course-not about it? Seems a perfectly logical question."

"You're missing the point."

"What's the point?"

"Why should I *have* to ask him? He should tell me."

"Why should he tell you that?"

I had her. Logic, right, and justice were all on my side. Richard should have told me MacAullif was on the case because he knew damn well it would matter to me. And he *deceived* me in not telling me MacAullif was on the case, because he knew it would make a difference in my decision whether or not to handle it. And he deceived me *deliberately* and *for a purpose*. Knowing I was a friend of MacAullif, he wanted me on the case so I would use that friendship to try to get information from MacAullif. So Richard's actions were devious, deceitful, and manipulative. Even Alice couldn't argue with that.

Could she?

"Okay," I said. "Richard should have told me because it would have made a difference to me."

"How?"

"What do you mean, how? In how I felt about it."

"You're making a fuss about your feelings?"

"Making a fuss?"

"Sorry. But isn't that the case? You may have feelings about MacAullif being involved, but how does that affect your decision?"

"I told you."

"No, you didn't. You just said you didn't like it. But suppose you knew that MacAullif was involved—would you have rejected the case?"

"That's not the point."

"Sure it is. You said Richard sucked you in by not telling you MacAullif was involved. So, what if he told you— would you have said, Oh, MacAullif's involved, sorry, I won't handle this?"

"No, but—"

"There you are."

"Alice, there's more to it than that."

"Like what?"

"Richard sucked me in. Got me hooked. Even gave me a raise, for Christ's sake."

"You don't want the raise?"

"Of course I do. It's just, the *reason* I got the raise was so he could ask me to do this."

"You think Richard's paying you extra because you're friends with MacAullif?"

"I know he is."

"So what's your gripe? You say trading on your friendship with MacAullif's distasteful. You say Richard *knows* you'll find trading on your friendship with MacAullif distasteful. Therefore, he's willing to compensate you by paying you extra to do it. Now, what is wrong with that?"

"He didn't tell me."

"Ah, a sin of omission. I'm not clear on where that ranks with a sin of commission."

"Alice—"

"How many years you been working for Richard? How many times you ask him for a raise? You finally got it. Any other man would be jumping up and down, taking his wife out to dinner to celebrate."

"Dinner?"

"You got a hundred-percent raise. Way overdue, but you got it. I would say that's damn fine work."

"Is that it? Is that why you don't care? Take the money and run?"

"Don't be silly," Alice said. "Look, if it was really bad, if it was something you couldn't do, you'd say, Sorry, and you'd turn it down. But this?" She shrugged. "How bad is this?"

"Are you kidding? I got Richard and MacAullif on opposite sides of a murder case."

"So what? Are you the defendant? No, you're employed by his attorney."

"I was employed without full knowledge of the facts. I was deliberately kept in the dark as to certain aspects of the case in order to manipulate me into a position where I'd be forced to abuse a friendship in order to gain an advantage for the attorney's client."

"Well said."

"What?"

"That was practically a tongue twister and you came right out with it."

"Alice—"

"How did you leave things with Richard?"

"Huh?"

"Did you quit?"

"No."

"Did you tell him you wouldn't do it?"

"No."

"Did you tell him you *would* do it?"

"I didn't tell him anything."

"You just walked out?"

"Yeah."

"Angry? Stormed out?"

I took a breath. A light glimmered. "Did he call you?"

"Huh?"

"Did Richard call you? Tell you what happened? Is that why you're so well prepared?"

"Of course not."

"He didn't call you and tell you to work on me?"

Alice put up her hands. "Stanley, you are really paranoid."

"Oh. Thanks a lot."

"Come back to earth. Richard's deceiving you. I'm deceiving you. It's a conspiracy."

"Alice, don't do that."

"Don't do what?"

"Lump yourself together with Richard. I know *he* set me up. I don't think *you* had anything to do with it. Let's not equate the two propositions."

"Fine. But can we look at the situation rationally for a moment?"

"Rationally. Good lord."

"No, that's what I mean. Putting all feelings aside, of who did what to whom, take the simple situation."

"What simple situation?"

"The case. The what's-his-name murder case."

"Anson Carbinder."

"Right. The Anson Carbinder murder case. Richard Rosenberg employs you to investigate. Never mind the money, the tricks, the inducements, or anything else. Just the simple fact that you're going to investigate. And the cop on the other side is Sergeant MacAullif. He's got information that you need. Now, are you going to ask him for it?"

"He wouldn't give me the time of day."

"That's not necessarily true. But it's neither here nor there. The point is, without all that emotional baggage, just the simple proposition, would you ask him, yes or no?"

"I don't know."

"Well, that would seem to be the question that needs an

answer. Once you resolve that, the rest should take care of itself."

"You don't understand."

"No, I don't. Which is probably better. I have no preconceived ideas. Which lets me look at this thing rationally. Just like you could, if you let go of everything else."

I exhaled. Rubbed my head. "Great. And if I looked at this rationally, what would I see?"

"It seems to me there's one basic question."

"What?"

"You've been asked to talk to MacAullif."

"So?"

"Suppose you did?"

"Yeah?"

Alice shrugged.

"How bad could it be?"

12

"Get the fuck out of here!"

Not exactly the greeting I was hoping for. But pretty much what I'd expected.

I had worked with MacAullif before. Though *worked with* doesn't really describe it. I'm not sure what does. But MacAullif and I had been involved in various cases. Usually, on the same side. At least, *I'd* assumed we were on the same side. What *he* assumed was anybody's guess.

But it was more than that. I'd done a favor for MacAullif once. And he'd done favors for me. Hell, last year, when I'd got a screenplay produced, he'd worked on the movie as a technical advisor and even wound up playing a small part in it.

So there was a relationship there.

Surely that should count for something.

"MacAullif—"

"Don't MacAullif me. Shut the fuck up and get out of my office."

"You're making this very hard."

"*I'm* making this very hard? Am *I* in *your* office? Am *I* interfering with *your* work?"

"I'm not interfering with your work."

"Damn right, you're not. You're not doing shit. You're

getting the fuck out of here and I'm pretending you never came."

I sat down.

MacAullif's mouth dropped open. He'd stood up when I'd come in. Now he lunged around the end of his desk, towered over me. His eyes blazed, his jaw muscles moved. I could tell he was restraining himself with a great effort.

"All right, listen, you son of a bitch. You're gambling. You're gambling I'm not gonna risk making the front page of the *New York Post* by picking you up and throwing you out. So you win. I'm not gonna do that. But I'm not talkin' to you, either. So what did you win? You can sit there till your fuckin' ass falls off, you're not gonna get anything."

I shook my head. "That's a bad attitude."

"Oh, yeah? A bad attitude? I got a bad attitude? Let me tell you about a bad attitude." MacAullif leveled his finger at me. "You work for Richard Rosenberg. Richard Rosenberg is Anson Carbinder's attorney. I'm investigating his wife's murder, and guess who's chief suspect number one? I know it, you know it, the whole fucking force knows it. And here you are in my office, and you know what that makes me look like?"

I opened my mouth. Stopped. "I can't. It's too easy."

"Very funny, asshole. Let me spell it out for you. There's an ADA assigned to this one. Had a real nice talk with Mr. Carbinder. When the gentleman couldn't find his fuckin' tongue. When he sat there like a dummy with Rosenberg sayin' No comment. Name is Wellington. That ring a bell?"

"As in Beef Wellington?"

"Great. That's just the image to throw at a working-stiff cop who's not on the take."

"I didn't know there were any."

"Fuck you. You ever heard of the ADA?"

"No."

"Well, he ain't heard of you, either, and that's just how I like it. The guy is young, tough, and eager, and he don't take no shit. Richard Rosenberg did not make his day."

"I can imagine."

"You would imagine right. Richard Rosenberg does not get on with cops. There's a personality clash. That goes double for an ADA."

"So?"

"So all I need is for Wellington to see you in here."

"He doesn't know me."

"So? What am I going to do, introduce you as my cousin from Des Moines?"

"You got a cousin in Des Moines?"

"I got a headache. I got a big fuckin' headache."

MacAullif glared at me, then walked around his desk, sat down in his chair. He opened his desk drawer, took out a cigar.

That was wonderful news. MacAullif had quit smoking cigars, but he often played with them when he talked. His picking it up was a good sign.

As if realizing this, MacAullif dropped the cigar and slammed the drawer. No matter. The intent was there. I was still in his office and we were both sitting down.

"This ADA," I said. "He close to an indictment?"

MacAullif cocked his head. "I am not talking about the case."

"I know you're not. I'm not talking about it, either. Just passing the time of day."

"You can pass gas for all I care. But pass it elsewhere."

I grimaced, shook my head. "Funny thing about the alibi."

"Alibi?"

"Yeah. Carbinder's alibi. That's got to be a kick in the teeth."

"What are you talking about?"

"Here you are, running around, trying to make a case against the guy. I bet this Beef Wellington ADA's looking to indict him, right? And you'll be a witness. Go before the grand jury, tell 'em what you know. Next thing you know, the guy's indicted and bound over for trial. Now, you tell me, how pissed off is Beef Wellington gonna be when we spring the alibi?"

"Stop calling him Beef Wellington."

"Why, you don't think it's funny?"

"No, you dumb fuck. I'm afraid *I'll* do it. Listen, is this alibi for real?"

"Damn straight."

"How solid is it?"

"Six witnesses."

"Six?"

"Give or take. At least five."

"For what time?"

"How's eight until two grab you?"

"Eight at night until two in the morning?"

"You got it."

"No shit."

"None. Now, how's your ADA gonna feel about that?"

"I've been a cop a long time. No alibi's airtight."

"This one is."

"So you say. You talked to all these people?"

"Not yet. But I will."

"Then do yourself a favor. Do a good job."

"I intend to."

"I'm sure you do. But you're not a cop."

"So what?"

"Even a cop will fuck it up—taking witness statements—and they're trained for it. You're an amateur. And you're pretty fuckin' gullible. Don't trust what you hear."

"Thanks for the tip."

"It's not a tip. It's a warning. This guy's relying on an

alibi you're supplying, you better make sure it's damn good."

"Will eight to two suffice?"

MacAullif cocked his head. "Is that what this is all about? You tryin' to find out the time of death?"

"You happen to know it?"

"Of course I happen to know it. You think I'm stupid?"

"You want me to answer that?"

"If you wanted to know the time of death, why didn't you just ask me?"

"Would you have told me?"

"No, I'd have thrown you out of my office."

"Sorry I didn't ask."

"I'm sorry you didn't, either. Then you'd already be gone."

"I'm goin', I'm goin'. I gotta check out this alibi."

"You do that."

"And if I nail it down, rock solid, eight till two—would you like to know?"

"Oh, sure," MacAullif said. "It would be a great personal favor. It would allow me to drop the case."

"You don't have to be sarcastic."

"That's not sarcastic. You wanna see sarcastic, wait'll you meet Wellington."

"Beef, baby?"

"Don't call him that."

"Oh, don't worry. I won't tell him you made it up."

MacAullif's eyes narrowed. "If you do that, I swear they won't find enough of you to bury."

"Don't worry. My lips are sealed. But this alibi."

"What about it?"

"You won't tell me the time of death and you're gonna throw me out of your office. That's fine. That's understandable. That's reasonable. But if I nail the alibi, from eight until two—will that do it?"

"Do it?"

"Don't be dense. You say no alibi's airtight. But if it is—if my client really wasn't there from eight till two—is he off the hook?"

MacAullif raised one finger. "You quote me on this, I'll cut your balls off."

"I'm not looking for a quote. I'm looking for a guideline within which to work."

MacAullif chuckled. Shook his head. "Oh, talk about set-ups."

"Come on, MacAullif. Off the record."

"Off the record?"

"Yeah."

He shook his head. "Fuck you. Not even off the record. You shouldn't even be in here."

"MacAullif—"

"No. That's it. No favors. Get the fuck out of here and let me work."

Shit. I'd done my best, but it hadn't worked. I stood up.

"Thank you," MacAullif said. "Now, you go do your work. But let me give you a little hint."

I'd turned to the door. Now I turned back. "Oh?"

"I think the guy's guilty. So, if I were you, I'd be very careful with those witnesses."

"Why is that?"

"You're not going to be able to prove an alibi from eight till two."

13

Richard wasn't impressed.

"You did *what?*"

"Hey, take it easy."

"Take it easy? You go blabbing to the cops and tell me to take it easy?"

"I didn't go blabbing to the cops."

"Oh, no? What's this you told MacAullif?"

"I didn't tell him anything."

"You told him we got an alibi."

"I wasn't specific."

"You weren't specific?" Richard threw his hands in the air. "Oh, well, it's all right then. You weren't specific. You went and told the cops our defense strategy, but, hey, don't worry, there was nothing specific."

"Richard—"

"What in the name of god induced you to tell MacAullif that? What, he's a friend of yours, you can't keep nothing back?"

"Give me a break. I thought you wanted to find out the time of death."

"I *did* want to find out the time of death. I *still* want to find out the time of death. So, tell me, what's the time of death?"

"I don't know."

"There you are."

"But I know generally."

"We knew generally before you went there."

"We know more."

"We know shit. What the hell is the big idea?"

"I told you. I had to tell MacAullif he had an alibi to goad him into giving us the time of death."

"Goad? You call that a goad?"

"Well, to finesse him, then."

"Finesse? You call what you did finesse?"

"Give me a break. I just did what you asked me to."

Richard held up his hand. "Whoa. Time out. Reality check. Do you recall me telling you to *goad* MacAullif, to *finesse* MacAullif, or anything of the kind? No. All I asked you to do was go find out the time of death."

"That's what I did."

"Oh, yeah? Did you ask him the time of death?"

"No."

"Why not?"

"It wouldn't have done any good."

"How do you know?"

"He told me so."

"He told you so?"

"Yeah."

Richard rolled his eyes, looked back at me. "Let me be sure I understand this. You didn't ask him the time of death, you asked him what he would say *if* you asked him the time of death?"

"It wasn't like that."

"What was it like?"

I took a breath, looked at Richard. "You know what it was like? It was like this conversation. It was like getting beat up. It was like getting pummeled by sarcasm. It was sparring and jabbing. Just between you and me, it was no fun at all."

"Fun? You think I'm paying you to have fun?"

"No. I think you're paying me to get what I can out of MacAullif."

"What's wrong with that?"

"He ain't givin'. As you might expect. If you were being reasonable here, you'd be happy for what I got, instead of grousing about what I didn't."

"I'm not grousing about what you didn't get. I'm ripshit about what you *gave.*"

"Oh," I said. "What a calamity. And how disastrous. An alibi's such a novel concept, the cops never would have thought of it."

"I'm sure they'd have thought of it," Richard said. "What they wouldn't have been able to do would be con- firm it and define it. We've already established that you've confirmed it. Just how well did you define it?"

"Not at all."

"No?"

"No."

"I thought you brought it up just to establish a time frame."

"Right."

"And what was that time frame?"

"Eight till two."

"You told MacAullif that?"

"Of course."

"Well, that defines it a little. An alibi from eight till two. Did you discuss how many people were supplying this alibi?"

I took a breath. Said nothing.

"Well, did you discuss that?"

"I told him at least five, maybe six people."

"So. The alibi is from eight till two, verified by five to six witnesses." Richard cocked his head. "I'm having a little trouble following your logic here. Would you mind point- ing out any way in which you *didn't* define this alibi?"

"I didn't say it was a poker game."

"You didn't say it was a poker game? Oh, well, then the cops have *no* idea what was going on. They happen to know Anson Carbinder was in the company of five to six people from eight until two, but they *don't* know that they were playing *cards*. These people might have been drinking, talking, or playing charades, but *cards* were never mentioned."

"Neither was a name or location," I pointed out.

"Oh, really? You didn't hint? You didn't even say Sounds like?"

"You want to gripe all morning, or you want to take a look at what I got?"

"What've you got?"

"Off the record I got MacAullif's assurance that, if the alibi holds up, Carbinder's off the hook."

"How do you know?"

"Because he told me it wouldn't."

"What wouldn't?"

"The alibi—it wouldn't hold up."

"How does he know that?"

"He *doesn't* know that. He was giving me something."

"What was he giving you?"

"Help with the time of death. He made two statements. Carbinder's guilty, and the alibi won't hold up."

"That tells you the time of death?"

"The way he said it, yes. It was cause and effect. If Carbinder's guilty, the alibi won't hold up."

"He said *if?*"

"No, he said it the other way around. He said it *won't* hold up because he's guilty."

"In so many words?"

"No, but that was the implication."

"You're giving me an implication?"

"No, I'm giving you what I got. For what it's worth, I have MacAullif's assurance the time of death's between eight and two."

"Okay," Richard said. "However it was arrived at, Mac-Aullif gave you this time of death?"

"That's right."

"Would he lie?"

"Huh?"

"Would he lie to you?"

"No."

"Don't be too sure. You've never been in this situation before."

"What situation?"

"You're working for the defense attorney. The cops are on the other side."

"The cops are always on the other side."

"No, they're not. You have this sort of storybook mentality, where you always feel like you're competing with the cops, but that's something else. This is a pitched battle. Two sides, diametrically opposed. My job is to do everything I can to get my client off. And their job is to do everything to nail the motherfucker." Richard shrugged. "Not that they necessarily think he's guilty, but once he's charged, that's their job."

"That's another thing."

"What?"

"Once he's charged. So far, he isn't even charged."

"Yeah, but he will be."

"How do you know?"

"Are you kidding me? He's the husband, he's got blood on his hands. And the cops got nothing else. You think they won't charge him?"

"No, I'm sure they will. That's the other thing I got out of MacAullif."

"What's that?"

"They're putting together a grand jury, getting ready to indict."

"Geez, what a surprise. I never would have guessed."

"Yeah, well, this ADA Wellington—"

"Beef Wellington? That's good. That's the only thing you've said today I've liked."

"Yeah, well, he don't like you."

"Oh?"

"That's what I got from MacAullif. The guy's a young hotshot, apparently you got on his nerves."

"He got on mine."

"I'm sure he did. Anyway, the point is MacAullif says it's personal."

"It always is."

"Always? How can you say that? I thought this was your first murder trial."

"A trial's a trial."

"Oh, that's nice. Does Anson Carbinder know that's your attitude?"

"Don't be dumb. The point is, personal injury or murder, you have an adversarial position where everyone's trying their best to win. I don't like opposing counsel and they don't like me. There's nothing new there. Anyway, the point is, we're in a fight and I intend to win. It's as simple as that." He shrugged. "And so far I'm winning. I sent you to MacAullif. Good move on my part. As badly as you botched the interview, we still got a lead on the time of death. If I'm to take your assurance that what MacAullif gave out is the truth."

"That's my opinion."

"Good. I like that. If it works, I'm a genius. If it doesn't, you're to blame."

"Richard—"

"But, for the time being, let's assume MacAullif was telling the truth."

"Okay. Say he was. What then?"

"Better nail the alibi."

14

"My friends call me B.B."

That was news to me. None of the other poker players had referred to Barry Brown as B.B. It occurred to me, maybe they weren't really his friends.

Barry Brown was one of those people who strike you as obnoxious right away. Well, I suppose I shouldn't speak for everyone. But he certainly struck *me* as obnoxious. Barry Brown, or B.B., as he imagined himself being affectionately referred to, was a chunky little man. Not fat, just solid. He had darting eyes, a piercing stare, and an insolent manner. Again, I'm projecting, but that's what I saw. Maybe it was just his body type. Maybe if he'd had a layer of blubber on him, he'd have seemed less threatening.

And someone might have called him B.B.

I wasn't about to.

"I understand you were in a poker game," I said.

"Yes, of course. I assume you've already spoken to the others?"

"You assume?"

"This happened two days ago. I wouldn't imagine I'm the first."

"You mean no one's called you?"

"Huh?"

"To tell you I was asking questions? That I'd be calling on you next?"

His eyes narrowed. "Then you *have* spoken to the others?"

"Did you get such a call?"

Barry Brown leaned back in his chair. "I don't like your manner."

I didn't like his. Barry Brown was the head of an advertising agency, which is probably why I resented him so much. When I was trying to make it as an actor, way back when, I remember I got a callback for a national TV ad. For once, I did a good audition, the casting director liked me, and it seemed as if lightning had struck and I was actually going to make some money. Then the head of the agency walked in, took one look, said, "No, I want a blond," turned on his heel and walked out, and that was it.

Which is probably why I was taking no shit from Barry Brown.

I stood up. "I'm sorry to offend you," I said. "I assumed you wanted to help Mr. Carbinder. I'll inform his attorney that such is not the case." And I folded my notebook and turned to go.

"Hey, just a damn minute here," Barry Brown said.

I turned back. "I beg your pardon?"

Brown had stood up. Now he pointed his finger at me. "Dont be stupid, now. Of course I want to help Anson. Come back and sit down."

"Will you answer my questions?"

"I'm perfectly willing to answer your questions. I just don't see why you can't answer mine."

"Would you like me to explain it to you?"

He blinked. "I beg your pardon?"

"My job is to collect information, not give it out."

"That's silly."

"No, it isn't. I'm taking witness statements. My job is to

get *your* impression and see how it compares with the others, not tell you what the others said and ask you if you agree."

"I didn't ask you what the others said. I just asked you if you talked to anybody else."

"And I asked you if anyone had called to tell you that I had."

We stood there glaring at each other for a few moments. Then Barry Brown exhaled and sat back down in his seat. "Sam Kestin called."

A small victory, but one's own. I tried not to smirk. "I had a feeling he had. Did he discuss what you're going to say?"

"It's not like that," he said irritably.

"Not like what?"

"Not like he told me what to say. He told me what *he* said, sure. But only generally. That someone was going around asking questions about the game."

"For the purpose of giving Anson Carbinder an alibi?"

"Of course."

"And can you give him one?"

Barry Brown scowled. He opened his mouth to say something. Stopped. "You know," he said, "this is the whole aspect I resent. Can I give him an alibi? Sounds so sleazy. I can tell about him being at the game. Is that giving him an alibi? Does he *need* an alibi? I mean, does anybody seriously think this man killed his wife?"

"The police might."

"That's absurd."

"Why?"

"Anson wouldn't do that."

I nodded. "Unfortunately, the police are not going to find that argument persuasive. Which is why he needs an alibi."

"Jesus."

"Are you going to take exception to the word again, or could we perhaps discuss it?"

"I'll discuss it. Just watch your tone."

"I'm sorry."

He stuck out his chin. "No, you're not. You've been insolent from the moment you walked in. I want to help Anson, yes, but I'm not going to put up with this shit. So change your tune or take a hike."

I wanted to in the worst way. But I had a job to do.

At two hundred bucks a day.

That was the thing hanging me up and pissing me off. Would I have walked out on this guy at ten bucks an hour?

I told myself, no, it's a murder case, you're doing it for your client, not because you've been bought. Perfectly easy to understand.

Intellectually.

"I apologize," I said. "What can you tell me about the poker game?"

"Nothing that Sam didn't."

"Right. But when you go on the stand, they won't let you answer that way. Speaking for yourself, what do you have to offer?"

"Not very much. We had a poker game. Anson was there."

"From when to when?"

"Sometime after eight until two in the morning."

"He was there the whole time?"

"That's right."

"Never went out?"

"Never went out."

"What about you?"

"What *about* me?"

"Did you ever go out?"

"No."

"You were there from eight till two?"

"That's right."

"How'd Anson do?"

"Huh?"

"In the game—how'd he do?"

"Oh. I'm not sure. I think he won."

"He didn't say?"

"What do you mean?"

"At the end of the game, when everyone cashes in—don't you usually discuss who won and lost, how everybody did?"

"Oh, yeah, sure. But it's not like it's important. Now, I know how *I* did."

"How *did* you do?"

"I was up sixty-six dollars."

"Sixty-six?"

"That's right."

"You know that exactly?"

"Sure."

"But you don't know if Anson Carbinder won or lost?"

"No. Why should I?"

I shrugged. "I don't know. But when you're in a game, you kind of get a general idea how the other people are doing."

"That's true." He frowned. "Now, in Anson's case, he was losing for a while. Then he won a few hands. Then there was one big hand when he took the whole pot. Now, whether that was enough to bring him all the way back, I really couldn't say."

"A big pot?"

"Yeah. It was a high/low pot, and he took the whole thing."

"Were you in the hand?"

"Sure."

"What did you have?"

"A straight. Queen high. Which was a kick in the teeth, because Anson had a full house."

"And everyone went high?"

"Right."

"Because Anson looked like he was going low?"

"Sure. He had ace, two, three, four showing."

"And Anson took the whole thing?"

"Right."

"How much was in the pot?"

"I don't know. Over fifty bucks."

"How many people in the hand?"

"You mean who stayed until the end?"

"Right."

"Just about everybody. I was in. And Sam and Marv. And I think Phil and Timmy."

I consulted my notebook. "That's Phil Janson and Timmy Hendricks?"

"That's right."

"And would you remember what they had?"

"No, I wouldn't. I'm not even sure they were in the hand."

"But you're sure Sam Kestin and Marvin Wainwright were?"

"Not for certain," Barry Brown said irritably. "I'm sure Sam was, because he reminded me on the phone. I think Marv was, but I could be wrong. I *know* Anson was, because he won the pot. That's the only thing I know for sure."

"I see," I said. "And how long have you known Anson?"

"I've known him for years."

"And there's no question in your mind that it was Anson Carbinder who was there that night?"

"None whatever." Barry Brown raised one finger, pierced me with his gaze. "Now," he said, "I've told you everything I know, and everything you need to know. And I happen to be a busy man. So, if you wouldn't mind, please close the door on your way out."

Under the circumstances, I didn't ask B.B.-baby if he might have any commercial work I could audition for.

15

Phil Janson made Ollie Pruett look like Superman.

In case you're having trouble keeping track of these names, Ollie Pruett was the Birdman of Central Park South, the fidgety little one who was so nervous he couldn't even sit still.

Phil Janson put him to shame.

Phil Janson was an actor, who probably specialized in *playing* people like Ollie Pruett. Apparently no such part was readily available, since I found him at home.

Phil Janson lived in the West Village in a studio apartment the size of a broom closet, a second-floor walkup over a boutique on Eighth Street that probably went for a thousand a month. It occurred to me, Janson most likely had lived there for years and paid closer to five hundred. It also occurred to me, the only reason I had that thought was because he was an actor, and actors on the whole are not notoriously wealthy.

But I hadn't come to discuss the rent. I'd come to discuss the poker game. And with Janson so nervous, it wasn't going to be easy.

"I don't want to testify," he said.

Phil Janson was a little man with red hair and glasses. I know that sounds like Woody Allen, but he didn't *look* like

Woody Allen. Actually, he looked more like Harrison Ford. I know that makes no sense. I guess you had to be there. Anyway, whatever he looked like, the guy was nervous, upset, and not at all happy.

"Okay, take it easy," I said. "No one's asking you to testify to anything yet. Right now, I just want to know what happened."

"Sure. So you can tell the lawyer and he'll make me testify. I tell you, I don't want to do it."

"There's nothing to worry about."

"Oh, no? Some smart lawyer trips you up, the next thing you know you're in contempt of court and you're in jail."

"I assure you that won't happen."

"Oh, *you* assure me? What, are you a lawyer?"

"No. I told you. I'm a detective."

"Right. Working for Anson's lawyer. Who wants me to testify."

"What's so bad about that?"

"I told you what's so bad about that. Look, why does he need me at all? There's other people in the game. Why don't you talk to them?"

"I *have* talked to them."

"So?"

"And now I'm talking to you."

"Aren't they enough?"

"No."

"Why not?"

Jesus. "Okay," I said. "Say the case goes to trial. And Anson has to prove his alibi."

Phil Janson shook his head. "Alibi. Jesus."

"Yeah, well, say that happens. The attorney will start calling the people in the game."

"Then he doesn't need me."

"Yes, he does."

"Why?"

"Because he'll ask who was playing in the game, and they'll name you."

"Why me?"

"I don't mean you specifically. I mean everybody. And then the attorney will call all these people. Well, if he leaves you out, the prosecutor will wonder why."

"So what?"

I took a breath. Was the guy really that dumb? Or was he just that nervous? "The thing is, if Anson Carbinder's attorney doesn't call you, the prosecutor will. To see why you weren't called. Well, Richard Rosenberg wouldn't let that happen."

"Who?"

"Anson Carbinder's attorney. Richard Rosenberg. There's no way he lets that happen. Not calling you builds up your importance. There's no way he doesn't put you on the stand."

"Suppose I don't go?"

"Then he serves you with a subpoena."

"Shit."

"Well, if he didn't, the prosecutor would. So there's no ducking it. One way or another, you're going on the stand."

"What if I didn't talk?"

"Then you'd be in contempt of court. Unless, of course, an answer would tend to incriminate you. Then you could refuse to answer on those grounds."

"Incriminate me?"

"In the crime."

"What crime?"

"The murder. If you killed her, you wouldn't have to say a thing."

Janson blinked. "That's not funny."

"No, it isn't. But it happens to be the case. That's the only way you're going to get out of this."

Phil Janson rubbed his head. "Jesus Christ."

"So there's no reason not to talk to me. Talking to me obligates you to nothing. And it's a good rehearsal for what's
to come."

Janson exhaled. "Oh, boy."

"Hey, come on," I said. "You're an actor, right?"

"Yeah. So?"

"So think of it as a dramatic exercise. "

"Yeah, right," Janson said. He rubbed his hand over his
face. "Okay, okay. What do you need to know?"

"You were at a poker game?"

"Yes, I was."

"This was three nights ago. The night Mrs. Carbinder
was killed."

"Jesus."

"I'm sorry. I'm just using it to pinpoint the date. But the
fact is, you were at the game?"

"Yes, I was."

"Where was this game?"

Phil Janson began tugging at his earlobe. I couldn't tell
if it was a nervous habit or if there was something wrong
with his ear. "Let me see, where was it?" he said. "Oh, at
Sammy's. Sam Kestin."

"You were at the poker game at Sam Kestin's?"

"That's right."

"Who else was there?"

"Well, Anson Carbinder, of course."

"Of course. Who else?"

"Well, Sam Kestin . . . Ollie Pruett . . . Ricky Pomerantz."

"Who?"

"Oh! Oh!" Janson said. He looked as if he were about to
tug his earlobe right off. "No, no. I'm wrong. Ricky was at
the *last* game, not that one." He looked at me, pleadingly.
"See? See? That's why I don't want to go on the stand. I'm

not *good* at details. I get confused. I'll say the wrong thing and screw everything up."

"No big deal. Anyone can make a mistake."

"Yeah, but like you said. The prosecutor will jump on it and crucify me."

"That won't happen."

"But if I make a mistake . . ."

"Hey," I said, holding up my hand. "That's why you're talking to me now. Getting it straight in your own head. So when the time comes, you won't make that mistake."

"Yeah. Whatever," Janson said.

"Anyway, *I'm* not going to cross-examine you. If you make a slip of the tongue, you just correct it and go on from there. Now, you mentioned this one guy who wasn't there who was at the previous game. No problem. Try again. So far, I got you, Anson Carbinder, Sam Kestin, and Ollie Pruett who were at the poker game. Now, who else was there?"

Janson exhaled again. "Marv."

"That would be Marvin Wainwright?"

"That's right."

"Okay. Who else?"

"Ah . . . Tim Hendricks."

"Fine," I said. "Let's see. That makes six. Who's the seventh?"

Janson thought a moment. "Christ, I don't know," he said. "See, I'm terrible at this."

"Then let me help you out," I said. "Just think back to the game, think of whose faces you saw around the table."

"Huh?"

"Who was sitting there? Who's to your left, who's to your right? Who's sitting across from you?"

After a moment Janson said, "Barry Brown."

"Oh?"

"That's who was across from me. Barry Brown."

"So that's the seventh player? Barry Brown?"

"Right."

"You call him Barry?"

"That's right."

"You ever call him B.B.?"

Janson frowned. "B.B.?"

"Never mind," I said. "Those are the players in the game. That's *who*. Let's do *when*. How long was the game?"

"In hours?"

"I don't mean how many hours. I mean from when to when."

"Oh."

"When did the game start?"

"I don't know. Around eight-thirty."

"When did you get there?"

"I don't know. Around eight-fifteen."

"When you got there, who was already there?"

"Oh. I don't know. Sam, of course."

"Who else?"

"I think Marv."

"What about Anson Carbinder?"

"He was there."

"When you got there?"

"I think so."

"You're not sure?"

Janson had been tugging at his earlobe again. Now he let it go and threw up his hands. "See? See?" he said. "See what I told you? It doesn't matter what I remember and what I don't. A simple thing like that, I don't remember and they tear me apart."

"Not at all," I said. "There's no reason why you *should* remember. If you say you got there around eight-fifteen, there were a few people there when you got there but you're not sure who, but everyone was arriving about then and by eight-thirty they were all there, who's to argue with you?"

"Are you telling me what to say?"

"Of course not. I'm just pointing out that the phrase, *I'm not sure,* is perfectly acceptable and will cover practically any lapse of memory. If you just say you're not sure, who's to argue with you?"

"Well, I'm *not* sure."

"Fine."

"No, it's *not* fine. I tell you I'm not sure, but you keep asking me questions."

"Which you can answer the same way," I said patiently. "Anything you're sure, you say. Anything you're not sure, you say you don't remember."

Janson stuck out his chin. "Fine. Then I don't remember."

"But you can't say that across the board."

"Why not?"

"Because it's not true. It's a lie. It's perjury. It's what you go to jail for. If you sit on the stand, stubbornly maintaining that you don't remember anything, the judge will see what you're doing and he'll order you to answer. And when you don't, you'll be in contempt of court. At which point he will throw you in jail until you *do* answer."

"Hey, come on," Janson said. He put up his hands as if warding off a blow.

"But that's silly," I said, "because it doesn't have to happen. All you have to do is tell what you know. If you forget some specific detail, you say you don't remember. But generally you do. You've already told me most of what you need to. It's the small details, like who came before who, that don't really matter. See what I mean?"

Janson looked at the floor. "I suppose so," he muttered.

"Fine," I said. "So, let's deal with some of the things you *do* know. The game started around eight-thirty. When did it end?"

"Two o'clock."

"That's when the game broke up?"

"Yes."

"And everyone went home?"

"Sure."

"And did Anson Carbinder stay till the end?"

"Yeah."

"That's two in the morning."

"Right."

"So Anson Carbinder was there from eight-thirty that night until two in the morning? Is that right?"

"Yeah. That's right."

"Did he ever leave?"

"Huh?"

"During the course of the evening—from the time he got there until the time he got home—did Anson Carbinder ever leave the poker game for any amount of time? Like to go out for a smoke, to go to the store, or what have you."

"Anson doesn't smoke."

"I'm glad to hear it. Did he leave the poker game for any reason?"

"No."

"See," I said. "You're doing fine. Now, was there anything about the game, any hand in particular, that you remember Anson being there?"

"No."

"No?"

"I don't remember."

"How about a big high/low hand where Anson took the whole pot?"

"Oh, that."

"See, you *do* remember."

"Not really."

"Yes, really. You said, Oh, that. Tell me about the hand."

"I don't remember."

"You remember it was a high/low hand and he took it all. Right?"

"Right."

"How did it happen?"

"I don't really remember."

"You must remember what you had."

"Not really."

"But you remember the hand?"

"I remember there was a hand. I don't remember it well."

"But it was a high/low pot and Anson took it all?"

"Right."

"Do you remember what *he* had?"

"No."

"Did he go high or low?"

"I don't remember."

"Do you know what time of night this was?"

"No, I don't."

I took a breath. "Look. When I said you could say you don't remember, that wasn't a blanket excuse to stop answering questions. Anson Carbinder's a friend of yours. I would think you'd want to help him."

Phil Janson had been fidgeting, tugging at his ear, and for the most part looking down at the floor. Now he looked up at me. "I *do* want to help him. I really do. It's just . . ." He broke off, shook his head. "It's just, I'm not going to make a very good witness."

No argument there.

16.

"I always leave at midnight."

I could buy that. Everyone I talked to told me Tim Hendricks left at midnight, like it was an event you could set your watch by. And the man himself gave that impression. Tim Hendricks was some sort of broker, who did something tremendously important on the floor of the New York Stock Exchange. He practiced early to bed and early to rise, so that he'd be bright-eyed and bushy-tailed every morning when the trading bell rang.

Hendricks was a tall, thin man, with precise manners and a snippy air. In that respect, he was not unlike Barry Brown, but where old B.B. merely got my back up, for some reason I found myself almost deferential to Mr. Hendricks. In retrospect, I guess he reminded me of a high-school teacher and made me feel like I was back in tenth grade.

"Midnight?"

"Absolutely," Hendricks said. "I've been doing it for years, no matter what they say."

"Actually, no one's said any different."

"Huh?"

"Everyone agrees you left then." He frowned, then raised his eyebrows. "No, no. You misunderstand." He raised one finger. "No, I mean I *leave* at midnight, no matter how they try to get me to *stay.*"

"They do that?"

"Yes, of course. It's always One more hand or Why don't we deal around to Sam? Or Why don't you deal off?"

"You ever do that?"

"Absolutely not. Midnight, I leave."

"What if you're in the middle of a hand?"

"I don't start a hand close to midnight. I cash in."

I was sure he did. I could imagine him doing it, too. Precise, proper, arrogantly pushing his stacks across the table, pissing the other players off.

"And on the night in question?"

"I left at twelve."

"Twelve exactly?"

"Close enough. I started cashing in at eleven fifty-five. By midnight I was out the door."

"People argue with you?"

"Huh?"

"You said people always try to talk you into staying. Did that happen this time?"

"Oh, sure."

"And who was that?"

"I think Marv said Play another hand. And Barry Brown made some crack. He didn't ask me to stay, just said something insolent."

"Uh-huh. But you ignored this and cashed out?"

"Sure."

"Did you win?"

"I beg your pardon?"

"In the game. How'd you do in the game?"

"Oh. I won."

"How much?"

"Does it really matter?"

"Probably not. But I'm trying to get a picture here. Do you have any objection to telling me what you won?"

"No. I won fifty-three dollars."

"Is that a lot?"

"I beg your pardon."

"For that game. Is that a lot to win in the game?"

"No, not a lot. I've won over a hundred. I suppose that's a lot, considering I don't stay for the whole game."

"Uh-huh. So on the night in question you won fifty-three dollars between the hours of eight-thirty and midnight?"

Tim Hendricks frowned. I could see his mind doing the math, figuring out if you spread it out over that amount of time, fifty-three bucks didn't seem that good. "That's right," he said.

"That *is* right—you were there from eight-thirty till twelve?"

"Yes, I was."

"Who else was in the game?"

"Don't you know?"

"Yes, I do. But I can't testify for you. You've already mentioned Marvin Wainwright and Barry Brown. Who else was there?"

"Well, Sam Kestin, of course. And Ollie Pruett. And the actor. Phil Janson. How many is that?"

"Counting you, six."

"Right. And Anson Carbinder makes seven."

"Mr. Carbinder was at the game?"

"Yes, of course."

"You remember when?"

"I can only speak for the time I was there."

"He was there when you got there?"

"Yes, he was."

"He was there when you left?"

"That's right."

"That would be from eight-thirty till midnight?"

"That's right."

"Did he ever leave the game for any reason?"

"No, he didn't."

"Not even to run out to the store?"

"For what?"

"I don't know for what, I'm asking if he did."

"And the answer is no."

"So you can give Anson Carbinder an alibi from eight-thirty till twelve?"

"That's right."

"You left the game at midnight?"

"Yes. I've said so. Many times."

"When you left the game, where did you go?"

"I went home."

"Here?"

"Yes, of course."

Here was Tim Hendrick's West Seventy-second Street apartment. I was calling on him at home rather than brave the floor of the stock exchange. Actually, I *had* braved the floor of the stock exchange earlier that afternoon, only to find, as I had feared, a swarm of people shouting in what to me might as well have been a foreign language. The fact that I'd located Tim Hendricks in that chaos was remarkable. The fact that he'd declined to speak to me there was not.

"How did you get home?"

"I took a taxi."

"Through the park?"

"Of course."

"How long did that take?"

"No time at all, that time of night. I was home by twelve-fifteen. I was asleep by twelve-thirty. Which for me is late."

"Uh-huh," I said.

I wondered if Tim Hendricks could prove that. His building did not have manned elevators. The doorman in the lobby might or might not remember him coming in.

Which was a crazy way of thinking. But he *was* the only person I'd questioned with no alibi from twelve till two.

"Anyway," I said, "getting back to the game. Was there anything about it that you remember particularly—relating to Anson Carbinder, I mean?"

"Sure. He won a big hand."

"Oh?"

"Sure. Didn't anyone else mention it? He won a big hand of high/low."

"He took the whole pot?"

"He sure did. It was a hand he looked like he was going low, but he had a full house."

"And everyone went high?"

"Sure did."

"It was a big pot?"

"Real big."

"A lot of people stayed in?"

"Sure did."

"Including you?"

"I'll say. I'd have won a lot more than fifty-three dollars if it wasn't for that pot."

"I see," I said. "You say Anson had a full house?"

"That's right."

"What did you have?"

"A flush. King high. What a kick in the teeth that was. Nothing like a second-best."

"You didn't have a low?"

"No. And even if I'd *had,* I wouldn't have *gone* low. Anson looked like a lock."

"Uh-huh."

I was out of there ten minutes later, without having learned anything else useful.

I was not happy.

Hendricks was the last of my witnesses, saved till last because he'd gone home early, making him the least important on the list. So, with his statement, I was ready to wrap the whole thing up.

Only, Tim Hendricks, who went home at midnight, had played in Anson Carbinder's big hand.

The hand Sam Kestin said had taken place at one o'clock.

17.

Richard seemed alarmed. "You didn't *say* anything?"

"What?"

"To this guy . . ."

"Tim Hendricks?"

"Right. You didn't say anything to him?"

"About what?"

"The hand. You didn't say, How could you have been in that hand if you left at midnight?"

"No, I didn't."

"Did you say *anything* to him?"

"Not about that."

"About what, then?"

"I asked him what time he got home, how he got there."

"But not in relation to the hand?"

"Not at all."

"You didn't give him any indication that there was any discrepancy with anything anyone else had said?"

"No."

"Are you sure?"

"Absolutely."

"And you didn't call this other guy up and say, How could the hand have taken place at one o'clock if the guy who went home early was in it?"

"No, I didn't."

"Really? It would seem a natural thing to do."

"Are you telling me I should've?"

"Certainly not. I'm just surprised that you didn't. And you didn't contact anybody else, call any other players, try to pin down the time of the hand?"

"No, I didn't. I brought it to you."

Richard frowned. "I see."

"You don't seem happy."

"A discrepancy of this kind is a major kick in the ass."

"Well, don't shoot the messenger. Aren't you glad I found it, rather than getting surprised with it in court?"

"I don't know," Richard said. "It's the type of thing, you don't ask, might never come up."

"Pardon me for doing my job."

Richard looked at me. "You're too quick to take offense. *You* will pardon *me* if I point out you have a rather self-centered viewpoint. Try and understand what is happening here. This is not a case of evaluate Stanley Hastings and grade him on the performance of his job. This is a case of defending a man accused of murder. If you could keep your ego out of it, you'd be a lot better off."

I nearly gagged. This, from the most arrogant son of a bitch ever to pass the bar exam.

"Now, then," Richard said. "Since what you are clearly looking for is praise, what you've done *right* here is backing off from the situation. I don't *want* you cross-checking stories, coordinating details, and getting accounts to conform. All I want you to do is gather the facts independently from each individual. And then lay them before me, so I can analyze them."

"You don't want me to point out discrepancies?"

"Don't be a moron. It's all right to tell *me*. I just don't want you pointing it out to *them*."

"Well, that's your major discrepancy. You can do with it as you choose."

"Is that the only one?"

"It's not the only discrepancy. But it's the only one that jumps out and bites you."

"Uh-huh. And, aside from that, what's your general impression?"

"Of the alibi?"

"Right."

"Holds up pretty well. I would say the DA'd be hard pressed to make a case. Unless, of course, she was killed some time after two o'clock."

"That's not a consideration," Richard said.

I looked at him in surprise. "You know she wasn't?"

"No. But if she was, all the work you've done is useless. So for the point of this discussion, we're assuming she wasn't. Now, making that assumption, you're telling me Anson's in the clear?"

"It would appear so. We have six independent witnesses. Well, five, actually, until two o'clock. The sixth only goes till midnight."

"Fine," Richard said. "Let's go over them now. I want to know what they said, plus your general impression of them and how you think they'd do on the stand."

"You haven't talked to any of them?"

"No."

"But you're going to, aren't you?"

"No, I'm not."

"You're kidding?"

"Not at all."

"You're not going to talk to your witnesses before you put them on the stand?"

"Not if I don't have to. I may have to straighten out this time element, but that's it."

"What's the idea?"

"I don't want a bunch of stories that sound like they're rehearsed. So I don't want to talk to 'em. Fortunately, I don't need to. Because I have you. Okay, so give me what you got."

I opened my notebook. "Okay, first up is Sam Kestin. He ran the game. Or, rather, hosted it. He's a bank executive and looks it."

Richard raised his eyebrows.

I put up my hand. "Sorry. That's a totally biased viewpoint."

"Not at all," Richard said. "That's the type of observation I want. I'm just surprised to hear you come up with it. Go on."

"Well, in my humble, biased opinion, the man looks well fed, prosperous, and smug. We've already been over the major discrepancy in his testimony. Aside from putting the big high/low hand at one o'clock, his story conforms nicely with all the others. Anson Carbinder got there between eight and eight-thirty and didn't leave until the game broke up at two.

"In terms of the big hand, he remembers it particularly because he had a nine low and could have won half the pot, but chose to go high with a three of a kind."

"Okay," Richard said. "Explain to me about this hand."

"You don't play poker?"

"I play *poker*," Richard said. "I don't play this high/low shit. I don't consider that poker. So why don't you fill me in?"

I gave Richard a rundown of the nuances of high/low poker.

"Okay," he said. "Let me be sure I understand this. The high hand, no problem, it's the same as straight poker. But the low hand is the worst hand you can get?"

"More or less."

"What do you mean, more or less?"

"Well, ace counts low."

"So?"

"So a hand with an ace in it can be *lower* than a hand without an ace in it. Even though, if you were going *high*, the hand with the ace would be the higher hand."

"But aside from that?"

"Aside from that, you would be correct if they were playing sixty-four low."

"You just lost me."

"Okay, there's two ways to play high/low. One, straights and flushes are only high hands, or, two, straights and flushes can also go low."

"What's that got to do with sixty-four?"

"If a straight can't go low, then the best low you can get is six, four, three, two, one. It's called a sixty-four low. If a straight *can* go low, then the best low is *five,* four, three, two, one. It's called a *fifty*-four low. It's sometimes called a wheel, because it can go both ways, as a low and as a straight."

"Uh-huh," Richard said. "And in this case?"

"They were playing straights and flushes swing."

"Swing?" Richard said. "You'll pardon me, but I have a *law degree,* and I'm having trouble following this."

"It's not you," I said. "I've *played* with people who can't figure it out. Swing means go both ways. In other words, they were playing fifty-four low. So if you had a five, four, three, two, one, you could declare it as a low, declare it as a high, or declare it both ways."

"How do you declare?"

"Actually, I didn't ask, but usually it's done with chips. After the last bet, everyone puts their fist in the middle of the table. Then you open your hand. If your hand's empty, you're going low. If you have a chip in your hand, you're going high. If you have *two* chips in it, you're going both ways."

"What if you go both ways?"

"Then you have to win both ways. If you lose either way, you lose the whole thing."

"People play this for fun?"

"Sure. I've played it myself."

Richard gave me a look that clearly conveyed that his opinion of me had just dropped another two notches.

"Okay," Richard said. "So the hand we're talking about was seven-card stud, high/low, where the best low was a fifty-four, which means a straight can go high or low or both?"

"That's right."

"And what did Anson have again?"

"He had ace, two, three, four showing. So it looked like he had a low."

"Or a straight."

"Right. But if he had a straight, it would also be a perfect low. So he'd either go low or both ways."

Richard's eyes were larger than I'd ever seen them. It was the first time I could recall him appearing to be not fully in control of the situation. "Okay," he said. "And Sam Kestin? What did he have again?"

"He had a nine low, and he also had three eights. He went high with the three eights, because nine low is not a very good low, and it looked like Anson would have it beaten. He was, incidentally, the only person at the table who *had* a legitimate low and who might have gone low on the hand."

"Is it at all strange that he didn't?"

"Not at all. As I say, nine's a poor low to begin with and looking at Anson's hand, there was almost no chance of it winning."

"So he went high with three eights and lost?"

"Right."

"And there's a lot of money in this pot, so he'd really remember, it would make a big impression?"

"Right."

"So the only thing he's apt to be wrong about is the time of the hand?"

"That's how I see it."

"Okay," Richard said. "Let's move on. Who's next?"

"Marvin Wainwright."

"Who's that?"

"He's a vice-president from Gladrags, Foster and Vale, a textile manufacturing company. He's another fat cat, chubby, well fed. At least in my humble opinion, that's how he'll come across to the jury. He was there from eight-thirty till two, says Anson was there the whole time, never left. The only discrepancy in *his* story is he said *everyone* stayed till the end. According to everyone else, Tim Hendricks left at midnight."

"You didn't point that out to him?"

"No, he was the first person I questioned."

"Uh-huh. And what about the big hand?"

"He was in it. He remembers it particularly because he had a flush and was hoping to get the whole pot."

"How could he do that?"

"If Anson had a low straight and went both ways, the flush would beat his straight, Anson would lose the whole pot, and the hand that beat him would take it all."

"I see," Richard said. "So he'd have reason to remember it particularly. And what time of night did *he* think the hand took place?"

"I don't know."

"You don't know?"

"I didn't ask him."

"Why not?"

"Like I said, he was the first person I talked to. At the

time, I had no idea there would be any dispute about when the hand took place."

"Even so, it would seem a natural question."

"Yes, it would," I said. "You want me to go back and ask him?"

"No. Let's move on. Who's next."

"Ollie Pruett. The Birdman of Central Park South."

"Huh?"

I filled Richard in on the state of Ollie Pruett's apartment.

"Great," he said. "A kook. Aside from that, what's he like?"

"Fidgety little man. Nervous, uncomfortable. Not going to make a good impression on the jury."

"Will they think he's lying?"

I frowned. "No, but they're going to think he's apt to be wrong."

"Just because he's nervous?"

"Well, he also has a tendency to misspeak himself."

"How so?"

"Well, referring to the hand again, everyone thought Anson was going low but he went high. Ollie Pruett said it the other way around. He told me Anson looked like he was going *high,* but he went *low.*"

"And when you pointed it out?"

"He fell all over himself correcting himself. He did *not* make a good impression."

"And the hand itself?"

"He had two pair, stayed in till the end. Which, considering the hand, doesn't say much for his prowess. He was beat all over the board."

"Did he know when the hand took place."

"No, he didn't, and I asked him. But he's the type of guy you wouldn't *expect* to remember."

"Great. Who else?"

"Also on the debit side, Phil Janson. He's an actor. Odd man out. How he got involved with this bunch is hard to say. He's the only one of the group doesn't have any money. He's like Ollie Pruett, only more so. So nervous it's hard to imagine him playing cards at all. And as a witness, he's the pits. This Ollie Pruett makes a slip like which way Anson's going in the hand. *Phil Janson* makes a slip like naming a player who wasn't even there."

"Oh?"

"Right. He names a regular who was at the *last* game, but wasn't at *this* one. Then has to sort that out for himself. If he's like that in front of the jury, it will be very bad news. You say you don't wanna talk to these guys, but here's one guy you might want to pin down."

"What's the rest of the story?"

"Nothing good, nothing bad. Basically, he's a yes man, agrees with everybody else. Anson Carbinder was there the whole night, never left. No one else left, except Tim Hendricks, who went home at twelve o'clock."

"And the high/low hand?"

"He doesn't remember."

"You're kidding."

"No. He remembers there *was* one, but he doesn't remember the specifics."

"Or when it took place?"

"He hasn't a clue."

"Great."

"Yeah. He's easily your worst witness." I turned a page. "Then there's Barry Brown. Ad-agency executive. Obnoxious, aggressive personality, puts people off."

"You're not exactly inspiring me with confidence," Richard said. "Do I have any witnesses you *like?*"

"Not really. But he's the only one I'd call antagonistic. He and I did not hit it off. Just a personality conflict, I'm sure. The only real bone of contention—and the only interesting part of his story—is the fact that he got a phone call from Sam Kestin telling him I was asking questions and attempting to coordinate what he said."

Richard frowned. "That's not good."

"Yeah, well, it probably doesn't matter. The guy has nothing significant to add. Anson Carbinder was there the whole evening, left at two o'clock, never went out. Anson won a big hand of high/low with a full house. Barry Brown was in till the end with a queen-high straight."

"Uh-huh. And what time does *he* think it was."

"I didn't ask him."

"Nice work."

"Look. You gotta understand. I spoke to Tim Hendricks last. Because he left early and was the least important. It was when I talked to him and he claimed to be in the hand that I knew we had a problem. If it weren't for that, it wouldn't be an issue and you wouldn't be giving me grief."

"Giving you grief?"

"Withdrawn. Anyway, it wouldn't be an issue."

"You happen to ask *Tim Hendricks* when the hand took place?"

"Yes, of course."

"Oh, now it's *of course?*"

"Of course. Because of the discrepancy."

"I'm surprised you even noticed it."

"Why? Isn't it obvious?"

"Yes, of course."

I gave Richard a look.

He put up his hands. "Sorry. Let's not get sidetracked. When does Tim Hendricks say the hand took place?"

"Somewhere around eleven o'clock."

"He's not sure?"

"No. But he thought it was about an hour before he went home. Now, that's just an estimate, but it's the type you'd expect to be right."

Richard frowned. "While that *sounds* reasonable, with that type of estimate the hand *could* have taken place as late as eleven-thirty, or even as early as ten."

"Maybe, but his impression was eleven."

"A jury's not going to be swayed by his impression. Especially with other people placing the hand much later."

"Exactly. So what do you want to do about it?"

Richard frowned again. "The only one who actually gave you a time was the guy who ran the game—what's his name?"

"Sam Kestin."

"Yeah, him. He's the only one?"

"That's right."

"Then he's gotta be wrong."

"Unless Tim Hendricks is."

Richard shook his head. "Not worth considering. Not with everyone saying, Tim Hendricks left at midnight, Tim Hendricks *always* leaves at midnight."

"So you wanna talk to Kestin, or you want me to?"

I never got an answer, because at that moment the phone rang, and when Richard picked it up it was Anson Carbinder, in a rather agitated state of mind.

The cops had just given him his one phone call.

18

Ever feel like a second-class citizen? I sure did, sitting in the corner of the booking room of the police station, while Richard Rosenberg was upstairs in the visitors room conferring with his client. As I sat there, watching the dregs of the earth being dragged in in handcuffs, it occurred to me that just once in the fucking case I would like to have the faintest idea what was going on.

All I knew at that point was that Anson Carbinder had been arrested for murder. No real surprise, of course—we always knew he would be—it was just a matter of when. Still, it would have been nice to know the details.

And it would have been nice to get them straight from the horse's mouth. As I watched a particularly tarty-looking hooker being booked, I realized that since our initial meeting I had had no contact whatsoever with my client.

Largely because he wasn't *my* client. He was Richard Rosenberg's client.

And I was Richard Rosenberg's employee.

A functionary.

A second banana.

That's what I'd been reduced to for two hundred bucks a day.

I wondered if it was worth it.

Three drunks, two prostitutes, four black teenagers, and one rather scary-looking Hispanic later, Richard Rosenberg came to get me.

"What's going on?" I asked.

"Let's get the hell out of here," Richard said in an unnecessarily loud voice, then stood in the middle of the room, hands on hips, looking around as if challenging anyone to try to stop him. There were no takers, and minutes later Richard and I were sailing out the front door.

"So, what's up?" I asked.

Richard snorted. "Sons of bitches. The grand jury's indicted Anson Carbinder for murder."

"Well, we always knew they would."

"Yeah, but it means they got something."

"Well, now you can find out what it is."

"Well, that's the other thing."

"What's that?"

"I'm entitled to the transcript. But they don't have it ready yet. They say I can have it tomorrow."

"Who says that?"

"The ADA Beef Wellington himself."

"He was there?"

"In person. Smiling, helpful, hearty. Makes me want to push his face in."

"What did Anson tell you?"

"Basically, nothing. Because he knows nothing. It's not like the cops told him anything, either. He knows he's under arrest for killing his wife. How the grand jury arrived at that conclusion, we have no idea."

"What about the time of death?"

"We don't know that, either. Presumably, we'll find out tomorrow when we get the transcript, but I'd like to know now."

I put up my hand. "No way."

"Huh?" Richard said.

"I'm not talking to MacAullif."

"Who asked you?"

"Well, whaddya want me to do?"

"I've hired you as an investigator. I'd like you to investigate."

"Investigate what?"

"The time of death."

"How would you like me to do that?"

"Any way you can."

"The only lead I have is MacAullif."

"Is that right?"

"Yeah, that's right."

"Makes it tough."

"Makes it impossible."

Richard put up his hand. "No, no. You're talking to a lawyer. Not *impossible*. It's just *hard*. I hired you to investigate. I'm *paying* you to investigate. And I'm *telling* you to investigate. And you *know* what I *want* you to investigate. Now, then, you tell me."

Richard cocked his head. "What you gonna do?"

19

MacAullif wasn't surprised to see me.

"Well, well," he said. "I was wondering when you'd show up."

"Oh?"

"Grand jury indictment came down, could you be far behind?"

"I wish I were."

"You and me both. Now I got you in my office, and what's it gonna take to get you out?"

"How about the time of death?"

"How about it?"

"Well, now it's no big deal. With Anson indicted, we'll get to see that grand jury testimony."

"What makes you think it's in there?"

"Are you saying it isn't?"

"No, I'm just asking why you think it is."

"Come on. Are you telling me the grand jury would indict without knowing when she died?"

"Why not? If you'll recall, your man wouldn't talk. Wouldn't say where he was that night. Which means he could have killed her anytime."

I put up my hand. "Hold on. You're swapping words

with me. Are you telling me the time of death *won't* be in the grand jury transcript?"

"I would not wish to be quoted as having told you anything of the sort."

"I'm not gonna quote you. I just wanna know."

"Yeah, sure. For all I know you're wearing a wire. To set me up to shake me down."

"I wouldn't do that."

"I'm glad to hear it. Because that would constitute blackmail. Which, the last time I looked it up, was against the law."

"We were talking about the time of death."

"*You* were talkin' about the time of death. Me, I'm just minding my own business, sitting here going over my case files."

"Including Anson Carbinder's?"

"I may have glanced at his."

"Did it mention the time of death?"

"You know, I didn't look at that."

"Yeah, but you know when it is."

"What makes you think that?"

"You're the investigating officer."

"I'm not the medical examiner."

"But you know what he said."

"Sure, but that's hearsay. I couldn't testify to that."

I looked at him. "Hey, MacAullif. What's your problem? Are you doing this to be a hard-on? Or have you had instructions from above? Or are you just covering your ass on general principles? I mean, what's the big secret about the time of death?"

MacAullif shook his head. "Schmuck."

"I beg your pardon."

"You're in here askin' me about the time of death. If you'll recall, it's the *second time* you've been in here askin' me about the time of death. Well, guess what? I'm not on your side. I'm the investigating officer. I'm working for the ADA. Responsive and responsible to him."

"What are you saying?"

"You come in here, he's gonna know. Why? 'Cause I'm gonna tell him. Why? 'Cause that may be bad, but if he heard it from someone else, it would be ten times worse. You got that?"

"It's a little convoluted, but—"

"Don't fuck with me. I'm tryin' to do you a favor here."

"How?"

"By explaining the obvious." He shook his head. "Jesus, what a moron. You ask me what's the big secret about the time of death." MacAullif waved his hand for emphasis. "There's *no* fucking secret about the time of death." He spread his hands. "Except, you come in askin' for it. Well, I gotta report that to the ADA. And he wonders why. Particularly since your client ain't talkin'. So he's thinkin', if the defense wants to know the time of death, fuck 'em, I ain't gonna tell 'em. So instructions to that effect go out, and you're hoist by your own petard."

"You're saying he won't tell 'cause I asked?"

"Bingo, right on the button. Geez, I thought you were dumb, but, no, you catch on just like that. How nice. Now you know how it is, you can leave me alone. And if you happen to be wearin' a wire, tough luck for you, you ain't gettin' a thing."

"MacAullif—"

"No, that's it. Too bad. Tough luck. You lose. Go on, get out of here."

"Can't you just—"

"No, I can't." MacAullif got out of the chair, came around the desk. He took me by the elbow and turned me around. Placing one hand in the small of my back and the other on my side, he smoothly and efficiently piloted me out the door.

"And do me a favor and do not come back," MacAullif said.

I couldn't tell if he was saying that for the benefit of the three cops who were close enough to hear. Or for the wire I might be wearing. Or if the son of a bitch really meant it.

Before I had time to give it any thought, MacAullif had ducked back inside his office and slammed the door.

As I stomped out the front door of One Police Plaza it occurred to me that Richard Rosenberg was paying me two hundred bucks a day for a friendship that wasn't worth a plugged nickel.

I stopped on the sidewalk to brush off my jacket and straighten my tie. MacAullif's push had not been gentle. He had given me a regular bum's rush out the door.

In fact, I was lucky he hadn't torn my clothes. As it was, the flap on one of my jacket pockets was askew. I put my hand in the pocket to straighten it.

And felt something.

A small, folded piece of paper.

I pulled it out, unfolded it.

On it was written "12–1."

20

"She was killed between twelve and one."

Richard frowned. "Are you sure?"

"Yes, I am."

"MacAullif tell you that?"

"No."

"Then how do you know?"

"That's not important."

"It may not be important, but it's certainly relevant. How do you know?"

"I can't tell you that."

"Why not?"

"I have a confidential source."

"Bullshit. You're working for me."

"That doesn't matter. If I violate the confidence, my source dries up."

"You're saying if you don't you'll get more?"

"I'm not promising anything. I'm saying it's possible."

"How can you know that?"

I put up my hand. "Richard. Back off. If you took a moment to stop and think, you'd realize I got you what you wanted."

"Yeah, but I can't vet it."

"You don't have to. It's gold."

"Twelve to one?"

"Right."

"That's what it's gonna say in the transcript?"

"No."

"No? Then what *is* it gonna say?"

"It's not gonna say a thing."

"They're gonna leave off the time of death?"

"You got it."

"And how do you know that?"

"*That* information came straight from Sergeant Mac-
Aullif."

"You're kidding. He said they left off the time of death?"

"That's right. And that's just for starters."

"What do you mean?"

"The *reason* they left off the time of death is because we
want it."

"Huh?"

"You sent me to MacAullif to find out the time of death.
The first time. He reported to Wellington. Beef-baby says,
If they're so eager to know the time of death, fuck 'em, they
can't have it. So the word comes down and the lid goes on,
and suddenly the time of death becomes a bigger secret
than the naval code."

"The naval code?"

"Oh. There was this movie, see, where—"

"Never mind. I get the picture. I'm wondering if *you* do."

"What do you mean by that?"

"Remember when you came back from MacAullif the
first time? I was upset that you'd told him too much—
hinted about an alibi—implied we might have one, depending on the time of death?"

"Bullshit, Richard," I said. "Whaddya crabbin' about all
over the place? It's like you gotta win the argument? Look,
if I hadn't done that, we'd have nothing now. As it is, I got

you what you wanted. I brought you the time of death. Whaddya say we take it and go on from there?"

"I don't know if I dare to."

"Why not?"

"Because I don't know if it's true."

"It's true."

"So you say. But I have just your say-so, and I don't know what you're basing it on."

"We're going around in circles."

"Yeah. 'Cause you won't talk."

"I'm talking. You're not listening."

"Yeah," Richard said. "Look. Did you ask MacAullif the time of death again?"

"Yes, I did."

"And?"

"He wouldn't say."

"So you got it somewhere else?"

"That's right."

"Where?"

"Richard, why are you doing this? Why can't you just drop it and let go? Accept this as a given and move on with the case?"

"*What* case?" Richard said. "That's the whole point. What *case?* Don't you see? If the time of death is twelve to one, there *is* no case. We got a solid alibi from twelve to one."

"That's great."

"Yes and no."

"Whaddya mean by that?"

"It's too easy. I don't trust anything that's that pat."

"Huh?"

"It's like they told me twelve to one because that's what I wanted to hear. They gave me exactly what I needed. They couldn't have planned it any better."

"Whaddya mean?"

"The guy's got an airtight alibi till two o'clock. Not one o'clock, two o'clock. So if the time of death was one till two, you could say, hey, there's a little gray area here, it's a close thing, it's not likely, but conceivably the guy could have killed her. But twelve till one it's ironclad. You've got a whole-hour buffer zone. If the alibi stands up, Carbinder walks."

"Which is great."

"No, it's not."

I blinked. Rubbed my head. "Pardon me, but why not?"

"Like I said. It's too pat. It's too perfect. It's like they threw me twelve till one to lull me into a sense of false security. I buy that, I let up on everything else, then I get into court and they jerk the rug out from under me."

"I swear by twelve to one. You have my personal assurance."

"Oh, yeah?" Richard said. "When Anson goes to jail, I'm sure that'll make him feel a lot better."

"That's not gonna happen," I said.

And immediately started having my doubts. Would MacAullif do that to me? Mislead me in that fashion? I couldn't really believe it. But could he put that paper in my pocket, knowing how I'd take it, if it wasn't true?

Nothing can stop the paranoid schizophrenic. My next thought was, had MacAullif really *put* that in my pocket? Or was 12–1 a note I'd put there myself sometime last year to remind me to do something on December first?

I exhaled.

No, it wasn't. It was a note from MacAullif, telling me the time of death. My only problem was Richard's stubborn refusal to accept that. Why was he being such a prick?

"Richard," I said, "I have not been privy to your conversations with Anson Carbinder, or I might be in better shape to understand your present position."

"Position? I don't have a position. I'm trying to formulate a defense for my client."

"Well, you just got one. His wife was killed between twelve and one and he couldn't have done it."

"I don't buy that," Richard said irritably.

And suddenly I understood.

It wasn't that Richard didn't trust me or MacAullif or the whole situation. Richard didn't buy it because Richard didn't *want* to buy it. Richard didn't *want* Anson Carbinder to have a legitimate alibi. Richard was living his lifelong dream, playing Perry Mason, and, damn it, Richard wanted to go to court.

Richard's attitude toward me was finally clear. He wasn't pissed off about what I told MacAullif. In fact, he couldn't have cared less. No, this was a simple case of shooting the messenger. In telling him Anson Carbinder had an ironclad alibi, I had become the bearer of bad news.

I was out of there half an hour later with instructions to shore up the discrepancy between Sam Kestin's and Tim Hendricks's testimony, to make sure Anson Carbinder's alibi was airtight.

At least, that's what I'd been *told* to do.

But I had a feeling Richard would have been much happier to have me break it down.

21

Sam Kestin was properly awed.

"Arrested?"

"I'm afraid so."

The banker frowned and shook his head.

I glanced over my shoulder and encountered smiles. Sam Kestin was seated at his desk, and the people I'd barged in front of to see him had taken his head shake to mean I'd just been turned down for a loan.

"Shocking thing," Kestin said.

"Yes, it is," I agreed. "But not unexpected. This is what we've been preparing for from the beginning."

"Right. So what's being done? Is Anson in jail?"

"For the time being. We're trying to arrange bail."

"What's the evidence against him?"

"We don't know. We haven't got the grand jury transcript yet."

"He's been indicted by the grand jury?"

"That's right."

"That looks bad."

"Yes and no."

"What does that mean?"

"An indictment isn't proof of guilt."

"Yeah, yeah, he's innocent until proven guilty," Kestin said impatiently. "Even so, it's bad news."

"Granted. What I meant was, an indictment doesn't necessarily mean anything because they're so easy to get."

Kestin frowned. "I beg your pardon?"

"The defense isn't there at a grand jury hearing. The prosecutor is the only one putting on evidence, and he tells the grand jurors only what he wants them to hear."

"Fine," Kestin said. "You can soft-pedal all you want, but the fact is, he's indicted for murder. Which is terrible. It's bad enough the guy loses his wife, then he has to go through this."

"Exactly," I said. "Which is why we have to get him off."

Kestin took that as a subtle rebuke. "Of course," he said. "What can I do to help?"

"Since it appears we are going to trial, I need to nail down your testimony."

"You got it. But I think I already gave you everything. I don't know what else there is to add."

"If you wouldn't mind going over it again, there are one or two points I'd like to clear up."

"Such as?"

I opened my notebook. "Okay. With regard to the big high/low hand—you say you could have gone low with a nine but went high with three eights?"

"Because of what Anson had on board. Sure." He looked at me. "Wouldn't you?"

"Probably," I said. "But we're not that concerned with the mechanics as with the *time* of the hand."

"The time?"

"Yes. As you'll recall, you told me the hand took place sometime around one o'clock."

"Well, that's just an approximation."

"Would that be an accurate one?"

"Why do you ask?"

"You also told me Tim Hendricks went home at midnight."

"Yes, he always does. But—" Sam Kestin broke off. Looked at me. "Was Hendricks in the hand?"

"You tell me."

Kestin frowned. "Yes, I believe he was."

"Are you sure?"

"No, I'm *not* sure. I'm trying to remember. It hadn't occurred to me. But when you pointed it out to me . . ."

"I didn't point it out to you."

Kestin smiled. "Don't be silly. You asked about the hand and pointed out Tim Hendricks left at midnight." He gestured around him. "One doesn't rise to this position without being able to make simple deductions."

"I'm sure one doesn't," I said. "But with regard to the hand."

"What about it?"

"Do you remember Tim Hendricks being in it? I'm talking now only about what you *remember*—not the fact that you *deduce* he was."

"I don't specifically remember him being in the hand. But then I don't remember him *not* being in the hand, either. I know that sounds stupid—I mean, I don't have a specific knowledge of him not being there."

"I understand. In view of that fact, I wonder if it's possible the hand could have taken place earlier than one o'clock?"

"Hell, yes. I told you, one o'clock was always an approximation. If Hendricks was in the hand, it had to take place before midnight. That's a given. It doesn't matter when I *think* it was, it matters when it *was.*"

"Right. So the hand might have taken place as early as eleven-thirty?"

"Absolutely. Hey, I'm glad you brought this up. Don't worry. If you put me on the stand, I won't blow it with the

time element. You won't find me up there stubbornly insisting the hand was at one."

"I'm glad to hear it. It's the type of thing the prosecutor'd pounce on and play up."

"Yeah, well, don't worry about it. So, was there anything
else?"

"Actually, yes." I referred to my notebook again. "I believe you mentioned this was a particularly big pot, even
though Anson had bumped half the people out."

"Did I say that?"

"I made a note."

"Then I must have said it. Is there a problem there?"

"It's just that practically everyone I talked to remembers
being in the hand."

"Well, they ought to know," Kestin said. "Once more,
my viewpoint is colored by events. You have to understand,
I threw half that pot away by making a wrong choice.
That's what I remember. Anson rolling over the full house.
And me, shooting myself in the head."

"I see. So when you say Anson had bumped half the people out? . . ."

Sam Kestin grimaced. "I'm generalizing. I know. I
shouldn't generalize. On the stand I'll watch it, and tell
only what I know."

"That would be best."

"No kidding. So, telling me—assuming we do a good
job and don't blow it—do we get Anson off?"

"I sure hope so."

"Hope so? Don't you know the time element?"

"So far the cops haven't released the time of death."

He stared at me. "You're kidding. You mean all this may
be worthless? The cops may be able to show he could have
killed her when he got home?"

I put up my hand. "Let's not jump to conclusions. At the
moment, we just don't know."

Sam Kestin scowled, which wrinkled up his pudgy face. It was like being glared at by a malevolent prune. "Well, what *do* you know?" he demanded.

I almost laughed. It wasn't just the way he looked. But the idea sprang to mind of what the people waiting to see him must have thought. Like the guy had loaned me a million bucks and I'd just admitted my collateral was phony.

I controlled myself, shook my head. "Frankly, Mr. Kestin, not a whole hell of a lot."

22.

"Shit."

I had hoped for more than that. I had been sitting in a chair in Richard Rosenberg's office for over an hour watching him read the grand jury transcript. No, he was not reading it out loud—then I would have known what it said and would not have been so disappointed by his one-word reaction.

"What's the matter?" I said.

Richard pointed at the transcript on his desk. "You should read this."

"Fine. Let's have it."

"Not *now*," Richard said. "I don't want to sit here and watch you read."

I knew the feeling. "Well, when did you mean?"

"Actually, I didn't. That was a figure of speech. You don't need to read it. I can tell you what you need to know."

I took a breath. The second-class-citizen counts were piling up. I don't need to talk to the client. I don't need to read the transcript.

"Fine," I said. "What do I need to know?"

"First off, they don't pin down the time of death."

"I told you they wouldn't."

"I know. But just because a cop tells you something

doesn't make it true. Anyway, now it's verified. No time of death."

"How can they do that?"

"Perfectly easy. They say the early-morning hours of October thirteenth."

"How can they get away with that?"

"Who's to say them nay? They can get away with anything they want."

"Right. I forgot. I mean, I didn't *forget*. It's just always hard to believe."

"Right. Anyway, no time of death."

"So what are you going to do?"

"Well, I could piss and moan and raise a stink and get them to divulge it, but I'm much happier to just let it go. As long as we're sure it's twelve to one? . . ." Richard gave me a glance.

"It's gold," I said.

"Then let that be their surprise, and let the poker game be mine. We got 'em there." He looked at the transcript. "And then the rest of it doesn't hurt so bad."

"The rest of what?"

"Well, the big stumbling block is Connie Maynard."

"What about her?"

"You met her."

"That I did."

"Then you know. The woman is sex on wheels. Now, I can lash down her tits and dress her up as a frump, but it isn't gonna fool anyone." Richard picked something up from his desk. "Not when the prosecutor can confront her with this."

"What's that?" I said.

"This?" Richard said. "Well, it seems Miss Maynard has worked as a photographic model. Not pornography, per se, but nude pinup art. Here, get a load of this."

I got up, went over to Richard's desk, and accepted what

proved to be an eight-by-ten color glossy photo of Connie Maynard. The woman had a dazzling smile. She also had large breasts with rather pointed nipples.

I handed the photo back to Richard. "The grand jury saw this?"

"That they did."

"Think you can keep it out of the trial?"

"I could try. The problem is, I lose more points than I win."

"What do you mean?"

Richard grimaced. "Don't be a schmuck. If you're sitting on that jury, and the prosecutor tries to show you that picture, how pleased are you going to be if I stop him?"

"I see your point."

"So there you are. The jury either sees the tits, or I'm the bad guy keeps 'em out. Either way I lose."

"What about the women on the jury?"

"They're the worst. They take one look at this and say the bastard killed his wife."

"Right. Aside from the photo, what have they got?"

"Largely insinuation and innuendo. They got the testimony from her doorman that Anson was a frequent visitor." Richard shrugged. "Big deal. What's it prove? Of course, you throw in that photo and they don't have to prove a thing. The jury's already sold. Anyway, that's the story on the babe."

"And what's the *real* story on the babe?"

"I beg your pardon?"

"That's the prosecution's smear. The insinuation and innuendo. So what's the truth?"

Richard gave me a look. "Stanley, what does it matter? The guy's not on trial for getting laid. He's on trial for killing his wife. Does it matter if he actually planked this broad—assuming he's innocent, I mean?"

"There you put your finger on it, Richard."

"What?"

"Assuming he's innocent. Tell me, is he innocent?"

"We've been over this before."

"Yeah, but I didn't get a satisfactory answer."

"Oh, yeah? Didn't I tell you he was innocent?"

"Yes, you did."

"That isn't satisfactory?"

"Not at all."

"Why not?"

"You're his lawyer. Of course you say that."

Richard grimaced. "You're a real pain in the ass."

"Why?"

"Asking me if he's innocent."

"It's a natural question."

"Which you've already asked. And I've already answered. Case closed. But here you are, asking me again. Do you know *why?*"

"Because I wanna know."

"Yeah. But why do you wanna know?"

"Do you have a point, Richard?"

"Yes, I do."

"What?"

"I'll tell you why you wanna know." Richard pointed. "Because of the damn photo. I show you the photo, you look at the tits, you say, Jesus Christ, he killed his wife. You're just like the goddamned jury." Richard snapped his fingers. "It prejudiced you just like that."

"Oh, come on."

Richard put up his hand. "Hey. I'm not pissed off at you. I'm pissed off at the situation. Your reaction is a normal reaction. It's the reaction I'm gonna get. Seeing it does not make my day, that's all."

"I don't think I'm prejudiced."

"No, of course not. But think about it." Richard raised one finger. "Anson Carbinder has an ironclad alibi." He pointed at me. "You investigated it. You spoke to all the witnesses. And you're the one who swears the time of death is twelve to one." He shrugged his shoulders, spread his hands. "And you're *still* asking me if he's innocent." He shook his head. "I rest my case."

I frowned. "Shit."

Richard nodded. "Yeah. So, believe me, the picture is damaging. In spite of anything else."

"Uh-huh," I said. But very grudgingly. I was not at all convinced that seeing the photo had prejudiced me into thinking Anson Carbinder had killed his wife. "So what else is there?"

Richard cocked his head. "After your reaction to the picture, I hate to tell you."

"Oh?"

"He bought insurance."

I blinked. "On his wife?"

"That's the ticket."

"He bought insurance on his wife?"

"Want me to say it again?"

"How much insurance?"

"Half a million dollars."

"Double indemnity?"

Richard grimaced. "See, there's the whole problem. Everyone knows the movie. All you have to do is say *double indemnity* everyone goes off the deep end."

"I'm not going off the deep end, Richard, but would you mind telling me when he bought this insurance?"

"Three months ago."

"Jesus Christ."

"See what I mean? If you didn't like the picture, you gotta love this."

"How does Anson explain it?"

Richard waggled his hand. "Well, there we have a little problem."

"Oh?"

"It was Connie's idea."

"What?"

"Yeah, I know. But there you are. According to Anson, Connie was afraid his wife would find out about their affair and cut him out of her will—she had all the money, by the way."

"This gets better and better."

"Doesn't it? So Connie figured he should protect against that happening by insuring her life."

"That's his story?"

"Yes, it is. You can see why I'm not too eager to have him tell it."

"Good lord."

"But again, it's beside the point. If the alibi holds, there's no case."

"Uh-huh," I said. "So what else have they got?"

"Actually, not that much. He had blood on his hands. As it happens, there's no way he *wouldn't* have had blood on his hands. But that doesn't matter. It's a catch phrase, for Christ's sake—blood on his hands. A jury hears that, and it's as bad as the picture or the insurance. Blood on his hands. Guilty of murder."

"Uh-huh," I said. "We knew that anyway. What else?"

"It's his knife."

"Huh?"

"Or *her* knife. Anyway, it's *their* knife. It was from the kitchen. Whether he ever used the damn thing or not, that's enough to make it his possession."

"Fingerprints?"

"None."

"Does that mean there weren't any, or they just didn't mention 'em?"

"No, no. There weren't any. They're not going to fuck around with that. It's one thing to be somewhat vague about the time of death—that could be either incompetence or an oversight. But to withhold the fact that his prints were on the knife—that would be prosecutorial misconduct. I doubt if Beef Wellington would stoop to that."

"How'd he kill her without leaving his prints on the knife?"

"He could have worn gloves."

"Then how did he get blood on his hands?"

"Good point. Unfortunately, there are a lot of ways that could have happened."

"Like what?"

"Well, if he wore gloves, he's gotta get rid of them before the cops come. He kills her, leaves the knife on the floor, and ditches the gloves. Then he has to set the scene of having come home, slipped into bed in the dark, and then discovering she was dead. According to his story, he knew something was wrong because he touched the blood. So he'd have to have blood on his hands, even if he killed her wearing gloves."

I shook my head. "No good."

"What do you mean, no good?"

"He killed her and got rid of the gloves? How? Where? Where's the gloves? If there were a pair of bloody gloves in the apartment, the cops would have found them. So what did he do with them? Did he incinerate them? Is there a furnace in the basement? Or did he run out and stash 'em somewhere at two in the morning? I would find that theory pretty hard to sell."

"I agree. Unfortunately, there's others."

"Oh?"

"Sure. Theory number two—he didn't wear gloves. He killed her, then he wiped the prints off the knife. And if he got blood on his hands, so what? He was going to have blood on his hands anyway. He set the stage, called the cops, and there you are."

"Same problem."

"What's that?"

"Where's the bloody handkerchief, rag, or whatever he wiped the knife off with?"

"It might not be bloody."

"Huh?"

"He kills her, the handle of the knife isn't bloody. He wipes it off with a handkerchief, which remains clean. He sticks the handkerchief in his pocket, in his dresser drawer, up his ass, I don't care where—then bloodies his hands and calls the cops."

"That's pretty thin."

Richard put up his hands. "Hey, don't take it personally, like I'm picking on you. These are perfectly good points and are probably ones I will even advance. You ask me how the prosecutor can argue that he's guilty—well, these are the arguments he'll make. I'm very happy to hear they're not strong."

"Uh-huh. Anything else?"

"Not really. Standard shit. Testimony of the cops at the scene."

"Uh-huh. So what you want me to do?"

"Do?"

"Yeah. You want me to run down these witnesses?"

Richard looked at me in surprise. "What on earth for? It's all simple, straightforward stuff. The guy's got a terrific alibi, so what's the big deal? The only problem now is getting him out on bail."

"How's that coming?"

"The hearing's this afternoon. No problem there. He's rich enough. If the judge can set it, he can make it. Then we just wait for the trial."

"How long is that?"

"Not long. Maybe a couple of months."

"You're kidding."

"Not at all. And that's if we're lucky. But it's no real problem if we're granted bail."

"Uh-huh. So you'll have him out by this afternoon?"

"I certainly hope so."

"You want me to talk to him then?"

Richard looked at me again. "What on earth for?"

"Well, I've interviewed all the witnesses. What do you want me to do?"

"Oh, right," Richard said. "I'm sorry. I'm so wrapped up in this, I've been thinking just of myself. You must forgive me. It's my first murder. I'm a little preoccupied."

Richard snatched up the phone. "Wendy? As of right now, start giving Stanley cases. He's back on the clock."

23

And just like that it was over. My new career as a special investigator for the defense team in a murder trial.

Done.

Over.

Finished.

And just in case there was any doubt in my mind, it turned out Wendy had a case for me right off the bat. So, not an hour later, there I was in Harlem in a fourth-floor walkup signing up the most enormous black woman you ever did see.

The woman, one Serita Jones, had fallen and broken her arm. She blamed uneven pavement. That might well have been. On the other hand, the fact that she had fallen was not nearly as surprising as the fact that she had ever been able to stand up at all.

Do I sound cruel, callous, and cynical? I suppose so. It was just such a comedown from a murder to a trip-and-fall. I had to keep reminding myself, schmuck, this is important to this woman. She's a client too, she needs your help, and it's your job to fight for her just as you would for Anson Carbinder.

You know how hard that was to buy? Well, just the fact I had to keep reminding myself of it would be a good indication.

So would the fact I didn't believe her.

She came downstairs—and what an adventure *that* was—took me outside, and showed me some broken sidewalk.

"Uh-huh," she said. "Tha's the place. Swear to god." Then, rolling her eyes, said, "Tha's the sidewalk. Tha's the one tha' made me fall. I swear it all day long. All night long. Tha' one right there. Uh-huh. Tha's the one."

Was it just overkill? Was it just a case of, methinks the lady doth protest too much? Or was it just me being pissed off at being back on the game?

Whatever the reason, my personal opinion was, Serita Jones didn't deserve one lousy cent. And the only thing that made her case bearable was the fact that I was getting twenty bucks an hour handling it.

Yeah.

Twenty bucks an hour.

And seventy-five cents a mile.

Hey.

Not bad.

As I drove to my next case in Jamaica, Queens, the odometer suddenly looked like a taxi meter clicking over.

Seventy-five cents a mile. Seven-fifty for ten. A fifteen-dollar bonus on top of my twenty-mile sign-up.

So, a twenty-mile, three-hour sign-up that had netted me thirty-six dollars at ten bucks an hour and thirty cents a mile, now pulled in a whopping seventy-five.

A thirty-nine dollar increase.

Son of a bitch.

And I must confess, most of the time that I was listening to Leon Roustabout's tale of woe—regarding his fractured hip and the causes thereof, which, if the truth be known, I don't really remember—I was mentally doing the math (add and subtract, compare and contrast) and figuring out under the new rate schedule just what the gentlemen was worth to me.

I did that all day long. And by the time I was driving down the West Side Highway, coming home from my last assignment in Yonkers, I had it all worked out.

I had put in an eight-hour day. At twenty bucks an hour, that's a hundred and sixty bucks. Forty less than the two hundred a day I'd been making.

But I'd gone over sixty miles. At seventy-five cents a mile, that's forty-five dollars.

So I'd take home two hundred and five. As opposed to the two hundred plus expenses I was making on the Carbinder case. Well, my expenses there were nil, there was no mileage to speak of, so, all in all, it was much the same thing.

With that thought to cheer me, I was not at all upset when my beeper went off as I turned off the highway onto Ninety-sixth Street. If Wendy/Janet had a case for tomorrow at twenty bucks an hour and seventy-five cents a mile, that was just fine with me. I pulled up next to a pay phone and called the office.

Only, Wendy/Janet didn't give me a case.

She put me on hold.

Moments later, Richard's voice came on the line.

"Get in here."

24.

I had expected to find Anson Carbinder in Richard Rosenberg's office, so the man who was actually sitting there was a bit of a surprise. He was one of the witnesses I had interrogated in the case. If I were better at names and faces, I could tell you which witness. But I'm not, and sudden confrontations with people I don't expect to see fluster me to begin with. So, at first glance, the best I could tell was that he was one of the two nervous, insecure, ineffectual ones. But what their names were, and which of the two he happened to be, totally escaped me.

Fortunately, Richard said, "Come in, Stanley. I believe you know Phil Janson. Mr. Janson, is this the man you were talking about?"

"Yes, of course. He came and questioned me."

"He's the one who gave you my card?"

"That's right."

"Well, I'm certainly glad you saw fit to call me."

"I didn't know what else to do."

"You did just right."

"Is this going to take much longer? I have an audition to go to."

Ah. That completed the picture for me. The name Phil Janson had certainly been a valuable clue. But, as I say, I'm not that good with names. But the fact he had an audition to go to allowed me to identify him as an actor, making him the last witness I had interrogated. The one with the Greenwich Village apartment. The one who was so nervous he couldn't remember what hand he was holding when Anson won the big pot. As opposed to the other nervous one, the Birdman of Central Park South, who *could* remember what hand he was holding, though I could not remember it now.

Anyway, nervous actor Phil Janson seemed even more nervous than usual. It struck me that his desire to leave for an audition might be based on the more fundamental desire just to get away, period.

Having deduced all that, I still had no idea what he was doing there.

"Now, Mr. Janson," Richard said. "Why don't you tell Stanley what you just told me."

"Again?"

"I'd like him to hear it from you."

"Did I do something wrong?"

"Absolutely not, Mr. Janson. *You* did exactly right."

Oh-oh.

From the stress on the word *you,* and the look on Richard's face, I had a feeling I was in deep shit. Why, I had no idea. But I assumed I had missed something in my questioning of Mr. Janson. Something the gentleman had recollected and decided to call Richard about. What that could be, I had absolutely no idea. But that had to be it.

Wrong again.

Phil Janson said, "Like I said, it was just this afternoon. I was at home preparing for the audition. Working on my scene, you know. Actually, I was doing it in front of the mirror. That's sometimes good, sometimes bad. I mean, you catch things you want to fix, sure. But your concentration's divided. So—"

"That's really interesting, Mr. Janson," Richard said. "Can you tell him what happened?"

"Oh. Sorry." Janson, who had actually been looking at me during his explanation of his rehearsal process, now seemed to find his fingernails fascinating. He began picking furiously at a cuticle. "Well, anyway, I was rehearsing and there was a knock at the door. Which shouldn't happen. There's a buzzer downstairs, and it hadn't rung. Sure, sometimes people leave the front door ajar. But they shouldn't. There's even a sign on the door about it. I'm sure none of the tenants do. But they have visitors. And the guy will go out and forget. And—"

"Mr. Janson."

"Yeah. Sorry," Janson said. He continued to attack his cuticle. "Anyway, there's a knock on the door. Frankly, I don't want to answer, because you never know who it might be. But I got a peephole, so I'm gonna look out, just in case it's my upstairs neighbor. Even though he would call first, because he knows I don't like that. Anyway, I'm going to the door to look out the peephole, I hear, 'Open up. Police.'"

Phil Janson looked up at me with a look that said, What did I do? Then returned to working on his fingernails. "So I look out the peephole and there's a big, beefy guy standing there. But he's not in uniform, so I don't open up. Then he holds up a badge. Well, even so, I'm not convinced, because I'm in the theater, and I know you can get a fake badge. Besides, what do I know what a real badge looks like. Then he says, 'Open up, Mr. Janson, it's about the Anson Carbinder case.'"

"Tell him what the cop said after you let him in," Richard prompted.

"Yeah," Janson said. "Well, I let him in, because if he knew about that he was probably a cop, right? So I let him in, but once he's in, it occurred to me I don't want to speak to him. And you know the first thing he says? He says, 'Where were you on the night of October twelfth?' "

Janson looked up from his fingers again. "Well, that's it. That's that night. That's when it happened. Anson's wife. So I know, this is it. If I tell him where I was, he's gonna want to know was Anson there. And when, and when did he leave, and who else was there, and the whole bit. So I tell him I'm not sure I'm supposed to talk to him, I want to call my lawyer."

"Which is just what you should have done," Richard said. "Tell him what the cop said then."

"Well, the cop said, 'Why do you need a lawyer if you're just a witness?' And he tried to talk me out of it, but I said no and I called you and you told me to come in."

"And what did the cop do then?"

"He gave me his card."

"Show him the card."

"Oh, where did I put it. Yeah, here it is. Right here." Phil Janson dug the card out of his pocket, held it up, and pointed. "Sergeant William MacAullif."

25.

"So," Richard demanded, after Phil Janson had gratefully scuttled out, closing the office door.

I flopped into the chair Janson had vacated, took a breath, and looked up at Richard. "I don't think I like this."

"*You* don't like this? How do you think *I* feel? So what's the story?"

"What story? You know as much as I do."

"Oh? Would you mind telling me how Sergeant MacAullif got a line on this witness?"

"I have no idea."

"Oh, no? What about your little chats with the sergeant? When you implied Anson might have an alibi? Hinted around about several witnesses?"

"I never said who they were."

"Oh, yeah? Are you telling me, if MacAullif got a line on this witness, it wasn't through you?"

"That's what I'm telling you."

"You sure of that?"

"Yes, I'm sure."

"Then how did he find him?"

"I have no idea."

"Oh, yeah? Well, I do."

"Oh, really? Then why don't you fill me in?"

"All right, I will. To begin with, this witness, Phil Janson—was he one of the first witnesses you talked to or one of the last?"

"One of the last. In fact, he *was* the last."

"Which means you talked to him *after* you talked to MacAullif?"

"Huh?"

"When you called on this witness—that was after the first time you talked to MacAullif about the case? After you hinted around about a possible alibi?"

"Yeah. So?"

"You watch your backside?"

"Are you saying I was followed?"

"Were you?"

"How the hell should I know?"

"I would expect a private detective to be able to spot a tail."

I looked at him. "Richard, this is stupid. You're pissed off because MacAullif found this witness, but it's got nothing to do with me."

"Oh, yeah. You think the cops would have found him if you hadn't talked to MacAullif?"

"You *sent* me to MacAullif."

"To get information, not to give it."

"We've been through this before."

"Yes, we have. At the time, you didn't think it could possibly make any difference. I trust that you know better now."

"Richard, this is childish."

"Childish? Stanley, this is not a game. This is a murder case."

"I'm aware of that."

"Are you? Then you realize how important it is to know if you were followed to this witness."

"I don't think I was."

"Oh, no? And why not? Are you telling me you *could* have spotted a tail?"

"No, I'm not. But I still don't think so. After all, this is just one guy. He's not the only witness I talked to after I spoke to MacAullif."

"Are you sure?"

"Absolutely. You pulled me in, sent me to MacAullif. I'd only spoken to two or three guys."

"Two *or* three?"

"That's off the top of my head. You want it exactly?"

"It would help."

I pulled my notebook out of my jacket pocket, found the page. "I covered three witnesses before you pulled me in. Then I saw MacAullif. I covered the rest of the witnesses the next day."

"How many was that?"

"Three. There were six in the game. Seven, counting Anson."

"You saw three before MacAullif and three after? And this Phil Janson was the last one?"

I looked in my notebook again. "Actually, I'm wrong about that. He was next to last. The last was Tim Hendricks. He was last because he was the least important because he went home at twelve o'clock.

"Uh-huh."

"I also saw Barry Brown, but I saw him before Phil Janson. I saw them in that order. Barry Brown, Phil Janson, Tim Hendricks. Phil Janson was right in the middle. Which is even better. If the cops were following me, there's no way they'd just find him. They'd get the other guys too."

"Let's see if they did."

"Huh?"

"You got the numbers there? Let's call them and see if they did."

"Wouldn't they call in?"

"Who knows?" Richard jerked his thumb. "This guy, he's a pantywaist. The cops lean on him he's got two choices, talk or yell for his mother. As it happens, we lucked out. But these other guys, who knows?"

"I don't think they'd talk."

"You'll pardon me if I'd like more than your assurances. You got their numbers there?"

"Yeah."

"Then let's give 'em a try. Who was the last guy you spoke to?"

"Tim Hendricks."

"Fine. Let's try him."

I checked the notebook. "Actually, that would be tough."

"Oh?"

"You'll never get him. He's on the floor of the stock exchange."

"Oh. Well, what about the other one?"

"That would be Barry Brown. Him you could get."

"Oh? What's he do?"

"Runs an ad agency."

"Got his number?"

"Yeah."

I gave Richard the number and he punched it into the phone. "Barry Brown, please. This is Richard Rosenberg." There was a pause, then Richard said, "Tell him it's Anson's lawyer and it's urgent." Moments later, "Barry Brown, this is Richard Rosenberg. I'm Anson Carbinder's lawyer. You've already spoken with my investigator, Stanley Hastings, concerning the poker game . . . Yes, that's right. The reason I'm calling is to ask if anyone *else* has contacted you concerning the game. In particular, the police or the district attorney's office . . . They haven't? You sure about that? . . .

Well, if they do, I believe my investigator gave you my card. Do you have it? . . . That's right. Richard Rosenberg. Now, listen, the first hint of a police officer, anyone sniffing around—would you give me a call? Believe me, you'd be doing Anson a big favor . . . Thanks a lot. I appreciate it."

Richard hung up the phone. "Nice guy."

Of course, he'd say that. Barry Brown had struck me as a prick. But I wasn't about to start another argument.

"So that's the story," Richard said. "If the guy's telling the truth, the cops haven't found him. Of course, you saw him *before* Phil Janson."

"But *after* MacAullif," I pointed out. "So if I were being followed, I'd have led the cops to him first. I didn't, which should rule out that theory."

"Unless."

"Unless what?"

"Unless the cops were working backwards and hadn't gotten to him yet."

"In which case they'd have started with Tim Hendricks."

"Whom we can't reach."

"Right. So maybe they couldn't, either. So they bypass him for Janson. That makes sense."

"Great," I said. "You happen to have any logical scenarios that *aren't* my fault?"

"Can't think of one. Can you?"

"How about an anonymous tip?"

"From whom?"

"I have no idea."

"Me, either. And it makes no sense."

"Makes as much sense as the cops follow me selectively to this one guy."

"We don't know that they did that."

"We sure don't."

"I mean, we don't know that it was selective. We still

haven't talked to what's-his-name—the guy on the stock exchange. You sure he's there now?"

"I should think so."

"Well, you got his number? Let's try."

Richard called Tim Hendricks's number, got an answering machine, left a message for him to call in.

When Richard hung up the phone, I said, "You want me to go down to the stock exchange, try to find him?"

Richard cocked his head. "Just in case you *haven't* led the cops to him yet?"

"That's not funny."

"No, it isn't."

"You think the cops are following me right now?"

"If they are, they're going to learn an awful lot about my negligence business."

"Are you telling me I'm off the case?"

"Don't be silly. There's no case to be on. Anson's out on bail and there's nothing to do until the trial."

"You got him out on bail?"

"Oh, sure. Nothing to it. The guy's got money, why should he stay in jail?"

"It's a good thing you're not running for public office."

"Don't be a schmuck. If the rich couldn't buy what they want, what would be the point of having all that money?"

"Yeah, fine," I said. "But the bottom line is I'm off the case."

"Stanley, you're not listening. This is not like on TV—they've only got an hour, so they gotta go right to court. This case won't go to trial for months. In the meantime, there's nothing to do. If the cops hadn't found that witness, I wouldn't be giving it a second thought."

I exhaled. "So you really just called me in here to bawl me out."

Richard gave me a look. "Stanley, you're taking this personally. The cops found this witness. I called you in here to see if we could come up with any logical way that might have happened. It was a long shot at best, but one worth taking."

"But—"

Richard put up his hand. "Stanley, you worry too much. Maybe you led the cops to this guy, maybe not. The point is, there's no way to find out."

Oh, yeah?

26

"Are you following me?"

MacAullif frowned. "What the hell are you talking about?"

"I want to know if you're following me."

"You're asking me on the theory that if I am I'll tell you?"

"That's right."

"Then I'm not following you."

"Son of a bitch."

"And talk about not following you, I mean, I'm not *following* you. What the fuck are you talking about?"

"Am I under surveillance? Am I being tailed? Are you, or anyone in your employ, following me around the city to see where I'll go. More to the point, have I *been* under surveillance at any time since this case began?"

"What case?"

"Don't piss me off, MacAullif, I'm in a very bad mood. The Anson Carbinder case. Have I been under police surveillance, either formal or informal, at any point in time since Anson Carbinder's wife was murdered? Is that specific enough for you? Does that pin it down?"

MacAullif frowned, squinted at me. "What the hell got into you?"

"What's the matter, can't answer the question?"

"I can, but it's not gonna help."

"Why not?"

"It's the policy of the department to deny police surveillance. I would tell you you weren't being followed whether you were or not."

I stared at him. "That's practically a confirmation."

"Not at all."

"Then why do you say it?"

"Why do I say it?" MacAullif got up from his chair, walked around, and sat on the front of his desk. "I say it because you're being a pain in the ass. I'm the investigating officer in the Anson Carbinder case. You're on the other side, but you're in my office almost every day. I've given you what I can, which may not be squat, but you're lucky you're not thrown out on your ear. But that's not enough. You're in here with a chip on your shoulder, wanting to know if I'm abusing our friendship—is that how you look at it?—by following you to see what you do?"

"And you know why."

"And I know why? What is that, some subtle trick to get me to break down and admit I'm doing it?"

"No, it's just a statement of fact."

"Good. State me a fact, why don't you, because as far as I'm concerned we're just talking around in circles."

"We're talking in circles because you won't give me a straight answer."

"Straight answer about what? I told you our policy about surveillance, and I still have no idea why you want to know." MacAullif snorted. " 'And you know why,' indeed."

"All right, I'll tell you why. Richard Rosenberg just chewed me out for tipping you off to a witness."

"What witness?"

"The one I supposedly led you to."

"Led me to?"

"Right. And that's the generous assessment. That's assuming I didn't just *tell* you about him."

"Tell me about who?"

"You know who. You gave him your fucking business card."

"Ah," MacAullif said. "I would assume you were referring to Phil Janson. The rather nervous young gentleman who wouldn't give me the time of day."

"Yeah, *that* Phil Janson. You wanna tell me how you got a line on him?"

"You know I can't do that."

"Was it by following me?"

"Would that have led to him?" MacAullif shrugged. "Obviously it would, or you wouldn't be asking the question. So, Janson *is* a witness, huh?"

Shit. Here it was, kick-myself-in-the-head time again. All my calling on MacAullif had done was to verify the fact Phil Janson was a witness, something the nervous young gentleman hadn't done himself.

But it was too late to worry about that now.

"Yeah, he's a witness," I said. "Didn't you get a hint when he refused to talk to you and called Richard Rosenberg?"

"That was a bit of a tip-off."

"Did he do it in front of you?"

"Actually, he did."

"You knew he called Rosenberg."

"Yeah. What's the big deal?"

"The big deal is, when I have to report *this* conversation I won't get beat up for telling you the guy called Rosenberg. That's something you already knew."

"And no big secret, either," MacAullif said. "Janson could have told you that."

"Yeah, but I'm not talking to Janson," I said. "I don't

know who I'm talking to anymore. Rosenberg's so pissed off at me for what I supposedly told you."

"That's hardly fair."

"You're telling me? Hey, why don't you call up Rosenberg and tell him?"

"Yeah, that'd go over big," MacAullif said. "Like getting a note from your mother for fucking up your homework. I could really see Rosenberg buying that."

"Good. Then you see my problem. Then you see how fucking frustrating this is."

MacAullif nodded. "I'll buy that."

"But you can't see your way clear to telling me if I'm being followed."

"Don't be a jerk. If you were being followed, you'd know it."

"In the past, that has not proven to be true."

"Right. So you learn from it. You become more cautious."

"Did you follow me to Janson, yes or no?"

"Grow up. I can't tell you how we found Janson."

"Can you tell me how you *didn't* find Janson?"

"Don't be an asshole."

"Me? You're the one playing word games."

MacAullif sighed, walked around, and sat down at his desk again. He leaned back in his chair, cocked his head. "Look. Suppose I told you I *didn't* follow you to Janson. You go to Rosenberg, you tell him that, you think that satisfies him? You think he's gonna believe me? You think that's the end of it?"

"I'd believe you."

"Big fucking deal. Whaddya after here? You trying to make things right with Rosenberg, or you trying to ease your conscience? Think about it. If you don't give a shit about what Rosenberg thinks, then you're in here because you feel bad that you might have led me to a witness and you wanna hear me say it isn't so. Well, get real. Every murder case doesn't happen to be a moral gymnasium built expressly for the purpose of testing your character."

"Son of a bitch."

"What?"

"That's practically a line from *Man and Superman.*"

"What's that?"

"You ever read Shaw?"

"Who?"

"Never mind. You wanna tell me what's so important about this witness?"

"You wanna tell *me?"*

"You know I can't."

"Same here. Why don't you do us both a big favor and leave me the fuck alone."

I sighed, shook my head. "You know what's unfair?"

"What?"

"It was Rosenberg sent me here in the first place."

"I know that. You know what else I know? I know you hinted around about Carbinder having an alibi. I know this guy Janson's probably one of the alibi witnesses." MacAullif shook his head. "That's the problem with this fucking case. If Carbinder's got a real alibi, he should have just come out with it. But Rosenberg's so hot to play defense attorney he's pulling all this cloak-and-dagger shit. And to what end? So he can hold the guy up for a big fee? So he can have fun in court? I tell you, just between you and me, it's a bad move. Wellington is pissed off, and Wellington is gonna take this one to the limit. You get in a situation where Carbinder wants to cop a plea, it's gonna be Katey, bar the door."

"I can imagine."

"Can you? Then imagine this. I don't like being in the middle on this one anymore than you do. But that's the way things are. Now, the trial is months away. In the meantime, as far as I'm concerned, this case is over. I'm into other things. If you weren't here, I'd be doing them now. Just in case you'd like to take that as a hint."

"You're through investigating the case?"

"Didn't I just say that?"

"Then why'd you look up this guy Janson?"

MacAullif sighed. "I've told you all I can. Why don't you get the fuck out of here?"

"Were you investigating the case yesterday?"

"Yesterday?"

"Yeah."

"Why do you wanna know?"

"Well, you say you wrapped up the case. And the grand jury indicted Carbinder. I'm just wondering why you would be working on the case after the grand jury indictment."

"Oh, you were wondering that."

"Yeah. Particularly, since you didn't get to Phil Janson till today."

"Well, well, well," MacAullif said. "Look who's made a deduction." He shook his head, said, "Finally."

He shook his head again.

"Maybe you're not as dumb as you look."

27

On the other hand, maybe I am.

Because, whatever MacAullif might think, I wasn't sure exactly what it was I had deduced.

What I *think* it was, was if he had completed his investigation and then got a line to Phil Janson, he certainly didn't get it through me. Because I'd called on Phil Janson *before* the grand jury indictment, and if he'd been following me, I'd have led him to him then. And if he knew about him then, why would he wait to call on him until later?

Unless *that* was the point. That the cops, at Beef Wellington's insistence, had deliberately refrained from running down the alibi witnesses until after the indictment was in.

What would be the point of that, I wasn't sure. But that could be his strategy—don't do anything to rock the boat until the grand jury indicts. Then, once the indictment's in place, start plugging every hole you can.

Could that be it? Was that the master plan?

And *was* there a master plan? Were MacAullif and I, as he had suggested, merely pawns in the game, being pushed out front by opposing counsel as part of some colossal mindfuck?

Or was this just a simple, straightforward murder case, and everyone was making too much of it?

I was not to know. I was not to care. I was not to hear
anything about it for a while.

A good long while.

For the trial, as everyone had said, was months off. And
in the meantime, apparently, there was nothing to be done.

Aside from negligence work. There was a whole moun-
tain of that. Trip-and-falls, hit-and-runs, medical malpractice, and automobile accidents were proceeding at record
pace, Richard Rosenberg's TV ads were steering the victims
to Rosenberg and Stone, and crack investigator Stanley
Hastings was on the job.

At twenty bucks an hour and seventy-five cents a mile.

But, you know . . .

There's nothing quite so disillusioning as getting what
you want.

Doubling my salary had seemed like a dream come true.
Suddenly, a forty-hour week isn't four hundred dollars, it's
eight. I was never hitting forty hours, as usual I was averag-
ing somewhere between thirty and forty. But still, that was
somewhere between six and eight hundred bucks. So at
least I could count on paying off my debts and getting out
from under.

Only it didn't happen.

As the weeks went by, slowly it dawned on me I was no
better off than I was before.

First off, more taxes. The extra money bumped me into a
higher bracket, so not only was I paying more tax because I
was paying tax on more money, but I was paying a higher
percentage of tax right across the board. This was com-
pounded by the fact that I'm self-employed and have to pay
quarterly estimated tax. A call to my tax accountant confirmed how much the estimated withholding would go up.
I hung up the phone with nerveless fingers.

Yeah, yeah, yeah. It was still more money. Don't get me

wrong. Even with the tax and the whole schmear. It was a lot more money than I was making before.

It just disappeared.

Somehow or other, it vanished into the gaping hole of inflation. Aside from taxes, it went for health insurance, Tommie's tuition, rent, Con-Ed, telephone, and the rest of the monthly madness. Not to mention a valiant but seemingly futile attempt to reduce the ever-increasing MasterCard bill.

But that was the bottom line.

For all my raise, we didn't have one whit more money.

And that was just part of it.

The other part was, for all my raise, I was still doing the same old draggy job.

All of which added up to just one thing.

I couldn't wait for the trial.

28

Huge disillusionment.

I'm talking about jury selection.

I had expected to see Richard Rosenberg pull a Perry Mason trick. I expected him to stand up and say, "Your Honor, the defense doesn't care *who* the jurors are, as long as they're willing to be fair. We're willing to accept, sight unseen, the first twelve jurors called into the box."

That would be dramatic, showy, and cause quite a stir. Moreover, it would expedite the selection process, empaneling a jury in a single day. Which might have the added kick of catching Beef Wellington asleep at the switch.

But Richard didn't do that. Instead, he seemed content to slog it out, haggling over each and every body. A tactic, which I knew from my stint on jury duty, which could make the selection process drag on for weeks.

That was a small disillusionment.

The big one was that even if Richard *had* pulled a stunt during jury selection, I wouldn't have seen it.

Because I wasn't there.

I was not, as I had envisioned, sitting next to Richard Rosenberg at the defense table, ready to run out at a moment's notice and bring back whatever valuable information the defense might require.

No, instead I was driving around New York City answering my beeper and signing up accident victims.

I couldn't quite believe it when Richard first told me, but actually he seemed rather surprised. Why would he need my help with jury selection? It was a simple, straightforward process, and why the hell would he want to pay me two hundred bucks a day to watch him do it?

So when the Anson Carbinder case went to court, I wasn't there.

By the end of the first day, I was disappointed that they hadn't gotten a jury.

By the end of the second day, I was somewhat *surprised* that they hadn't gotten a jury.

By the end of the third day, I was beginning to suspect they *had* gotten a jury, but Richard just wasn't telling me.

And so it went, day after day, with me driving around the five boroughs answering my beeper, each time thinking maybe this will be it, and each time getting another accident case.

Until finally Wendy/Janet beeped me to tell me they'd started the trial.

29

Next morning at a quarter to ten I found myself in a crowded courtroom on the fourth floor of the Criminal Court Building at One Hundred Centre Street.

I was somewhat overwhelmed.

There was so much to take in at once. It was like everyone else in the courtroom had a two-and-a-half-week jump on me. I was the new kid on the block, who didn't know the ropes.

First off, I wasn't at the defense table. Richard and Anson Carbinder sat there alone. I could go up and confer with them while court was in recess, but during the actual proceedings I had to sit with the spectators.

And not in the first row, either. That was reserved for the press. They sat there with the tags around their necks, the photo IDs that identified them as members of the media. I sat right behind them, second row, center aisle, so I could slip out quick if Richard needed me during a recess. From there I surveyed the rest of the court.

At the other table, the prosecutor's table, ADA Wellington sat with his young trial deputy. It occurred to me the nickname Beef was apt—Wellington was yet another chunky man, with a large belly poking out over his low-slung pants. He was in such sharp contrast to his young, slim trial deputy, who looked as if he were just out of law school, that I couldn't help wondering why Richard had never commented on his size.

The answer was simple. I had leapt to the wrong conclusion. The fatter, older man was the trial deputy. Beef Wellington was the kid.

On the other hand, the judge was a hundred and five. His name was Judge Blank, and he looked as if he had spent his entire life trying to live it down. The man had the most expressive face I've ever seen. He had a full head of snow-white hair, bushy white eyebrows, craggy features, piercing eyes, and the deepest frown lines ever seen on the face of the earth. It was as if the man had been born scowling. I was intimidated just sitting there as a spectator. How the lawyers felt, I couldn't imagine.

Then there was the jury, the sixteen men and women who had been chosen to hear this case. Twelve regulars and four alternates. I have to tell you, as I sat there looking at them I couldn't help thinking, two and half weeks for this? They were sixteen of the blandest, most ordinary people you'd ever want to see. Half black, half white, half men, half women, your basic instant jury, just add water and stir.

There was one more player in the game. You couldn't miss her. She sat in the second row, behind the defense table. Richard had obviously coached her well and dressed her down, but I doubt if he was fooling anyone. There was no way to make Connie Maynard inconspicuous.

I had just had time to sort all that out, more or less, when court was called to order and away we went.

ADA Wellington rose to his feet, strode out in front of the jury box, bowed, and said, "Ladies and gentlemen of the jury, we expect to prove that Anson Carbinder killed his wife, Barbara Carbinder, by stabbing her with a carving knife."

And suddenly, bang, we were under way.

Wow.

Pretty impressive.

ADA Wellington had opened up with the punch line. It was a short, snappy opening, throwing down the gauntlet and promising a knock-down-drag-out fight. On the whole, an excellent beginning.

It was all downhill from there.

A hour later ADA Wellington was still droning on about what he expected to prove. And not only was *I* having trouble focusing on it, but, from their appearance, at least half the jury were either daydreaming or had actually fallen asleep.

I have to tell you, I was shocked. After the huge buildup from Richard and MacAullif about the young dynamo Beef Wellington, I had expected something better. I had thought this guy was gonna be good.

But he wasn't.

Oh, he was still striding around out there, pointing his finger, shaking his fist, cocky and self-assured.

But nobody gave a flying fuck.

Because he'd been at it for over an hour now, and he was going over the same points again and again.

I couldn't understand it, how he could be that stupid as to let his case slip away from him. He had the jurors in the palm of his hand, and here he was, turning them off. And the longer he talked, the better I felt, because the surer I was he was gonna blow his case. There was no way this guy could win. Carbinder was going to walk out of here a free man.

I glanced over at the defense table, where Anson Carbinder sat with Richard Rosenberg, and I couldn't help thinking, just wait till he gets up to bat.

Big difference.

When Richard finally got his turn, he came striding out, eyes flashing, challenging the entire courtroom. He stopped in midstride, spun around facing the jury, stuck his finger in the air.

"Ladies and gentlemen of the jury," he declaimed, then turned and, with his other hand, pointed straight at ADA Wellington. "I have been listening to that man for over an hour and a half, and I have yet to hear one scintilla of evidence linking my client to the commission of this crime. The prosecutor has certainly shown that the decedent, Barbara Carbinder, was viciously and brutally murdered. On that matter, there is no dispute. What he has *not* shown is that her husband, Anson Carbinder, had anything to do with it. Oh, he tried. I think I counted fourteen times in his opening statement that he mentioned the fact that Anson Carbinder was covered with blood when the police arrived. What he glossed over in that statement is, the *reason* the police arrived is that Anson Carbinder called them and asked them to come.

"Which is not surprising. Having found his wife brutally murdered, it was the natural thing to do.

"And what about the blood on his hands? Well, having found his wife brutally murdered, his first reaction was to see if he could help her. To see if she was still alive. It never crossed his mind, No, no, I shouldn't do that, that might make me a murder suspect. And why should it? It doesn't occur to an innocent man that the police might suspect him. But, no, this man embraced his wife, took her in his arms, tried to see if there was anything he could do.

"Of course there was not. The woman was dead."

Richard paused, looked around. "Indeed, she had been dead for some time." He held up one finger. "As we shall demonstrate when we put on our case.

"And what else does that prosecutor have? Well, the main thing he seemed to harp on is the fact that my client wouldn't talk. You will notice how obliquely he alluded to that fact. That's because, under the law, my client is not required to talk. Nor is he, you, the judge, or anyone else on god's green earth allowed to assume any indication of guilt from the fact that he did not choose to talk.

"However, since it has been brought up, and doubtless will be referred to whenever possible during the course of the trial, I would like to dispose of that matter now. The reason Mr. Carbinder would not talk is that immediately after calling the police, and before they arrived, Mr. Carbinder called me. And, as his attorney, I naturally advised him not to say anything until he had talked to me. I say *naturally* because, not knowing what the facts were, there was no way I could offer him advice. And, until I knew what the facts were, I was certainly not going to allow my client to talk."

Richard turned and bowed ironically to the prosecuting table. "The police and the district attorney's office, in their infinite wisdom, took his silence to be an indication of guilt, and proceeded to build their case from there. Although precisely the type of wrong thinking one would expect from a bureaucracy, it is shocking nonetheless."

I smiled. Good for Richard. For my money, everything he just said was right on, and ADA Beef Wellington and the cops had it coming. There was no doubt about it, Richard Rosenberg had won the opening argument hands down.

Only he didn't stop there.

He went on.

And on.

And on.

As I watched with mounting misgivings, Richard Rosenberg went over the same ground ADA Wellington had, seizing on each minor point and arguing it again and again and again. And, as with Wellington, he gradually lost his audience. By the time the judge interrupted him to say we had to break for lunch, the jurors looked positively numb.

I figured we'd have lunch with Anson Carbinder, that after all this time I'd finally get to talk to the guy, but, no, as soon as court adjourned, Connie Maynard swooped down on him and the two of them, thick as thieves, slipped out of court together, and Richard and I wound up having sandwiches at a small deli near the courthouse.

"So how do you think it's going?" Richard said, as we seated ourselves at a table.

It was not exactly the question I was hoping he would ask.

"Oh. Okay, I guess."

"You guess? Why do you say that?"

"Well, we ran into the lunch hour."

"What about it?"

"It interrupted your opening argument in the middle."

"Yeah, but no big deal," Richard said. "I suppose I could have delayed, told the judge I didn't want to start till after lunch, but I'm trying to speed things along."

"I see," I said.

But my face betrayed me.

"What's the matter?" Richard said.

"Oh. Well, you're talking about speeding things along."

"Yeah. So?"

"So, don't you think your opening argument's a bit lengthy."

"Oh," Richard said. "Is that what's bothering you? It isn't at all. I doubt if I'll have more than half an hour after lunch."

"Another half an hour?"

Richard looked at me. "Believe me, that's nothing. I probably won't even talk as long as Wellington."

"I thought Wellington's opening was pretty long."

Richard frowned. "What, are you nuts? His opening was sketchy because he hasn't got a case. Give the guy some facts to play with and I wouldn't even be on yet."

"But . . ."

"What?"

"It seemed long to me."

"Of course it did. And you know why?"

"No. Why?"

"Because you're not a lawyer and you don't spend any time in court. All your ideas come straight from TV. That's the problem. You think it's like on "L.A. Law." Where every opening and closing argument you've ever heard is one to two minutes, tops. You know *why* it's that long? It's that long because they're on an hour TV show. And they gotta wrap the case up and sell some soap." Richard shook his head. "That's the whole problem with you. You can't divorce fiction from reality. You read detective books, so you think detective work is like that. Some asshole in the books makes two hundred bucks a day, so you think you gotta make that." He raised his hand. "But never mind. The point is, your perception of a courtroom is based on courtroom *drama*. And courtroom drama is distilled and edited down to the few flashy moments that grab your attention and give you the gist of the case. Real life is a little different. In real life, we deal with the case, the whole case, and nothing else but the case. Some of it happens to be boring. Well, unfortunately we can't just say, well, we're not going to deal with this part of it because it doesn't happen to be good theater. You see what I mean?"

"Yeah, but . . ."

"But what?"

"What you said. Grab your attention and give you the gist of the case. Why isn't that exactly what you want to do for the jury?"

Richard looked at me a moment, then smiled ironically. "Because they're stupid."

"What?"

"The jurors. They're stupid people. They're not real bright."

"How can you say that?"

"Because it's true. Why do you think the jury selection process took so long? I'm fighting to get intelligent people on the jury, the prosecutor's fighting to keep them off."

"Why?"

"Because he doesn't *want* intelligent people on the jury. He wants a bunch of morons who'll do exactly what he says. He wants people whose perception of the law is, if the guy wasn't guilty he wouldn't have been charged."

"That can't be true."

"Grow up. Of course it's true. You know how many people on that jury have a college degree?"

"None?"

"Bingo, right on the button. If there were, they'd have been kicked out right on their Phi Beta Kappa."

"You're a cynical son of a bitch."

Richard shrugged. "I'm a lawyer. Anyway, the prosecutor packed the jury with sheep, and sheep need to be led. Flashy moments may grab their attention, but it's not gonna convince them of anything. I gotta spell my theories out. In most cases, many times."

"Jesus."

"Hey, it's not the end of the world. Don't look so glum."

"It's not just that. "

"Oh? What is it then?"

"I don't know. It's just, you got the grand jury transcript. Then there's discovery. You've got the list of the prosecution's witnesses. You know everything they intend to do."

"So?"

"So?" I said. "That's the whole problem. There's no surprises."

Richard looked at me. Cocked his head. Grinned.

"Oh, yeah?"

30

"State your name."

"Sergeant William MacAullif."

That marked, to the best of my recollection, only the second time I'd ever heard MacAullif refer to his first name. The first had been when we'd been working on the movie and he'd been forced to give it to the script supervisor in order to sign out a script. *Forced* is the wrong word. Actually, the young lady had charmed him out of it.

Such was not the case here. ADA Wellington was all crisp efficiency. Snapping out a staccato series of questions, he led MacAullif through a recitation of his qualifications as a homicide sergeant.

It was, I had to admit, rather impressive. It turned out MacAullif had three citations, including one for bravery. Which was news to me. I happened to know he'd never been shot, which I somehow equated with bravery in the line of duty.

Anyway, it went down well with the jury, who were eating MacAullif up. He was big, beefy, looked like a cop, and seemed natural and self-assured on the witness stand. It occurred to me what he had to say was going to be convincing.

Which was too bad for our side. I had to keep reminding myself of that.

MacAullif was on the other side.

"Now, then, Sergeant MacAullif," ADA Wellington said. "Directing your attention to the early-morning hours of October thirteenth, did you have any occasion to go to a town house on East Sixty-second Street?"

"Yes, I did."

"What time was that?"

"Approximately 2:30 A.M."

"And what did you find when you arrived?"

"Two radio-patrol officers were already on the scene."

"They were inside?"

"That is correct."

"Was anyone with them?"

"Yes, sir. The defendant, Anson Carbinder."

"Did you notice anything about the defendant's appearance at that time?"

"Objection, Your Honor," Richard said. "Leading, suggestive, and calls for a conclusion on the part of the witness."

"Sustained."

"Now, sergeant, you say you arrived to find Anson Carbinder in the company of two police officers?"

"That's right."

"Could you *describe* his appearance at that time?"

"Objection."

"Overruled. Witness may answer."

"He was covered with blood."

"I see. Now, when you say covered? . . ."

"I'm sorry," MacAullif said. "That's a figure of speech. He was not *covered* with blood. But he certainly had enough blood on him."

"And just where was this blood?"

"He had blood on his hands. He had blood smeared on his face. He had blood on his shirt. On the sleeves and on the front of the shirt."

"On the sleeves?"

"That's right."

"This was a long-sleeved shirt?"

"Yes, it was."

"What kind of shirt?"

"A white shirt."

"You mean a dress shirt?"

"That's right."

"When you arrived at the house at two in the morning, Mr. Carbinder was wearing a white dress shirt with blood on it?"

"That's right."

"What else was he wearing?"

"Gray slacks."

"Gray slacks?"

"That's right."

"Was he wearing shoes?"

"No."

"Socks?"

"No."

"Just a white shirt and gray slacks?"

"That's right."

"And did you question the defendant at that time?"

"Yes, I did."

"What did you ask him?"

"I asked him to tell me what happened."

"Did he answer?"

"He did not."

"Objection. That's a conclusion, Your Honor."

ADA Wellington appeared nettled. "Nonsense. How is that a conclusion? It's a fact."

"What he *said* is a fact. Whether he *answered* or not is a conclusion the *jury* can draw from *what* he said."

Judge Blank banged his gavel. "That will do. Gentlemen, we will argue objections at the side bar, not in front of the jury. I will thank you to remember that."

"Yes, Your Honor."

"In this case, the objection is sustained. That question and answer will be stricken from the record. Please rephrase the question."

"Yes, Your Honor," Wellington said. "Sergeant, when you asked the defendant what happened, what did he say?"

"He said his attorney had advised him not to talk."

"So he wouldn't answer your questions?"

"That's right."

"What did you do then?"

"Since the defendant was not responsive, I asked the officers to direct me to the crime scene."

"Which was where?"

"In the upstairs bedroom."

"You went to the upstairs bedroom?"

"That's right."

"What did you find?"

"The place was a mess." MacAullif grimaced. "I'm sorry. That's a conclusion. But there was a lot of blood, and it was all over. There was blood on the floor. Or rather, the carpet. There was blood on the sheets. The sheets were half on, half off the bed. The decedent was lying in bed at an angle. That is, her head was on the pillow, but her feet were almost over the side of the bed. Her right arm was down at her side. Her left arm was flopped up over the head of the bed. She was wearing a sheer negligee, which was in tatters. She had been stabbed several times in the chest. There were what appeared to be defensive wounds on the hands. And her throat had been cut."

"Was she alive or dead?"

"I'm not a medical examiner, and that's not my determination to make. But there was no question in this case. The woman was clearly dead."

"What did you do then?"

"About that time the medical examiner arrived, in addition to the crime-scene unit. The medical examiner took charge of the body. I sent the crime-scene unit to process the bedroom. And I took the defendant into custody."

"You brought him in for questioning?"

"That's right."

"And did he make a statement at that time?"

"He did not. He refused to make a statement unless his attorney was present."

"Did his attorney show up?"

"Yes, he did."

"Did he make a statement then?"

"He did not."

"Thank you, sergeant. Now, then, with regard to the crime scene, did you find anything you considered significant?"

"Yes, I did."

"And what was that?"

"There was a large carving knife lying on the floor, with blood on it."

"Blood?"

"That's right."

"And did you notice anything with regard to the size of the knife in relation to the wounds in the body of the decedent?"

"Objection."

"Sustained."

"How big was the knife?"

MacAullif shrugged. "It was your standard carving knife." He held his hands apart. "About so big."

"And was there anything about the size of the knife that was inconsistent with the wounds in the body?"

"No, there was not."

ADA Wellington nodded. "I see. And was there anything else significant you observed at the time?"

"No, there was not."

"And, to refresh my recollection, can you please tell me
again everything significant that you observed at the crime
scene?"

"There was blood on the carpet. There was blood on the
sheets. There was a bloody knife on the floor next to the
bed. The mutilated body of Mrs. Carbinder was lying askew
in the bed with her throat cut."

"I see," ADA Wellington said. He nodded gravely. "And
after you observed these things, what did you do?"

"I took the defendant into custody."

"Thank you, sergeant. That's all."

I grimaced.

Damn.

That was neat and effective. ADA Wellington's examination of Sergeant MacAullif had been standard fare, dwelling
on the horror of the crime and rubbing the jurors' noses in
blood.

The last two questions were something else.

They were perfectly reasonable questions, simple, straightforward, nothing to object to. Taken singly, they didn't
mean a thing.

But taken together?

What a killer.

Particularly coming from MacAullif. It occurred to me,
Wellington had been wise to lead with him. Because his
whole manner carried conviction. He was a seasoned pro,
not the type to make mistakes. An honest, straightforward,
no-nonsense cop, telling it like it is.

I wondered how Richard was going to deal with that.

Well, first off, he didn't appear the least bit upset. He
got up from his seat next to Anson Carbinder, gave Anson

an encouraging pat on the shoulder, strolled over to the witness stand, looked up at MacAullif, and smiled.

"Now, then, sergeant, you say you took the defendant into custody?"

"That's right."

"You brought him downtown?"

"Yes, I did."

"And I believe you stated that when you found the defendant he was wearing a white shirt and gray slacks, but no socks and shoes?"

"That's right."

"You brought him in without socks and shoes?"

"No, I did not."

"You allowed him to put on socks and shoes?"

"That's right."

"Where did you get the socks and shoes?"

"From the upstairs bedroom."

"You mean the crime scene?"

"That's right."

"You let the defendant up to the crime scene?"

"No, I did not."

"Then how did he get the shoes?"

"I got them for him."

"You went up to the bedroom, brought back the socks and shoes?"

"That's right."

"And how did you know where they were?"

"I asked him."

"You asked him where his socks and shoes were?"

"That's right."

"What did he say?"

"He said they were on the floor of the bedroom, right inside the door."

"And were they?"

"Yes, they were."

"Did he tell you how they came to be there?"

"No, he did not."

"But he did answer that one particular question as to where his socks and shoes were?"

"That's right."

Richard smiled. "So when you say he made no statement, that's not exactly true, is it, sergeant?"

MacAullif's eyes narrowed. "Yes, it is."

"I thought you said he told you nothing. He refused to answer."

"When I asked him what happened," MacAullif said. "He refused to tell me what *happened.*"

"You mean he made no statement as to the actual crime. But he did make a statement as to the location of his socks and shoes?"

"That's right."

"So when you said he made *no* statement? . . ."

"I was referring to what he said when I asked him what happened. That is the question he declined to answer. It is the relevant question one is concerned with in a murder investigation. If the suspect declines to answer it, that is what we mean when we refer to his refusing to talk." MacAullif exhaled. "But that does not mean the suspect said *nothing.* A suspect under interrogation may ask to go to the bathroom. We do not take that to be an admission. Nor contend that it in any way alters his decision not to talk. We try to differentiate between what is relevant and what is not. If you want to make a big deal about the fact he told me where his shoes were, I suppose you can. As far as I'm concerned, that does not alter the fact that your client declined to discuss the crime. And just between you and me, I think you're beating a dead horse."

I thought so too. For my money, Richard's cross-examination of MacAullif wasn't working. It certainly wasn't winning him any friends on the jury. It was nit-picking, plain and simple. And MacAullif's obvious contempt seemed well deserved. Rather than rattling MacAullif, Richard's questions were actually building him up. MacAullif was coming off as rational, dignified, and intelligent.

Richard was coming off as a jerk.

It didn't seem to bother him, however. He merely nodded and said, "Thank you, sergeant. Now, getting back to the socks and shoes, you say you found them right inside the door?"

"That's right."

"The bedroom door?"

"Yes. The bedroom door."

"And when you say the bedroom, you are referring to the crime scene?"

"Yes. As I said before."

"Uh-huh," Richard said. He rubbed his forehead. "And when you found these socks and shoes, what did you find?"

"I beg your pardon?"

"Could you please describe what you found?"

"They were a pair of men's black dress shoes. The socks were either black or dark gray."

"Where were the socks?"

"Stuffed in the shoes."

"Had they been worn?"

"Objection," Wellington said. "That calls for a conclusion on the part of the witness."

"And one I think he's qualified to draw," Richard said. "However, I will withdraw the question. Sergeant, what was the condition of the socks?"

"They were wadded up and stuffed in the shoes."

"Did you remove them from the shoes?"

"No, I did not."

"What did you do with them?"

"I brought the socks and shoes downstairs to Mr. Carbinder."

"You gave them to him?"

"That's right."

"Did he remove the socks from the shoes?"

"Yes, he did."

"You saw him do that?"

"That's right."

"What was the appearance of the socks that he took out of the shoes?"

"As I said before, they were crumpled up. And I believe one of them was inside out."

"Inside out?"

"That's right."

"And what did Mr. Carbinder do with the socks?"

"He straightened them out and put them on."

"So, without giving us your conclusion as to whether the socks were worn, they were rumpled, stuffed in the shoes, and one was inside out?"

"Oh, Your Honor," Wellington said.

"Exactly," Judge Blank said. "Mr. Rosenberg, if we could avoid such side comments."

"Sorry, Your Honor," Richard said. "Now, then, sergeant. I believe you stated Mr. Carbinder was covered with blood, is that right?"

"That's right."

"Correct me if I'm wrong, but, according to your statement, I believe he had blood on his face, on his hands, and on his white dress shirt. Is that right?"

"That's right. On the sleeves and on the front of the shirt."

"Was there blood on the pants?"

"I beg your pardon?"

"On the gray slacks. Was there blood on the slacks?"

"I don't recall seeing blood on the slacks."

"You don't recall?"

"No. The slacks were dark gray. The blood wouldn't show up as well on them. On the white shirt of course it was plain as day. But on the slacks it wouldn't be as readily apparent."

"Are you saying there was blood on the slacks but you didn't see it?"

"Objection," Wellington said. "How can he testify to something he *didn't* see?"

"Exactly," Richard said. "Sergeant, I'll rephrase the question. Was there blood on the slacks, yes or no?"

"Objection, Your Honor. How can he answer that?"

"He can say yes, he can say no, or he can say, I don't know," Richard said.

"The objection is overruled. The witness may answer."

"Was there blood on the slacks, yes or no?"

"I don't know."

"You don't *know?*" Richard said. His voice had a baiting, taunting quality, as if trying to goad the witness into getting mad.

MacAullif didn't take the bait. "I'm not certain," he said calmly. "And that's the way you told me to answer if I wasn't sure."

"You're not sure if there was blood on the slacks?"

"That's right."

"You don't remember seeing blood on the slacks?"

MacAullif smiled. "If I remembered seeing blood on the slacks, I'd be sure."

"So you don't recall seeing blood on the slacks?"

"That's right."

"To the best of your knowledge, was there blood on the slacks?"

"Objection. Already asked and answered."

"Overrruled."

"To the best of your knowledge, was there blood on the slacks?"

"Frankly, I don't know. I don't recall seeing blood on the slacks. On the other hand, I don't recall *not* seeing blood on the slacks."

"Uh-huh," Richard said. "And what about the lights in the room?"

"I beg your pardon?"

"I don't believe you mentioned the lights in the bedroom. What can you tell us about them?"

"The overhead light was on."

"The ceiling light?"

"That's right."

"Were there other lights in the room?"

"Yes. There were lights on the end tables on either side of the bed."

"Were those lights on or off?"

"They were off."

"But there was still plenty of light to see?"

"Oh, yes. Quite sufficient."

"And it was in that light that you observed the murder scene?"

"Yes, it was."

"I believe you stated there was blood on the carpet, there was blood on the sheets, the victim was lying half in, half out of the bed, and the knife which you presumed to be the murder weapon was lying by the bed on the floor. Is that right?"

"Yes, it is."

"And you found Anson Carbinder's shoes and socks just inside the door?"

"That's right."

"What about his jacket and tie—did you happen to find Anson Carbinder's jacket and tie anywhere in the room?"

"Actually, yes. They were draped over the back of a chair."

"The back of a chair?"

"That's right."

"Was the jacket *hung* over the back of the chair?"

"No. This was not a straight chair. It was an overstuffed chair. The jacket was lying over the back of it."

"What about the tie?"

"The tie was on top of the jacket."

"And did you give Anson Carbinder his jacket and tie when you took him into custody."

"No, I did not."

"You did not?"

"No," MacAullif said. He added dryly, "It was not a formal occasion. He needed his shoes and socks to walk. He did not need a jacket and tie."

"Uh-huh," Richard said. "But you did find his shoes and socks inside the door, and his jacket and tie draped over an overstuffed chair?"

"That's right."

"And you did notice blood on his white shirt, but can't recall whether or not there was blood on his gray slacks?"

"That's right."

Richard smiled and nodded. "Then, sergeant," he said, "wouldn't your findings seem to indicate that Anson Carbinder returned home at approximately 2:00 A.M.; that he found the bedroom dark; that he removed his shoes and socks just inside the door; that he removed his jacket and tie and tossed it over the back of a chair; that he then slipped into bed, trying not to wake up his wife; that he immediately noticed something was very wrong—his hand encountered something wet and sticky; that he tried to rouse his wife, couldn't, sprang from the bed in mounting horror, and switched on the overhead light; that he discovered his wife's body lying murdered in the bed; that his first impulse was to go to her, grab her, attempt to revive her; that he did so, getting blood on his hands, face, and shirt; that when he was unable to revive her, he called the police; that after calling them, he pulled on his pants and went downstairs to wait for them to arrive—which is why, when you got there, there was blood on his shirt but not on his pants—isn't that what your findings show, sergeant?"

ADA Wellington was on his feet. "Objection, Your Honor!" he shouted. "This is outrageous. Counsel is making an argument in the guise of a question. He—"

Judge Blank's gavel cut him off. "That will do," he snapped. He pointed. "Attorneys. To the side bar."

Richard and ADA Wellington moved off to the side of the judge's bench. The court reporter picked up his stenographer's machine and moved over there with them to record the conversation. Judge Blank came down from his bench and joined the attorneys, and they conversed in low tones.

I couldn't hear a word, but I could see their lips moving. Richard appeared quite composed, while ADA Wellington appeared animated and vehement. Judge Blank, for the most part, looked stern.

When they resumed their places, Judge Blank said, "The objection has been sustained on the grounds that it calls for a conclusion on the part of the witness for which no proper foundation has been laid. Should the proper foundation be laid, it might be asked at a later date. However, at the present time you are to dismiss it from your minds, give it no weight. For all intents and purposes, the question was never asked.

"Mr. Rosenberg, you may proceed."

"Thank you, Your Honor," Richard said. "Sergeant MacAullif, I believe you stated your qualifications as a police officer?"

"Yes, I did."

"You're with homicide?"

"That's right."

"And how many homicides have you investigated in your career?"

"I really couldn't say."

"Would it be hundreds?"

"Yes, it would."

"Thousands?"

"*Over* a thousand is possible. I really couldn't say."

"Would it be fair to say you've had extensive experience in investigating homicides?"

"Yes, it would."

"I believe in your direct examination you stated your work in the last few years has been exclusively homicides?"

"That is correct."

"Your only work in the past few years has been homicide work?"

"That's right."

"You did no work in any other areas?"

"No, I did not."

"Is that so?" Richard said. He crossed to the defense table, picked up a manila envelope, and took it to the court reporter's desk. He pulled from the envelope a small, rectangular box, handed it to the court reporter. "I ask that this be marked for identification as Defense Exhibit A."

"One moment," Wellington said. "Let me see that."

"You'll have an opportunity to inspect it when I offer it into evidence," Richard said. "At the moment, I'm merely marking it for identification."

When the box had been marked, Richard took it and approached the witness stand.

As he did, I could see the box more clearly. My mouth dropped open.

It was a videotape.

One I knew.

"Sergeant MacAullif," Richard said, "I hold in my hand Defense Exhibit A, which consists of a videocassette of a movie entitled *Hands of Havoc, Flesh of Fire.* I hand you that videotape and ask you if you have ever seen it before?"

Sergeant MacAullif's calm, competent assurance was gone. A number of conflicting emotions took its place: surprise, anger, embarrassment, rage.

I couldn't blame him. The cover of the videocassette he'd just been handed couldn't have been worse. It looked like it was straight out of a fifties grade-B movie. It depicted the young hero in a martial-arts pose. Clinging to his arm was a voluptuous blonde with her bosom spilling out of her dress.

"I ask you, sergeant," Richard said, "if you are not familiar with the movie *Hands of Havoc, Flesh of Fire*? I ask you if you have ever worked on the movie? More specifically, if you worked on it just last year? I ask you, if we were to play that videocassette, if we would see your name listed in the credits as the technical advisor? Is that not a fact, Sergeant MacAullif?"

"Objection," Wellington roared. "Incompetent, irrelevant, and immaterial."

"This is cross-examination, Your Honor," Richard said. "The man stated he held no other job."

"Objection overruled. Witness will answer."

"Were you a technical advisor on the movie, *Hands of Havoc, Flesh of Fire*?"

MacAullif's face was granite. I swear his teeth never moved. "Yes, I was."

"So when you stated you had worked no other job but homicide? . . ."

"I assumed you were referring to police work," MacAullif snapped. "I had no idea you were referring to this. Frankly, I didn't even think of it."

"You simply didn't remember?"

"That's right."

"But you remember now that you worked on the movie

Hands of Havoc, Flesh of Fire as a technical advisor just last year?"

"Yes, I do."

"How long did you work on the movie?"

"For four weeks."

"You worked for four weeks on this movie?"

"That's right."

"As a technical advisor?"

"Yes."

"Was that your only job?"

Oh, shit.

"I beg your pardon?"

"I'm asking if that was your only job on the movie? Or is it not a fact, that if we were to play this videocassette, we would see you, in person, in uniform, playing a scene with the young star, Jason Clairemont, a scene in which he, as a fugitive on the lam, dupes you and makes good his escape? Is that not a fact, sergeant?"

I now know what is meant by the phrase, *if looks could kill*.

31

"I can't believe you did that."

"I beg your pardon?"

Richard and I were in a cab heading back to his office. Court had broken immediately after MacAullif's testimony, ADA Wellington being quick to intercept the sergeant as he left the witness stand, so as to forestall any possible confrontation between him and Mr. Rosenberg, probably a wise move considering the presence of both the jurors and the press. Anyway, MacAullif had been whisked out the exit, the jurors had been instructed, and court had been adjourned. At which point Anson Carbinder had pulled his own vanishing act, hopping into a Mercedes driven by the renowned chauffeur Connie Maynard. Believe it or not, Richard and I had not been offered a ride and had been forced to hail a cab.

"Come on," I said. "I mean, Jesus Christ, Richard. That was MacAullif."

"I know that was MacAullif."

"So how could you do that?"

"You didn't like my cross-examination?"

"Are you kidding me?"

"No, I'm not. I thought it was short, snappy, and effective. And what about my summary of the evidence—didn't you think that was rather neat?"

"That was stricken from the record."

"Oh, sure," Richard said mockingly. "Jurors will disregard. Right, like they'll just forget about it like it never happened. I suppose you think a juror's decision was never influenced by something he was told to disregard?"

"Never mind that," I said. "I was talking about Mac-Aullif."

"I'm talking about MacAullif. He was a hell of a good witness, and I had a hell of a tough job."

"Yes, and you did it, didn't you?"

"I sure did."

"That was not meant as praise."

"I know that. You're all pissed off at me for making a fool of MacAullif. Which is stupid. He's trying to convict, we're trying to acquit. I was just doing my job."

"It's more than that."

"No, it isn't. You just think it is because you know the guy. If it was anyone else, you'd be pleased as punch."

"I don't think so."

"Sure you would. Suppose it was that other sergeant— the stupid one that you kept getting involved with—what's his name?"

"Sergeant Thurman."

"Right. Sergeant Thurman—suppose it was him."

"It *wasn't* him."

"Yeah, but if it was, you'd be laughing your ass off."

I frowned. "That's not the point."

"Sure it is. And if you didn't know the guy at all, you'd just think it was a neat trick. Look, just this morning you were grousing, Oh, this is so boring, oh, there's no surprises. I give you one and you're pissed off and you don't like it."

I turned around in my seat. "Richard, that was my fucking movie."

"So?"

"I think that's the point here. You say, how would I like it if it was some other cop I didn't know? Well, it wouldn't *happen* if it was some other cop I didn't know. The point is, the only reason you *had* this information to shoot at MacAullif is because he's a friend of mine."

"Yes, of course."

"What do you mean, yes, of course? You can't agree with me. That's my whole argument."

"Stanley, I'm a lawyer. I'm a paid partisan. I use anything I can get my hands on to help my client."

"Yeah, I know that."

He shrugged. "So what's the big deal?"

"So what's the big deal?" Alice said when I got home and went in the kitchen to tell her about it.

To my surprise, Alice agreed with Richard. I say *to my surprise*. I shouldn't. Over the years I've gotten used to Alice's reactions being a hundred and eighty degrees from what I thought they'd be. So a surprise was no surprise. What would have surprised me would have been if she'd agreed with me.

No risk of that.

"Come on," Alice said from the stove, stirring something that smelled delicious. "This is not the end of the world."

"You should have seen MacAullif."

"I take it he was angry?"

"You could say that."

"Who was he angry at?"

"Huh?"

"Was he angry at you?"

"You better believe it."

"Oh? What did he say?"

"He didn't say anything."

"Oh?"

"I didn't see him after court. They hustled him out the door."

"So how do you know he was angry?"

"Alice, give me a break. I told you what Richard did. Don't you think he's angry?"

"Sure, but at Richard. Why would he be angry at you?"

"It's my movie. I got him into it. If it weren't for me, Richard wouldn't know about it."

Alice looked up from the stove. "When?"

"Huh?"

"When did Richard know about it? Was it something he learned just now, during the trial? Or did he know about the movie then?"

"Don't be silly. He was at the filming. He saw the dailies, for Christ's sake."

"Did he see MacAullif when you were filming?"

"Of course."

Alice smiled. "Then Richard knew about the movie then. And MacAullif *knows* Richard knew about the movie then. It's not like this was some secret bit of information you suddenly supplied Richard with because you were working as his detective for the trial."

As usually happens when I argue with Alice, my mind was becoming mush. "Alice," I said feebly.

"So you see," Alice said. "There's no reason for MacAullif to be mad at you at all."

If only life were so simple.

32

"State your name."

"Dr. Melvin Fleckstein."

"What is your occupation?"

"Medical examiner."

I was not surprised. Dr. Fleckstein looked like a medical examiner. He was an older man, with white hair, pudgy cheeks, and steel-rimmed glasses. *Why* that looked like a medical examiner, I couldn't tell you. I guess I must have associated him with some doctor I knew when I was a child, though I can't remember any such doctor—but that was the initial impression I got, and for once I turned out to be right.

Dr. Fleckstein ran through a list of his qualifications, which were extensive, including twenty-three years as a medical examiner for the city of New York.

ADA Wellington nodded his approval. He included the jury in his gaze, inviting them to share in his appreciation of the doctor's credentials. "Thank you, doctor," he said. "Now, then, directing your attention to the early-morning hours of October thirteenth, were you summoned to a residence at One-thirteen East Sixty-second Street?"

"Yes, I was."

"And what time was that?"

"I arrived there at precisely 2:50 A.M."

"And what did you find?"

"I found the body of a woman in the upstairs bedroom."

"Was she alive?"

"She was dead."

"How did you make that determination?"

"It was not particularly hard. Her throat had been cut."

"Was that the only readily apparent wound on the body?"

"Not at all. The woman had been stabbed repeatedly. There were stab wounds on the chest and defensive wounds on the hands."

"Defensive wounds?"

"Yes. The type of wounds that would have occurred had she put up her hands to fend off the blows."

"The blows?"

"By the blows, I mean the blows of the knife."

"Did you determine the cause of death?"

"Not then. The apparent cause of death was obvious, but I didn't verify it till I got her back to the lab."

"The apparent cause of death?"

"Yes. Her throat had been slit. No one can live with their throat slit. It is a fatal wound."

"Then why do you say *apparent* cause of death?"

Dr. Fleckstein smiled. "Because I'm under oath, and I have to be accurate. The wound was sufficient to have caused death. The question was whether it actually had. You must remember there were other wounds on the body. It was conceivable one of them could have caused death, and the body could have been already dead when the throat was slit.

"That was one possibility. Another was that the cause of death could have been by entirely different means. The woman could have been poisoned, for instance, and all these wounds administered only after death."

"Are you saying such was the case?"

"No, no, no. Absolutely not." Dr. Fleckstein held up his hands. "Don't get me wrong. None of those were the case." He smiled again. "All I'm saying is, it was necessary for me to *eliminate* those possibilities in determining the cause of death."

"Which you were eventually able to do?"

"Absolutely. The woman died from having her throat slit."

"On what do you base that conclusion?"

"Several factors. For one thing, the defensive wounds on the hands. The woman was obviously alive when she was stabbed, because she attempted to fend off the blows of the knife.

"Then there was the loss of blood. Which was considerable. There was blood on the bed, blood on the floor. The body had bled profusely."

"Indicating what?"

"That she was alive when she was stabbed. That the heart was still beating, pumping out blood. If she had been dead when she was stabbed, the blood would have merely seeped from the wounds. Clearly, it had spurted."

"And how do you know the cut on her throat was the fatal wound?"

"Again, from the way the blood flowed. She lost a huge amount of blood from the wound in her neck. Much more than would have flowed had she died first from the other stab wounds. There's no doubt about it. She died with her throat cut, gasping for air that would not come as her blood gushed out of her."

Jesus Christ.

I'd been wondering what Wellington was getting at with this testimony. It was obvious what killed her, so why was he making such a big deal?

The answer lay in the faces of the jurors. One glance at

those men and women—shrinking in horror and revulsion from the repugnant testimony—told the tale. ADA Wellington had seized the opportunity to drench them in gore.

After standing there several moments to prolong the effect, ADA Wellington nodded and said, "Thank you, doctor. That's all."

Richard Rosenberg got up from the defense table. His eyes never left the doctor as he strode out into the center of the courtroom. He chose a position in relation to the jury box and the witness stand so the jurors could see his eyes fastened on the doctor. And he stood there, stone-faced, unblinking, just as long as ADA Wellington had stood at the end of his examination.

Finally, he spoke.

"Twenty-three years, doctor?"

"I beg your pardon?"

"You've been a medical examiner for twenty-three years?"

"Yes, I have."

"How many autopsies have you performed in that time?"

"I don't know. Hundreds, I'm sure."

"As many as a thousand?"

"Oh, easily. Most likely two or three."

"Two or three thousand homicides."

The doctor raised his finger. "Now, now," he said. "I didn't say that. Not all violent deaths are homicides. Or all suspicious deaths, for that matter. Some are accidents. Others turn out to be from natural causes." He smiled. "That's one of the main things an autopsy is used to determine."

Richard didn't return the smile. "That's fine, doctor," he said. "Let's talk about the percentage of your cases that *were* homicides. And just how large a percentage was that?"

Dr. Fleckstein frowned. "I really couldn't say."

"Is it as much as half?"

"Oh, yes. More than half."

"Fine, doctor. Since you say you've handled over two or three thousand cases, half that would still give us over a thousand to work with. Now, in those cases that turned out to be homicides, can you tell me how many times you were asked to appear in court?"

"Once again, I would—"

"Approximately, doctor. Would that be more than half?"

"I'm really not sure."

"Well, let's get at it another way. Have you appeared in court a hundred times?"

"Oh, yes."

"More than two hundred?"

"I would say so, yes."

"More than five hundred?"

"I'm not sure."

"That's all right, doctor. Two hundred will do. You feel you've testified in court two hundred times?"

"I would say so, yes."

"Uh-huh," Richard said. "What was the time of death?"

The change of subject was so abrupt that Dr. Fleckstein blinked. "I beg your pardon?"

"What was the time of death, doctor? When did the woman die?"

"She died in the early-morning hours of October thirteenth."

Richard stood, his face deadpan, his eyes on the doctor.

A beat.

Two.

"No kidding," Richard said dryly. "Do you know why I asked that question, doctor?"

"Objection. Argumentative."

"Sustained."

"The reason I asked that question, doctor, is that on direct examination you didn't mention the time of death. I am wondering, doctor, on those two hundred occasions that you've given medical testimony in court, did you ever once give testimony and not mention the time of death?"

"Objection."

"Overruled."

"I can't recall."

"You can't recall, doctor?"

"No, I cannot."

"You can't remember one other occasion where you didn't testify to the time of death?"

"Objection. Already asked and answered."

"Sustained."

"Doctor, in response to a direct question by me, you stated that the time of death was the early-morning hours of October thirteenth, is that correct?"

"Yes, it is."

"Can you be more precise?"

"Not with any degree of certainty. I can make an *estimate* as to when the decedent probably met her death."

"Isn't that what you do in every case?"

"Yes, of course."

"Then why are you having so much trouble doing it now?"

"Objection."

"Sustained."

"Doctor, on those two hundred occasions you referred to, when you've given testimony in court, don't you always do so specifically in terms of certain hours? Don't you say, Death could have occurred between six and eight? Or, death could have occurred between eight-thirty and nine-thirty? Isn't that the effect of medical testimony, to erect parameters within which death could have occurred?"

"Yes, of course."

"Then why can't you do so now?"

"Objection."

"Sustained."

"Doctor, in this case I asked you when death could have occurred. You told me the early-morning hours of October thirteenth. Since you yourself saw the body at 2:50 A.M., all your statement does is limit the time between midnight and that time. Which is somewhat less than helpful."

"Objection."

"Sustained."

Richard's eyes blazed. He raised his arm, pointed at the prosecution table. "Doctor, were you instructed by the district attorney's office *not* to divulge the time of death?"

ADA Wellington lunged to his feet, spouting objections until I figured it was side bar time again, but I got lucky. Judge Blank, either figuring this would be a long discussion, or tired of whispering, or both, sent the jury out of the room and had the argument in open court. So I got to hear it.

So did the spectators.

So did the press.

Big victory for Richard.

As things turned out.

"Now, then," Judge Blank said. "Just what is the objection here?"

ADA Wellington's face was still red. "That man," he said, pointing at Richard, "just asked the witness if I instructed him to withhold testimony."

Judge Blank nodded. "Right. What's your objection?"

ADA Wellington almost gagged. "It's an insult. A gratuitous attack on my reputation."

"I'd appreciate a legal argument, counselor."

"Damn it, it's false."

"Then the witness will say so," Judge Blank said calmly. "Do you have any legal grounds for your objection?"

"What I told the witness is incompetent, irrelevant, and immaterial."

"It's always relevant to establish bias, Your Honor,"

Richard said. "What the prosecutor may have told his witness may not be relevant. But if the witness *acted* on those instructions—if it should turn out the doctor deliberately withheld portions of his testimony at the instructions of the prosecutor—well, that would certainly be an indication of his bias, and I have every right to bring it out."

"Are you saying such is the case?"

Richard spread his hands, palms up. "I have no idea. Faced with the rather unique situation of a medical examiner failing to disclose the time of death, I have to make some attempt to discover the cause. The first logical question is whether he was instructed to do so. If he was, it's entirely relevant. If not, he can merely say so. Frankly, I don't see what's the big deal."

"I don't either," Judge Blank said. He turned to the prosecutor. "Mr. Wellington, do you have anything further."

Wellington didn't.

He *said* he did, and he *acted* like he did, and he made several attempts to *speak* as if he did, but it was clear that he didn't, and Judge Blank lost no time overruling the objection. The jury was brought in, told of the decision, and the question was read back by the court reporter. "Now, then, doctor, were you instructed by the district attorney's office not to disclose the time of death?"

Dr. Fleckstein, who had remained on the witness stand, listening to the entire argument, was bristling with indignation. "Certainly not," he snapped.

"What *were* you instructed to do?"

"Objection."

"Sustained."

"Doctor, you have just testified that you were not instructed to withhold the time of death. *Were* you instructed, if you were asked for the time of death, to give it in as general terms as possible and, more specifically, to avoid mentioning the actual hours during which death might have taken place?"

Dr. Fleckstein squirmed on the witness stand. He cleared his throat.

"Objection," Wellington put in.

"Overruled."

"Well," Dr. Fleckstein said grudgingly. "It wasn't like that."

"Oh? What was it like?"

"Objection."

"Overruled."

"What was it like, doctor? *You* define the situation for us."

"Well," Dr. Fleckstein said, "it wasn't like I was to withhold anything or in any way alter my medical findings."

"Well, I'm certainly glad to hear that, doctor. What were you instructed to do?"

"Only to listen to questions carefully and answer only what I was being asked."

"Really," Richard said, grinning. "Was that on direct examination?"

"That's right."

Richard's grin grew wider. "What about cross-examination? What were you instructed to do then?"

"Objection to the words *instructed to do.*"

"Overruled. The witness may qualify his answer if he wishes."

"I wasn't instructed to do anything. Naturally, I discussed my testimony with the assistant district attorney. That is standard procedure for any witness who is going to testify in court. So there's nothing sinister about it, no matter how much you want to make of it."

"I don't want to make anything of it," Richard said, "but I'd certainly like to know what it is. I don't believe you answered my question, doctor."

"I certainly did."

"I asked you what you had been instructed to do, the prosecutor objected to the word, then you decided you hadn't been *instructed* to do anything. Even though I believe before he made the objection, you responded to a question as to what you had been *instructed* to do on direct examination. But be that as it may, I don't really wish to get involved in a discussion of semantics, doctor. So, if you please, what did the prosecutor say with regard to your testimony on cross-examination?"

"Objection."

"Overruled."

"What did he say, doctor."

Dr. Fleckstein hesitated. He looked around, then blurted, "Don't help him."

A murmur ran through the courtroom.

Richard smiled, "Don't help him, doctor? That's what you were told?"

"That's right."

"And who told you that, doctor? Who was it who said, Don't help him?"

"Objection, Your Honor. Incompetent, irrelevant, and immaterial."

"Overruled."

"Who told you that, doctor."

"Mr. Wellington."

Richard's smile was enormous. "The prosecuting attorney, Assistant District Attorney Wellington, who just objected to that question on the grounds that it was incompetent, irrelevant, and immaterial?"

Laughter rocked the courtroom. This time ADA Wellington's objection was sustained. But the damage had been done. As far as the press was concerned, Richard had won the day.

And he wasn't through.

"And what did you take that to mean, doctor—the words, Don't help him?"

"Objection. Calls for a conclusion."

"Sustained."

"Doctor, when you testified just now, in your own mind, did you come to a conclusion as to how you were going to answer on cross-examination, based on the conversation you had had with the prosecuting attorney in which he had said the words, Don't help him?"

Dr. Fleckstein took a breath. "As a witness for the prosecution, I am aware that I've been called to the stand to advance the theories of the prosecution. It is my duty to present the facts accurately and fairly. It is not my duty to volunteer information that might be favorable to the defense."

Richard's eyes widened. "Are you saying you would deliberately withhold such information?"

"Absolutely not," Dr. Fleckstein snapped. "I just got through saying I would try to be as fair and impartial as possible. I was pointing out that while I would not volunteer information, I would certainly give you anything you asked."

"I'm glad to hear it. What are the hours during which death might have occurred?"

Dr. Fleckstein sucked in breath, exhaled. "If you want to put it that way, death might have occurred anytime between midnight and 2:50 A.M."

Richard shook his head. "Oh, dear," he said. He chuckled ironically. "And after such a fine speech about being fair and impartial."

"Objection."

"Sustained. Mr. Rosenberg, please avoid such side comments."

"Sorry, Your Honor. Dr. Fleckstein, I think we're into semantics again. Are you basing your answer on my use of the word *might?*"

"I'm telling you what's conceivable."

"I'm sure you are, doctor," Richard said. "Let's get at it another way. What is the main method used for determining time of death?"

"There are several methods."

"Yes, but isn't body temperature the generally accepted method?"

"It's *one* of the main methods."

"Let's not quibble. It is *a* main method, is it not?"

"Yes. I just said so."

"Would you please explain to the jury the method of using body temperature to determine time of death?"

"Certainly." Dr. Fleckstein seemed relieved to be able to escape the cross-examination and discourse on a subject. He turned to the jury. "As you know, during life, the normal body temperature is ninety-eight point six degrees Fahrenheit. When a person dies, the body cools. The rate of cooling is a constant. So, by taking the body temperature, we are able to determine when a person met their death."

"That constant is approximately one and one-half degrees Fahrenheit per hour, is it not, doctor?"

"That's right."

"And, in this case, did you take the body temperature of the decedent, Barbara Carbinder?"

"Yes, I did."

"And what time did you take the temperature?"

"Approximately 3:00 A.M."

"What was the body temperature at that time?"

"Ninety-four point nine."

"Ninety-four point nine, doctor? Well, let's do that math. Let's see. Ninety-eight point six minus ninety-four point nine is three-point-seven degrees. At one-point-five degrees per hour, three degrees would be two hours, and point-seven would be approximately one-half. So, the body temperature would indicate that death occurred two and one-half hours before you took it. If you took the body temperature at 3:00 A.M., that would put the time of death at approximately half-past twelve."

"Which you cannot do," Dr. Fleckstein said petulantly, shaking his head. "Which is why laymen shouldn't try to play with these figures. Do the math and say, Well, she died at twelve-thirty. It simply isn't so. All taking the body temperature does is allow you to set up the parameters during which the woman probably died."

"Exactly," Richard said, snapping his fingers. "Which is the question I asked you to begin with. You said between midnight and 2:50 A.M. Now, granted, you said that prompted by the prosecutor's advice, Don't help him. But still, I suddenly find those figures quite interesting. Midnight is just half an hour before twelve-thirty, the mathematical midpoint for the time of death indicated by the body temperature. However, between twelve-thirty and two-fifty A.M. there are two hours and twenty minutes. Quite an imbalance, wouldn't you say? Midnight is the earliest time the decedent is most likely to have met her death. Wouldn't one o'clock be the latest time she would be likely to have done so?"

"You're twisting my words," Dr. Fleckstein said. "Now you're saying *most likely*. Before, you were saying *possible*."

Richard smiled. "And you, taking Mr. Wellington's *Don't help him* to heart were taking my words as literally as possible in order to divulge no information?"

"Objection."

"Sustained."

"I am asking you now, doctor, based on your medical findings, based on your autopsy, based on the body temperature which you took, is it or is it not a fact that the most likely time the decedent met her death was between the hours of midnight and 1:00 A.M.?"

Dr. Fleckstein took a breath. "That's right."

"Thank you, doctor. No further questions."

ADA Wellington was immediately on his feet, asking the doctor a million questions in order to demonstrate that there had been no impropriety on his part in the instructions that he had given the doctor regarding his testimony.

But it didn't matter.

As far as the press was concerned, Richard Rosenberg had kicked his ass.

33

Wellington fired back with Connie Maynard.

First he called two doormen from her building. Both of them testified that over the past six months Anson Carbinder had been an increasingly frequent visitor.

Then he called Robert Tessler.

"State your name."

"Robert Tessler."

"What is your occupation?"

"I'm a private detective."

"Are you acquainted with a young woman by the name of Connie Maynard?"

"Yes, I am."

"How do you happen to know her?"

"I was hired to place her under surveillance."

"Who hired you to do that?"

"Barbara Carbinder."

"Objection!" Richard shouted, but the damage had been done. The court was in an uproar and some of the reporters were actually on their way to the exits.

It was no surprise that Anson Carbinder had had an affair with Connie Maynard—everyone had known that since the beginning of the trial—but it certainly was news that Barbara Carbinder had hired a private eye to spy on them.

"Now, then," Judge Blank said after the jury had been led out and order had been restored. "What is your objection, Mr. Rosenberg?"

"My objection is that I've been ambushed by surprise testimony," Richard said. "Without any prior notice, I am suddenly confronted with this private detective."

"Not at all, Your Honor," ADA Wellington said smoothly. "Mr. Tessler is on our witness list, and has been all along."

"Is that true, Mr. Rosenberg?"

"In a manner of speaking, Your Honor," Richard snapped, holding up the paper. "If you look over the prosecution's list of witnesses, you will find Detective Robert Tessler sandwiched between Detective Raoul Velez and Detective Sean Grady, who are doubtless police officers. The fact that Robert Tessler is *not* a police officer is deliberately obscured."

"Be that as it may," Judge Blank said, "do you maintain that it is incumbent on the prosecution to make sure that the defense is not confused about the identity of any of their witnesses?"

"No, Your Honor. But I maintain that this was done deliberately to circumvent discovery and catch the defense by surprise."

"Have you proof of that?"

"How can I have proof of that when I'm taken by surprise?" Richard said in exasperation.

It was an unfortunate situation, and a fight that Richard was not destined to win. Realizing that, he backed off as quickly as he could, rather than put up a big fight and lose. While this was a good tactic, still the whole thing was a bitter pill to swallow.

As well as a hell of a shock.

Barbara Carbinder had known about her husband's affair. Barbara Carbinder had hired a private detective to spy on

Connie Maynard. Barbara Carbinder, in all likelihood, had been preparing to sue her husband for divorce. And have enough hard evidence on him when she did so to take him to the cleaners.

All of which furnished an excellent motive for murder.

I sat there in court and watched the jury buy it.

First off, Robert Tessler got to testify, and what a witness he made. I thought that after the bombshell about Barbara Carbinder hiring him to spy on Connie Maynard, the rest of his testimony would be anticlimactic.

Wrong again.

First off, Wellington handed him a picture and asked if this was the young woman he'd been asked to spy on, and damned if the picture didn't turn out to be one of the cheesecake photos Wellington had used way back when to sway the grand jury. That left Richard in the no-win situation of letting the jury see it or fighting to keep it out.

He opted not to fight. After his initial resistance to the surprise testimony, Richard, in giving in, seemed to adopt the position of let's get it over with. At any rate, he didn't object to the evidence or anything the detective had to say.

Which was a mouthful. During the time he'd had Connie Maynard under surveillance, Anson Carbinder had been a frequent visitor. Moreover, the two had taken a trip to Atlantic City, where they had registered together as husband and wife.

The surveillance of Connie Maynard had lasted five weeks and terminated the week before Barbara Carbinder was killed.

Which couldn't have added up better. She hires the detective, gets the evidence, confronts her husband, and bam.

Richard let it all go in. He didn't object to anything. Didn't even offer a token resistance.

Still, I was sure he had some trick up his sleeve. Some

secret plan to trip this detective up. To nail him on cross-examination.

I hoped it would involve me. I had a feeling it might. After all, that was what I was here for. I'd been waiting in court for days for just this opportunity. To run out and nail the one pertinent fact that would trip up the witness. Somehow, it just seemed the stage was set for that to happen.

First off, it was near the end of the day. So even if Richard couldn't make the charge of surprise-witness stick and get an adjournment on that account, surely he could talk the judge into postponing his cross-examination until the following morning.

Which would leave me time to do the job, whatever it might be. What, exactly, I wasn't sure, but there had to be some way this witness could be undermined. And if there was, Richard would know it. Not the fact, but the principle, if that makes any sense. He would know how to go about it. What ammunition he needed to shoot. And he would send me out to get it.

I was so much anticipating that that it absolutely floored me when it happened.

It was near the end of the afternoon, the witness's testimony was winding down, and we had a break in the action while ADA Wellington returned to the prosecutor's table to consult his notes. During the pause, Richard caught my eye and motioned me over.

I was thrilled.

I was also scared. That if I got up from my seat in the spectators' section and entered the gate into that arena, into the sacred ground where attorneys sparred, the judge would immediately stop me and demand, "Where do you think you're going?"

But it didn't happen. I came through the gate and

walked over to the defense table where Richard sat with Anson Carbinder, bent down, and whispered, "What's up?"

Richard pushed a folded piece of paper into my hand.

Good god. His message was so important he didn't even dare whisper it.

I looked at the folded paper.

It was a dollar bill.

I looked up at Richard.

He leaned over. Whispered.

"Get me a Coke."

34

"Let's look at the evidence," Richard said.

It was a week and a half later, and ADA Wellington had just rested his case.

Are you surprised I just skipped a whole week and a half of testimony? Don't be. Remember what Richard said about opening arguments—that you only get a two-minute snippet on "L.A. Law," that it isn't like that in real life? Well, that goes double for the actual trial. Trust me on it. That week and a half was boring as hell.

Which was amazing, considering it included: the introduction of the murder weapon; the introduction of the bloody garments worn by Anson Carbinder on the night of the murder; the introduction of photographs of the crime scene, including gross-out photos of the victim; evidence that the knife was the property of Anson Carbinder, or at least had come from his kitchen; and the evidence that Anson Carbinder had taken out a half-million-dollar, double-indemnity life insurance policy on his wife.

Does that sound exciting? Spread it out over a week and a half. Cover with a thin layer of bullshit—irrelevant objections, arguments, and rulings, legal nit-picking, maneuvering, tugs-of-war—none of which amounted to a goddamn thing except to delay, obscure, confuse, and drag out whatever issue was being discussed to the point where, had I been a member of the jury, by the time the prosecution rested its case, my only concern would have been when I could go home.

At any rate, it was over, court had adjourned for the afternoon, and now Richard and I were back in his office planning strategy. Since I had done nothing for a week and a half but sit in court listening to testimony and fetching an occasional Coke, it was nice to know my opinion was at least being sought.

If it indeed was.

I had a feeling I was there not so much to advise as to cheer.

"Okay," Richard said. "As far as I can see, they have nothing new. Not that it isn't damning, but it isn't convicting, either. The point is, when I put on my alibi, he has nothing so far to contest it."

"What *could* he have?"

"Not much, really. He tried his best with the medical examiner, but I pinned him down to twelve to one. Granted, that's only the *most likely* time of death—Wellington could still try to argue he killed her at two-fifteen. But if he does that, we're home free. No one on the jury's going to buy it. The way I see it, the case is going to stand or fall on the alibi."

Richard looked at me. I realized a comment was needed. All I could think of to say was, Right. I did, and Richard nodded and went on.

"So let's look at what we got. Six independent witnesses. Some better than others but, taken collectively, a pretty sure bet. The only question now is how to play them."

"What do you mean?"

"Like I say, some are better than others. Therefore, the order becomes important."

"I assume you've already worked this out?"

"Yes, of course. But I need to say it out loud. Put it in words. See if there's anything I forgot. I value your opinion, you know."

I did my best to keep a straight face. It occurred to me that if I had any comment other than, Good idea, Richard, the value of my opinion would sink like a stone.

"Fine," I said. "So what's your plan?"

"Okay," Richard said. "Here's how I see it. We have three witness who are relatively strong, two who are relatively weak, and one who is all right but unimportant—the one who left at midnight."

"You're basing that on my assessment?"

"Don't be silly. I've personally talked to them all."

I frowned. "Wait a minute. I thought you said you didn't want to talk to them. That you didn't want their stories to sound rehearsed."

"Right. And I certainly don't. On the other hand, I'm not going to put them on the stand without knowing what they're going to say."

"But . . ."

"But what?"

"You said you *weren't* going to talk to them. That that was your strategy."

"Right. And that sounded good?"

"Yes, it did."

Richard nodded. "See? That's because I'm a lawyer. What I say is *supposed* to sound good."

"Richard, I'm not a jury, I'm your investigator."

"Yes, but you bought it, right? Sounded good to you?"

"Sounded fine."

"There you are. Look, I can't be in court all the time. And I've never been in court on a murder case before. I don't get to practice much. This isn't like when you're in a play you get to rehearse and then you go on. I'm in there on my feet, improvising on the spot. How'd you like to be in a play where you didn't know the lines?"

"I have that nightmare all the time. Most actors do."

"Yeah, well, that's what trial work is. A drama where you improvise the whole script. So, you wanna give me a didn't-I-say-something-else? Well, maybe I did in dress rehearsal, but nothing counts until the trial starts. If I contradict myself on something I say *in court,* there is something I need to know. Got it?"

I got it. Richard, in addition to relegating me to the position of a cheerleader, had just undercut all my investigative work by interviewing the witnesses himself. While I always thought he *should,* it was a kick in the head to find out he *had.* I wondered if I wouldn't take it so personally if in the last week and a half I hadn't fetched so many Cokes.

"Uh-huh," I said. "So, what's your plan?"

"Lead off strong and end strong. I figure this to take two, possibly three days. The first day's gotta be good. I figure to start off with two winners right in a row."

"Two?"

"Yeah," Richard said. He consulted the pad on his desk. "That would be Sam Kestin and Barry Brown. The banker and the ad executive. Good solid witnesses, aren't going to rattle."

"Yeah, but why waste 'em both? You only got three winners. Don't you wanna spread 'em out?"

Richard nodded. "Exactly. Good point. I'm glad you asked that, because that's just the point I wanna make. Now, the first witness has gotta be strong. You can see that."

"Of course."

"Now, the second witness, same thing. Here's how I see it. I lead off with this banker. My direct examination will be short. Then Wellington gets a crack at him. His cross-examination will be long but ineffective. The guy's not the type to rattle, Wellington won't get a thing."

Richard held up one finger. "The next witness is key. So far, you got one man's unsubstantiated testimony. Corroborate it, you win. Blow it, you lose. If I put on a strong witness who holds the line, then I got a strong alibi, and everything Wellington does after that will look like whistling in the wind. But if I put on someone weak and he tears him to shreds . . ." Richard held up his hands, made a scale, ". . . then it's one to one. Equally balanced, could go either way. Since he's probably the last witness of the day, the jurors go home with that impression. So there I am the next morning, starting from scratch again."

"Uh-huh," I said. "Okay, I see what you're saying. But even so, you've blown two of your three best witnesses. I can understand your not wanting to have a weak follow-up. But what about the other guy? The one who went home at midnight. What's-his-name? Tim Hendricks. He's a stock trader, cold, methodical. He's not going to rattle. Wellington won't be able to do a thing with him."

"Yeah, but he went home at midnight. One's a good alibi and one isn't. I don't want to follow up a good alibi with a bad one, no matter how good the witness is. To go from 2:00 A.M. to midnight would be a sign of weakness. Even more so than putting on the guys who are going to rattle."

Richard went back to the list. "Let me give you the order the way I see it. First up is Sam Kestin, the banker. As I said. He's a logical first. Not only is he a good witness, but the game was at his house.

"Next up, Barry Brown. The ad executive." Richard consulted his notes. "The one you particularly didn't like." He looked up at me. "Is that why you object to him going second?"

My eyes widened. "It never occurred to me."

"Maybe not," Richard said. "Sometimes these subconscious motivations come into play nonetheless."

Good god. I blinked. That's what the cheerleader got for disagreeing.

"Anyway," Richard said, "he goes second. At this point we go with someone weak."

"Why?"

Richard shrugged. "I got to put 'em somewhere."

"Why?" I said. I think his subconscious-motivation crack had made me quarrelsome.

"What do you mean, why?"

"Why do you have to put 'em somewhere? Why use 'em at all?"

Richard looked at me, pityingly. "Stanley, use your head. It's a poker game. One of the first questions is, who was there? All of them are witnesses. If I skip one, it's like a red flag. If I don't call him, Wellington will. If *he* does, it's ten times worse."

"Fine," I said. "Granted. So you put a weak one third."

"Right. In fact, I put the weakest one third. That would be the actor—Phil Janson. Undoubtedly, Wellington will tear him apart."

"You'll let him?"

"Sure."

"Why?"

"In the first place, I couldn't stop him. In the second place, it will make Wellington look bad."

"Why?"

"You met the guy. He's basically defenseless. He'll tell his story, then Wellington will get him so confused he won't know which end is up. He'll contradict himself, he'll tie himself in knots, but it will be all right. The jury will already have two solid versions of what happened. So the perception will be of a poor, weak individual, being persecuted by a heartless bully who's twisting his words."

"I see," I said. I wondered if it was that simple.

"Now, you come back with the guy who left at midnight. Doesn't help, but doesn't hurt. Actually, it *does* help, because it solidifies the fact that these guys are telling the truth and the prosecutor's an asshole. Particularly if Wellington goes overboard getting the actor confused and gets so fired up from it he tears into this guy for going home early. At any rate, that witness, this Tim Hendricks, should get us back on solid ground."

Richard shrugged his shoulders, spread his hands. "Then we're back to weakness again, but look what we've done. The witness isn't all that bad. This is the guy owns the camping equipment store. The Birdman of Central Park South. Ollie Pruett. He's another nervous, fidgety type, gonna get tied up in knots, *but*—" Richard raised one finger. "He's not as bad as the stupid actor. Compared to him, he'll come off pretty well. And by now the jury will have no sympathy with Wellington going after these guys, so whatever he makes him say, it won't be that bad."

Richard smiled. "And then we're home free. I got the vice-president of the textile manufacturing company to close with. This Marvin Wainwright. Solid, substantial, back on track. Another one Wellington can't budge." His eyes gleamed. "And you can bet he'll go overboard, knowing he's the last one in the game. Knowing this is his last shot. That if he can't break this one, it's over. So he'll put up a huge fight, which eventually he'll lose.

"And the moment he does—the moment he says, No further questions—I rest my case."

Richard spread his hands. "And that's that. Wellington is in a no-win situation. If he doesn't put on rebuttal witnesses, I've won. If he does, the only way he can break this alibi is to manipulate the time of death. And once he does that—once he starts trying to show there's a slight possibility she was killed as late as two o'clock—once again I'm home free. Because, by doing that, he's conceding the alibi's unbreakable. Either way, Anson Carbinder is out the door."

"Uh-huh. So that's it?" I said.

"What do you mean, that's it?"

"All you've got is the alibi?"

"What do you mean, all I've got?"

"You got a second string to your bow?"

Richard, who had been tipped back in his desk chair, ready to discourse on the subject, stopped in mid-pontification. He frowned, crinkled his nose. "A second string to my bow? Did you really ask me that?"

"Well, I was just wondering—"

"If I was putting all my eggs in one basket?" Richard said. "Do you have any more clichéd idioms you'd like to throw at me?"

"Not at the moment," I said. "The point is, what have we got besides this alibi?"

"What *should* we have?" Richard said. "You'll pardon me, but if the guy didn't do it, what else is there?"

"Well, who did?"

Richard's eyes widened. "Oh," he said. "Of course. I'd forgotten about your TV mentality. Stanley, look. I'm an attorney. I don't solve crimes. I represent clients. I try to keep them out of jail. If I do a good job, they don't go there. If I do a bad job, they do. But solving crimes is not my department. It is the function of the police. If you think it's my department, it's because you grew up on a steady diet of Perry Mason. But guess what? No one is going to break down on cross-examination and say they did it. The way it works is, the prosecutor puts on his case, I put on mine, and the jury says who wins. It's as simple as that."

I knew it was.

I knew everything Richard said made perfect sense. That he was, as usual, right, and that I was just being silly.

But I couldn't help it. I'd had a problem with this case

from the beginning, and my problem was exactly that. That we weren't trying to prove who did it, only who didn't.

That was the whole problem.

Richard didn't care who did it.

I did.

35

"Your name is Sam Kestin?"

"That's right."

"What is your occupation?"

"I'm a banker."

Well, that certainly *sounded* impressive. Sam Kestin wasn't a person who *worked in* a bank. He was a *banker*. And he certainly looked the image—chubby, well fed, in his custom-tailored three-piece suit. Instead of answering Richard's questions, he could just as well have been turning him down for a loan. I found that reassuring.

And I needed reassuring. My talk with Richard the night before had left me very ill at ease. And it wasn't just that Richard had no interest in solving the crime. It went deeper than that.

In all the years of my association with Richard, I had always seen him as a sort of mythical figure, rushing in where angels fear to tread, confronting the upholders of the law, and beating them to a standstill. In all the times he'd interceded for me, he'd never been at a loss as to a course of action, as to what to do. And I, for one, had never doubted him. Argued with him sometimes, yes, but never doubted him. I guess what I'm trying to say is, I had never doubted that Richard had total confidence in *himself*. That *he* was always sure that he was doing the right thing.

That's what was bothering me now.

In every other case, Richard had interceded with the police or the district attorney's office in a short, snappy, effective manner, expediently accomplishing whatever needed to be done. But it had always been a simple, single task—get investigator released from jail, negotiate immunity in exchange for statement, or what have you. This was the first time Richard had ever taken a case to trial, and, while I knew it was his lifelong dream, it also seemed to me that, having achieved it, he wasn't quite sure what to do.

Of course, like most of my opinions, I was in no way sure it was correct. For all I knew, Richard was totally in control and the course of action he had chosen to pursue was absolutely right.

At any rate, I had to agree with his choice of Sam Kestin as his opening witness.

His direct examination wasn't bad, either.

"Mr. Kestin, where were you on the night of October twelfth and the early-morning hours of October thirteenth?"

"I was in my town house on East Sixtieth Street."

"Did you happen to see the defendant, Anson Carbinder, at that time?"

"Yes, I did."

"When did he arrive at your house?"

"Around eight o'clock."

"Eight o'clock on the evening of October twelfth?"

"That's right."

"And what time did he leave?"

"Two in the morning."

"And did he leave your house at any time between the hours of eight o'clock and 2:00 A.M.?"

"No, he did not."

"The defendant, Anson Carbinder, was in your house from eight o'clock until 2:00 A.M.?"

"That is correct."

"Thank you. No further questions."

My mouth fell open. No further questions? I hadn't known Richard was going to do that. He'd left out the poker game, the big hand, and all the other witnesses. In short, all the information I'd worked so hard to get.

And, in a flash, I realized what a great move it was.

ADA Wellington couldn't leave the testimony unchallenged. He had to cross-examine. And it would be like walking through a mine field. Sam Kestin would get all the damaging information in. And ADA Wellington would be the one bringing it out.

My faith in Richard's abilities soared.

ADA Wellington got to his feet, stalked the witness stand. The man did not look happy. He stood so the jury could see his face, as his eyes bored into the witness. His expression was classic. It instantly conveyed the idea that he was a man confronted by a habitual perjurer, incapable of telling the truth.

"You're a banker, Mr. Kestin?"

"That's right."

"Just what do you *do* in your bank?"

"I'm an executive."

"Uh-huh," Wellington said. Kestin might as well have told him he was a car thief. "And as an executive, what is it you do?"

"I approve loans."

"You approve loans? By that you mean automatically, anyone who applies for a loan gets one?"

"Objection, Your Honor," Richard said. "Incompetent, irrelevant, and immaterial."

"It was brought out on direct examination, Your Honor," Wellington said. "Counsel asked him what he did."

"Overruled," Judge Blank said. "But do try to move it along."

"Yes, Your Honor. Is that the case, Mr. Kestin? That you approve every loan you get?"

"Certainly not."

"Then your job isn't to *approve* loans, it's to decide whether they should be approved or not."

"Yes, of course."

"Some you approve, some you turn down."

"That's right."

"What percentage do you turn down?"

"Objection."

"Sustained."

"But you do turn down some?"

"Yes, I do."

"So, when I asked you what you did, and you said you approved loans, you weren't being entirely honest, were you?"

"Objection."

"Overruled. Witness may answer."

Sam Kestin did not appear the least bit ruffled. "I was being *entirely* honest. My job is to approve loans. That is the way it is generally referred to by me, by my associates, and by every other banker I've ever met. To approve loans automatically carries with it the converse, to reject loans. So it is not necessary to say it." Kestin smiled. "Believe me, I was not attempting to deceive you or the jurors in stating that I approve loans."

"Maybe not," Wellington said. "But is it or is it not a fact that the *reason* bankers refer to what they do as approving loans is because it puts them in a positive light?"

"I really couldn't say."

I could almost feel sorry for ADA Wellington. He was obviously feeling his way along, testing the waters, trying to work up the nerve to dive in.

Finally, he did.

"Mr. Kestin, you have stated that the defendant was in your house from eight o'clock on the evening of October twelfth until 2:00 A.M. on October thirteenth? Is that right?"

"Yes, it is."

"And just what were you doing at that time?"

"I refuse to answer on the grounds that an answer might tend to incriminate me."

And the place went wild.

36

Oh, boy.

Good move.

I had to hand it to Richard. What he'd done was obvious, but I hadn't even thought of it.

Sam Kestin had been playing poker.

That's illegal.

That's gambling.

By saying so, Sam Kestin would incriminate himself in the commission of a crime. He had a constitutional right not to do that, Richard had so advised him, and he had just invoked it.

Of course, no one in the courtroom except Richard and I knew that. For all *they* knew, Sam Kestin was guilty of the goddamn murder.

Hence the uproar.

At any rate, Judge Blank banged for silence, which was not quick in coming. When court finally quieted down, he ordered counsel into his chambers, turned on his heel, and stalked off, with Richard and ADA Wellington trailing along behind.

This abrupt departure left the jurors in the box and the witness on the stand. With the judge gone, no one was quite sure what to do with them. I saw a couple of the court officers confer and then glance in the direction of the judge's chambers, but it was clear neither one of them would have dreamed of disturbing him.

So there we sat, in suspended animation, for a good three-quarters of an hour, until the door finally banged open and Judge Blank returned to the bench. I can't say he looked any happier than he had when he left. Neither did ADA Wellington.

Richard looked positively serene.

When they had all resumed their positions, ADA Wellington approached the witness and said, "Mr. Kestin, you have refused to answer my question as to what you were doing on the evening of October twelfth on the grounds that an answer might tend to incriminate you. Is that correct?"

"Yes, it is."

"May I ask if you have consulted an attorney who has advised you of this constitutional right?"

"Yes, I have."

"Did you make a full and frank disclosure of the facts to this attorney?"

"Yes, I did."

"And the attorney advised you that you did not have to answer this question on the grounds that an answer might tend to incriminate you?"

"Yes, he did."

"Mr. Kestin, at this time, in my official capacity as a representative of the district attorney's office, I hereby grant you full immunity from any crime other than murder that may be disclosed by the answer to this question, and ask you again what you were doing in your town house on the evening of October twelfth."

"One moment," Judge Blank said. "Before you answer, Mr. Kestin. Let me make sure you understand the situation. Are you aware that the prosecutor is granting you immunity from prosecution for any crime that your answer might disclose?"

"Yes, Your Honor."

"Are you aware that, by so doing, he is removing the need for you to protect yourself by invoking your constitutional rights against self-incrimination?"

"Yes, I am."

"Are you further aware, that since he has made this concession, that since you need no longer fear any prosecution for such crimes as might be disclosed in your answer, that you are no longer eligible to invoke your constitutional privilege against self-incrimination and that you are therefore required to answer—in fact, should you now fail to do so, you could be held in contempt of court?"

"I understand, Your Honor."

Judge Blank nodded. "Fine. You may proceed, Mr. Wellington."

"Thank you, Your Honor. Now, then, Mr. Kestin. What were you doing on the evening of October twelfth and the early-morning hours of October thirteenth?"

"I was playing poker."

After all that, the admission was quite an anticlimax. But Wellington didn't seem a bit fazed. Obviously, it had been discussed in chambers. "You were in a poker game?"

"That's right."

"Who else was at this poker game?"

Sam Kestin ticked them off on his fingers. "Marvin Wainwright. Ollie Pruett. Barry Brown. Phil Janson. Tim Hendricks. And Anson Carbinder."

ADA Wellington just stood there glaring at him. His distress was obvious. Sam Kestin had just blown his case out of the water. The only question was, did he dare try to salvage it?

Not that big a question. The way things stood, he didn't dare *not* to.

"Mr. Kestin. The people you've just named—they were all there from the hours of eight o'clock until 2:00 A.M.?"

"I didn't say that."

"Well, you certainly implied it. But if that's not the case, would you kindly tell me who was there when?"

"All the people I named were there from eight o'clock until 2:00 A.M., with the exception of Tim Hendricks. Tim always leaves at midnight. This night was no exception. He left then. Everyone else stayed until the game broke up at two."

"Including Anson Carbinder?"

"That's right."

"And did Anson Carbinder leave the poker game at any time during the course of the evening?"

"No, he did not."

Wellington frowned, thought a moment. "Mr. Kestin, this poker game was in your town house?"

"That's right."

"Is this the *only* poker game you've ever had in your town house?"

"Objection, Your Honor," Richard said. "Incompetent, irrelevant, and immaterial. Also, that question is on its face an attempt to get the witness to incriminate himself by disclosing other crimes not included in the stipulation of immunity."

"Overruled," Judge Blank said. "But the witness will indeed be warned that he has not been granted immunity from any other crimes his answer might disclose."

"Then I decline to answer on constitutional grounds," Kestin said.

Wellington's frustration was evident. "Your Honor," he said. "I would like to pursue this matter, for reasons that will become clear. I therefore stipulate that my grant of immunity shall be extended to include any and all poker games in which the witness has participated, which took place in his town house. With this stipulation in place, I would like that question answered."

"So ordered," Judge Blank said. "Mr. Kestin, do you understand that you may now discuss poker with no fear of incrimination?"

"Yes, Your Honor."

"Proceed."

"Mr. Kestin, was that the only poker game you have ever had in your town house?"

"Of course not."

"You've played there several times?"

"Yes, we have."

"This year, for instance—have you played there other times this year?"

"Yes, we have."

"How often do you play cards?"

"Usually once a month."

"Was it always at your house?"

"No. But it often is."

"Prior to October twelfth—had you recently hosted other games?"

"That depends what you mean by recently?"

"I mean within the last few months."

"I believe I had, yes."

"You named half-a-dozen people who played in this game. Tell me, is it always the same people who play?"

"I beg your pardon?"

"The people you named—are they the only people who ever play?"

"No, of course not."

"Why not?"

"Everyone is not always free. People have engagements, they're out of town."

"I see. So when some people are busy, other people play?"

"That's right."

"So there are other regulars who have been to your house, besides the six you just named?"

"That's right."

"Then, let me ask you this. Is it not possible, is it not conceivable, that when you mention Anson Carbinder as having been at your poker game, you are remembering him being there, not from the game in October, but from some *previous* game? And that on October twelfth, the date that you mention, it was some *other* player who was there instead?"

"No, that is *not* possible."

"How can you be so sure? This happened over a month ago. How can you tell you're not confusing what happened then with what happened at some other time?"

Sam Kestin smiled. "It may be over a month ago *now,* but when it was brought to my attention it was fresh in my mind. Anson Carbinder's wife had just been killed. My first reaction when I heard that was, *My god, he was just here.*"

"But not necessarily that night," Wellington said. *"Just here* is a relative term. You might feel that way, even if the game had taken place last month."

Kestin shook his head. "No, no. I remember particularly, because of the high/low hand."

And there it was again. ADA Wellington either had to let that go or cross-examine.

He tried, for all the good it did. Because Sam Kestin cheerfully launched into an explanation of the big high/low hand, when Anson Carbinder had ace, two, three, four showing, and everyone expected him to go low, only he'd had a concealed full house and gone high. Sam Kestin remembered it particularly, because he'd had a nine low, and could have taken half the pot, but had chosen to go high with three eights.

I'm not sure ADA Wellington followed that, and I'm

pretty sure none of the jurors followed that. The poker part, I mean. But it didn't matter.

Not after Sam Kestin got through telling about how guilty he felt for thinking how lucky Anson was to have won that hand, and then finding out his wife had been killed.

The jurors might not have understood the intricacies of high/low poker.

But they sure knew Anson Carbinder had been in the game.

37

When court resumed after lunch, Barry Brown took the stand, and proved just as good a witness as Kestin. As much as I disliked the guy, I had to admit he came off well. His testimony was brief and to the point—he'd been at the game, Anson Carbinder had been at the game, and he had not left until the game had broken up at two.

Then Wellington went to work on him. You'd think there wouldn't be anything to work on, but actually there was. See, at Wellington's insistence, all the witnesses were under the rule. What that means is, they were not allowed to sit in court and listen to the other witnesses give testimony. So Barry Brown hadn't heard what Sam Kestin said.

Which left Wellington his opening. He could pick Barry Brown's testimony apart, looking for an inconsistency. So that's what he did.

"Tell me, Mr. Brown, who were the other people in the game?"

(And, oh, yes, Barry Brown had also been granted immunity.)

"Anson Carbinder. Sam Kestin. Ollie Pruett. Tim Hendricks. Phil Janson. And Marvin Wainwright."

"Were they all there the entire time?"

"Tim Hendricks left at midnight."

"Did anyone else leave early?"

"No, they did not."

"Did Anson Carbinder leave the poker game at any time for any reason?"

"No, he did not."

"Is it not a fact, Mr. Brown, that Anson Carbinder was not at that poker game, but he was there on a previous night?"

"No, it is not a fact. He was there that night."

"But not on a previous night?"

"He's been there on previous nights also."

"Then isn't it possible you confused the two events—no, let me finish, Mr. Brown. Isn't it possible that you're *remembering* Anson Carbinder from having been there at a previous game, and that is why you are now mistaken in placing him at that one?"

"No, it is not possible. He was there that night. I happen to remember particularly, because of the big high/low hand."

"Ah, yes," Wellington said. "And would that be the hand where Sam Kestin beat him out of a large pot?"

"No, it would not," Barry Brown said. "It was the other way around. Anson won the pot. He had a full house and he took it all."

"How is it you remember it so particularly?"

"Are you kidding? I was in the hand. I had a queen-high straight. Thought I had a good shot. It turned out I didn't."

"What hand did Sam Kestin have?"

"Three of a kind. Big deal. I beat *him.*"

"I see," Wellington said. "So, even if Anson Carbinder hadn't had a full house, Sam Kestin wouldn't have won?"

"No. Like I say, I had a straight."

"Then Anson Carbinder didn't beat Sam Kestin out of the pot. That doesn't make any sense. Because Kestin couldn't have won it anyway."

"No, no, you're missing the point," Barry Brown said. "Sam could have gone low. He'd have gotten half the pot if he had. No one else had a low. Anson beat him out of it by *looking* low and forcing Sam high. See what I mean?"

Wellington clearly didn't. It was almost comical, watching him trying to understand the nuances of high/low poker, and realizing, if he couldn't, he was going to lose his case. He put Barry Brown through a wringer. And I have to give the guy credit. Barry Brown, I mean. Grueling as the cross-examination was, he never lost his cool. And, finally, Wellington gave up.

It would have been great if court had adjourned just then. Richard would have accomplished his purpose—two solid witnesses, nailing down the alibi, locking it into the jurors' minds.

Unfortunately, Barry Brown was too good. Wellington gave in too soon. There was too much time left.

"Call your next witness," Judge Blank said.

For the first time all day, Richard did not look pleased.

"Call Phil Janson."

38

As Phil Janson took the witness stand, the thought that ran through my mind was, oh, my god.

He'd dressed for the part.

He was in costume.

Phil Janson was wearing a suit and tie, circa 1940, obviously ripped off from the wardrobe department of some summer theater somewhere. The wide-lapeled, pin-striped jacket had seen better days. It had also seen larger men. On him it was huge. Almost grotesquely so.

And the wide-striped tie didn't go. I must admit I'm no good at clothes—Alice always has to tell me if things match—but even I could tell the tie clashed. It wasn't close.

Then there was the shirt. I swear to god there was a tan ring around the collar of the shirt. And I knew exactly what it was. It was makeup. Theatrical base makeup. I don't think he was wearing it then. I certainly *hope* he wasn't wearing makeup then. But this was obviously a white shirt he had worn in plays. The makeup on the collar was quite visible, and what a bizarre touch *that* added to the scene.

Then there was the man himself. Janson, you will remember, was the one who kept fidgeting with his fingers. As if figuring that alone wasn't enough, he had now taken to biting his lip. And he was doing it at such a steady pace, the damn thing was bound to start bleeding before we were done.

Richard was on his feet before he was even sworn. I immediately recognized the strategy—get him on and off as fast as he could.

"Mr. Janson, were you at a poker game on the evening of October twelfth and the early-morning hours of October thirteenth?"

"Yes, I was."

"Who else was in the game?"

Phil Janson almost tore his hands apart and bit through his lip. But he managed to croak out the answer, listing all the usual suspects, Anson Carbinder chief among them.

"And from eight o'clock until two in the morning, did Anson Carbinder ever leave the game?"

"No, he did not."

"And do you recall a large high/low hand, where Anson won the whole pot?"

"Objection. Leading and suggestive."

"Sustained. Mr. Rosenberg, kindly avoid leading the witness."

"Sorry, Your Honor," Richard said. But he wasn't. This was one witness Richard intended to lead as much as he could. "Ah, Mr. Janson, do you remember any hand in particular?"

"Yes, I do. There was a big high/low hand, and Anson won it all."

"And what can you tell us about that hand?"

"Just that. Anson looked like he was going low, but he went high. We all went high, and he took the whole pot."

"You went high too?"

"Yes, I did."

"What did you have?"

"I had a straight to the jack."

"Do you know when this hand took place—what time of night, I mean?"

"No, I don't. I just remember the hand."

"But you do remember Anson Carbinder won the hand?"

"Yes, I do."

"And that Anson Carbinder was at the game from eight o'clock until two in the morning when the game broke up?"

"That's right."

"Thank you, Mr. Janson. That's all."

I'll never forget the look on Janson's face when Richard said that. He had stopped tearing at his own fingers. Now his hands gripped the sides of the witness stand, his fingernails digging into the wood. He was sitting very erect, with his back slammed against the back of the chair, his head up, his eyes wide. And his chin tucked in. It was quite a position. Defensive, defiant, terrified out of his mind. He looked for all intents and purposes like a man tied to a stake, about to be torn apart by a ravenous lion.

He go to his feet, that ravenous lion. ADA Beef Wellington. After Sam Kestin and Barry Brown, he was practically salivating at the chance to get at this one.

But it was not to be.

Before he could commence his cross-examination, Judge Blank took notice of the time and adjourned court until ten o'clock the next morning.

39

"What's the matter?"

"I don't know."

I really didn't. Something was bugging me about the day in court, but I couldn't put my finger on it. And Alice couldn't help me because she hadn't been there.

Well, that's not quite true. Alice could probably help me fine if I just knew how to let her. I sometimes think of Alice as a computer, capable of solving anything if just fed the right data. I was the one not up to the task of knowing what data to feed.

"Tell me again," Alice said.

"Tell you what?"

"Tell me everything. Anything that strikes you. Anything that made an impression."

"I think it's the last witness."

"The nervous one?"

"Yeah. The actor. Phil Janson."

"You said he wasn't that bad."

"His *direct examination* wasn't that bad. Richard helped him along, asked him easy questions and accepted whatever he said. Wellington will make him jump through hoops."

"I thought you already knew that."

"I did."

"I thought that was part of the plan. Isn't that what you told me last night? Two strong witnesses, then the weak one. They tear him apart, but it doesn't matter. Isn't that what you said?"

"That's what Richard said."

"And you don't agree?"

"It isn't that."

"What is it, then?"

"I don't know."

Which is where you came in. And would seem a suitable stopping place. Only Alice wouldn't leave it at that.

"All right," she said. "What about the other witnesses?"

"What about them?"

"You said they were good?"

"They were perfect. Couldn't be better. If court had adjourned after them, everything would have been fine."

"So, it isn't them."

"No, it isn't."

"And their testimony took most of the day?"

"That's right."

"And this actor—how long was he on the stand?"

"Just a few minutes. That's all."

"And if it hadn't happened—if he hadn't gone on—everything would have been just fine?"

"Everything would have been aces. The jury would have gone home sold on the idea Anson Carbinder was at that game."

"And they didn't?"

"No."

"Why not?"

"I told you. Because of the actor."

"Yes, but what *was it* about the actor?"

"I told you. He's nervous, he's insecure."

"So what?"

"What do you mean, so what?"

"Lots of people are nervous and insecure. They don't necessarily make a bad impression."

"He did."

"Why?"

"Why do you keep asking why?"

"Because I don't get an answer. And I need an answer,
because I wasn't there. So I don't have my impression, I
only have yours. You need to translate your impression for
me. Look, here's how I see it. We have a day here that is basically good. We have one small element that is slightly
bad. It's not even bad yet, it's just *potentially* bad. And yet
you choose to evaluate the entire day in terms of that one
small potential bad element."

"Are you telling me I'm a manic depressive?"

"No, I'm telling you there must be a reason. Why did
the bad witness make more of an impression on you than
the two good ones?"

"How about the fact he came last?"

"Not good enough. It's still only potentially bad. Put
yourself in the jurors' place. You've heard testimony all day
long establishing the fact Anson Carbinder has an alibi.
And then you hear this guy. It doesn't confirm it, but it
doesn't deny it, either. At worst, you go home wondering,
What's eating him? But you're still sold on the alibi. See
what I mean?"

"Yeah, but—"

"Aha!" Alice said, pouncing on it. "You're not sold on
that premise. Which means there *is* something more to it.
Now, what is it about the witness that disturbs you so
much?"

"I don't know."

"Come on. Think," Alice said. "This isn't that hard."

I stared at her. "Are you telling me you *do* know?"

"Yes, of course."

"What, then?"

"Okay," Alice said. "What is it about this witness—"

I broke in. "Excuse me, but fuck the Socratic method. Just tell me what you think."

"He's lying."

"Huh?"

"The witness is lying. This actor."

"Lying? How can he be lying?"

"He isn't, necessarily. What I mean is, he gives that impression. That's what you're reacting to. And that's what disturbs you so much. Not the fact he's insecure, but the way it translates to you, and the way you're afraid it translates to the jury. *The witness is lying.* That is the last impression that was left in everyone's mind when court broke up. Not that this was an insecure witness. Not that the prosecutor was going to rip him apart the next day. The impression was that Janson was lying. Which doesn't necessarily have to be true—it's just an impression. It's an impression formed by all the mannerisms you recognize as nervousness, but it translates subconsciously into a person who's not telling the truth. So, even if you *know* he's telling the truth—which I assume you do?"

"Yes, I do."

"Subconciously, you're still left with that impression. Which is why it's bothering you."

I frowned. "I suppose."

"Well, what else could it be. Was there anything he said?"

"He hardly said anything."

"Was his memory bad?"

"No. It was better than I expected. He remembered who was in the game, when they were there, and the fact Anson won the big high/low hand."

"He hadn't remembered that before?"

"Yeah, but not what he had. Richard must have worked on him. When I questioned him, he wasn't sure if he was in the hand or not. Now he remembers he stayed in with a jack-high straight. Maybe that's what's bothering me."

"What do you mean?"

"Well, in his case, the more he remembers, the worse it is. On cross-examination, I mean. If he simply says he doesn't remember, there's nothing Wellington can do. The more he remembers, the more Wellington can pound him with—if you remember this, how come you can't remember that?"

"Uh-huh," Alice said. "So you think that's what's bothering you?"

"I don't know."

Yes, we had come full cycle again. Still, I think we went around at least two more times. Even after that, the thing kept revolving in my head. Right through the eleven o'-clock news, right through my suggestion of marital bliss (denied), then right through David Letterman's monologue and top-ten list, after which I turned off the TV and lay there in the dark, unable to stop my mind.

Phil Janson. Walking disaster Phil Janson. Playing in the big game with his relatively well-to-do friends. A wonder the guy could even play cards, assuming he had the spare cash to do so. He seemed to lack the brains and the nerve. Typical of him, that he'd stayed in the big hand with a jack-high straight. Beaten by Barry Brown's queen-high straight. Not to mention Anson's full house, and someone else's flush besides. What did that make him, fourth best? Granted, he beat Sam Kestin's three eights, but Sam Kestin could have and probably should have gone low.

Easy for me to say, not being in the game. Not sitting there, looking at the ace, two, three, four. Would I have gone low with Kestin's hand? With a nine? With that much money in the pot?

An impossible question to answer. I hadn't been there. I hadn't seen what everyone had on board. What cards were showing around the table. The flush, for instance. Who was that, Tim Hendricks? Had he had a four flush showing? Or only three? Either way would be scary. Particularly with him staying in. Or had his cards looked low as well? Would that be another reason to go high?

And what about Barry Brown's straight. How good had it looked on board? Or Phil Janson's, for that matter. Without knowing what he saw, could I really fault Sam Kestin for going high with three eights?

Not on your life.

As I drifted off to sleep, the thought that occurred to me was, that jury was going to learn more about poker than any human being could ever wish to know.

I fell asleep, dreamed I was a high roller playing in the big game.

It was not a happy dream. I had a jack-high straight, and I was beat all over the board.

But I wouldn't fold. Even knowing I was beaten, I kept throwing money in.

I awoke in a cold sweat, sat bolt upright in bed.

There were five eights.

40

Richard wasn't impressed.

"Stanley, do you know what time it is?"

Yes, I did. It was two in the morning, and I'd called Richard at home. After Anson Carbinder did it, I'd pried Richard's home number out of him as part of the new deal.

I don't think he expected me to use it.

"It's important, Richard. There's five fucking eights."

"So you say. I don't see what's the big deal."

"He's lying, Richard."

"Not necessarily."

"Oh, yeah? Add it up. Sam Kestin went high with three eights. Barry Brown had a straight to the queen. That's eight, nine, ten, jack, queen. Phil Janson had a straight to the jack. That's seven, eight, nine, ten, jack. Any way you slice it, that's five eights."

"So he made a mistake. What's the big deal?"

"Wellington will crucify him with it."

"Wellington may not even notice it."

"Are you kidding? I noticed it."

"After a considerable length of time," Richard said dryly. "Are you aware of the fact that it's two in the morning?"

"Yes, I am. Richard, we've got to do something."

"Just what would you like to do?"

"This Phil Janson—we've got to see him."

"Now? Are you out of your mind?"

"Richard, Phil Janson lied. If I figured it out, other people can too."

"You're making too much of this."

"You don't want to talk to him?"

"Of course, I want to talk to him. I'll see him before court."

"That may not be enough."

"Enough? Stanley, I worked with bad witnesses before. I can straighten this out."

"If he's mistaken, yes. But what if he's lying?"

"About what hand he had?"

"About the whole thing."

"Stanley, give it a rest. Whatever the guy's situation, it's not gonna change between now and this morning. I appreciate your concern, but give it a rest. If I don't get some sleep, I'll be no good in court. I'll see you tomorrow."

And he hung up.

Damn.

I slammed down the receiver, grabbed my notebook off the kitchen table, flipped through.

I'd been calling from the kitchen so as not to wake up Alice. Nice try. She came padding in from the bedroom, rubbing her eyes. "Stanley. What the hell are you doing?"

I found the number, punched it into the phone.

"Calling a witness."

"What?"

One ring.

Two.

"Stanley?"

"Just a minute."

Three.

Come on, come on, wake up, you son of a bitch.

Four.

Click.

"This is Phil Janson. I'm not in right now, but please leave a message after the beep."

"Stanley?"

Beep.

"Phil, this is Stanley Hastings. The investigator. Anson Carbinder's investigator. Phil. Can you hear me? Pick up the phone. If you hear this, pick up the phone. Please."

Nothing.

Damn.

I slammed down the phone.

"Stanley, what's going on?"

"There's five eights."

"What?"

"Hang on, Alice. I gotta make another call."

"To who?"

But I was already flipping through the notebook. I found the number, punched it in.

41.

Sergeant MacAullif slammed his car to a stop in front of the building on Eighth Street, opened the door, and got out. He stomped to the sidewalk, blew on his freezing hands.

"I can't believe you came," I said.

"Don't be silly."

"Silly? After what Richard did in court?"

"Exactly," MacAullif said. "After what he did in court, you wouldn't call me unless it was life or death. So what's up?"

"You know who lives here?"

"Of course, I do. I was here myself, remember?"

"That was a while back."

"Yeah, wasn't it. So what's the deal?"

"You hear this guy's testimony?"

"No, I didn't. I'm a witness, and I'm under the rule. Damn stupid rule, a cop can't sit in court."

"Hey, don't look at me. It was Wellington asked for it."

"You get me here three in the morning in the freezing cold to debate technical rules of law?"

"No. The thing is, this guy testified today."

"Yeah? So what?"

I jerked my thumb at the door. "Let's find out."

MacAullif's eyes narrowed. "You're not going to tell me?"

"I didn't say that."

"Three o'clock in the fucking morning and you're not going to tell me?"

"I think the guy's in trouble. I hope I'm wrong."

"Trouble how?"

"What'd you hear about the testimony?"

"The guy's a chickenshit, Wellington'll tear him apart."

"Yeah. Well, I don't think he wants that to happen."

"No kidding. Oh, you mean bad?"

"Yeah."

"How bad?"

"Bad."

"You think he'd kill himself?"

"I think he might. I hope I'm wrong."

I was wrong.

Phil Janson hadn't killed himself.

Someone else had done it for him.

42.

Judge Blank frowned down from the bench. "Why wasn't I informed of this in chambers?"

"It just happened, Your Honor," Wellington said.

"The witness is unavailable?"

"The witness is dead, Your Honor."

"So you said. And you wish a continuance?"

"No, Your Honor. I wish to proceed."

"How can you proceed without the witness?"

"I mean with the trial."

"And what is the defense position? Does the defense wish a continuance?"

"I move for a mistrial, Your Honor," Richard said.

ADA Wellington nearly gagged. "Mistrial? Did he say mistrial? What a perversion of justice that would be. When Your Honor hears the facts of the case—"

"I don't wish to hear the facts of the case," Judge Blank said. "I would like to hear arguments regarding procedure. You want to proceed, and the defense wants a mistrial. I am concerned with the grounds."

"There are several," Richard said. "The witness, Phil Janson, has been murdered. Once the jury hears that, how can the defendant get a fair trial? Every juror's perception must be altered by this event. And you can't keep it from them.

Phil Janson testified yesterday. He was to be cross-examined today. If he's not cross-examined, they'll want to know why. If you tell them, it's bad. If you don't tell them, it's worse. Either way, it colors their perception. There's no way they can be fair and impartial. I move for a mistrial."

"Unbelievable," ADA Wellington said, shaking his head. "Absolutely unbelievable. Your Honor, without going into the specifics of the case, let me go into the facts regarding the death of this witness. The witness, Phil Janson, was discovered dead in his apartment at three in the morning by Sergeant MacAullif, the police officer who has already testified here in court. Acting on allegation and belief, Sergeant MacAullif entered Phil Janson's apartment at 3:00 A.M. and discovered him lying dead on the floor. He had been killed by multiple stab wounds from a kitchen knife. The knife was found on the floor beside the body. It was apparently a knife from the kitchen of the decedent. Your Honor will note that this is identical to the method by which Barbara Carbinder was killed."

"Objection," Richard said. "That's a conclusion on his part."

"Yes, but we're not taking evidence now," Judge Blank said. "Proceed, Mr. Wellington. What else have you got?"

"The answering machine, Your Honor."

"What about it?"

"There was one message on Phil Janson's answering machine. It was from one Stanley Hastings, whom I understand is a detective in the employ of the defense. On the tape you can hear him identifying himself and asking the decedent to pick up. You can hear the voice, tense, urgent—"

"Objection," Richard said.

"We have the tape. You can hear for yourself."

"What was the time of this call?" Judge Blank said.

"The defense is not communicative on this point. But according to Sergeant MacAullif, he received a phone call at approximately two-thirty this morning from the investigator, Stanley Hastings."

Judge Blank held up his hand. "One minute. The *defendant's investigator* called the police officer?"

"That's right, Your Honor. When he couldn't reach the witness himself he became concerned, he communicated with Sergeant MacAullif, and he was present when Sergeant MacAullif entered the apartment."

"And just how did the officer enter the apartment?"

"As it happened, the door was ajar," Wellington said. "If I could continue, all these matters are somewhat secondary to what has actually happened here."

"Which is what?"

"I already mentioned the answering machine. Perhaps even more interesting is the phone itself. We are in the process of tracing Phil Janson's phone calls. But one we already know. The last one. Phil Janson's phone had a redial feature. You know, you press a button and it automatically calls the last number dialed. Well, that number happened to be Anson Carbinder's apartment."

"You see, Your Honor," Richard said. "This is exactly the type of insinuation and innuendo that will prejudice the jury."

"Insinuation? Innuendo?" Wellington said. "I just stated a simple fact. The facts of the matter are somewhat damning, but they are nonetheless facts."

"That may well be," Judge Blank said. "But I've not heard anything yet to justify your position. The death of this witness, sensational as it is, is certainly prejudicial and will make it difficult for the jury to evaluate the case."

"No, it won't, Your Honor," Wellington said. "If I may be allowed to continue. There have been other developments that leave the matter in no doubt."

"Other developments?"

"Yes, Your Honor. Which I am eager to get to. Only, it's

difficult with this spectacular elimination of a witness to handle first. The fact is, another witness has come forward who can shed some light on this matter."

"Another witness?"

"Yes, Your Honor."

"May I point out that you have finished your presentation. The defendant is putting on witnesses now."

"This *is* a defense witness, Your Honor."

"I beg your pardon?"

"This is a defense witness. I am referring to Mr. Ollie Pruett, who is one of the witnesses on the defense witness list. He has come forward and offered to shed some light on the situation."

"Objection, Your Honor!" Richard shouted. "He can't do that. That's tampering with a witness."

"Nothing of the sort," Wellington said smoothly. "This witness came forward of his own accord."

"I take it the defense knows nothing of this?"

"Your Honor, not only do I know nothing of this, but I find it indicative of highly unethical conduct."

"You watch your ethics and I'll watch mine," Wellington snapped.

Judge Blank frowned. "Gentlemen, we will have none of that."

"I'm sorry, Your Honor," Wellington said. "But once you understand the situation . . . Well, the fact is, this witness came forward because he doesn't wish to lie."

"Objection, Your Honor!" Richard shouted. "That's an outrageous statement!"

"One moment, Mr. Rosenberg. I assure you, you will get your chance. But I am going to hear this charge." Judge Blank held up his finger. "Mr. Wellington, I warn you to watch your tongue. But I am going to ask you now exactly what you mean."

"Exactly what I say, Your Honor. The witness, Ollie

Pruett, does not wish to perjure himself, as the other witnesses have done."

"Other witnesses?"

"The other defense witnesses. Their testimony is per-
jured, Your Honor. That is why a mistrial would be a gross
miscarriage of justice. For the defense attorney to suborn
perjury, and then cry mistrial when his perfidy is found
out."

"Your Honor, Your Honor!" Richard cried. "I know you
told me to be quiet, but this is too much!"

ADA Wellington raised his voice to drown him out.
"That's what the witness, Ollie Pruett, will testify to, Your
Honor. That he was asked to lie. That *all* the witnesses were
asked to lie. About Anson Carbinder being at the poker
game. Because, in point of fact, Anson Carbinder was never
there at all."

43

"What a mess."

I had to agree with Richard there. It certainly was a mess.

We were alone in Richard's office. It occurred to me, it seemed like we were *always* alone in Richard's office. Ever since this case began. That's because Anson Carbinder never sat in on our little meetings. He always had something better to do.

I must say, I resented him for it.

I couldn't resent him for it now. After ADA Wellington's showing, Judge Blank had rescinded bail, and Anson Lover-Boy Carbinder had been unceremoniously hauled off to the hoosegow.

It occurred to me, it was about time. Is that vindictive? You bet. I'm sorry, but it was my first murder trial. The first case I'd been asked to gather evidence for. And what had I been allowed to do? Aside from bug MacAullif about the time of death, absolutely nothing except take witness statements from a bunch of yuppie poker players.

All of whom were lying their ass off.

"How bad is it?" I said.

Richard looked at me, cocked his head. "That's like asking the hangman if it's going to hurt. It's bad. It's real bad."

"Wanna fill me in?"

Richard had just come from a post-trial conference with his client. I sure would have liked to have been a fly on the wall. I didn't know what was said, but I had an idea as to the tenor of the conversation. Richard's shirt collar was unbuttoned, and his tie was pulled down. I can't recall ever seeing him like that. Except when I asked him for that raise.

"I can give it to you in a nutshell," Richard said. "Anson's alibi was faked, as you know. As the whole fucking courtroom knows. As anyone who watches the evening news is going to know. It may even be the goddamn lead story."

"Where was he?"

"Where do you think?"

"With the bimbo?"

"Bingo. Right on the button. And what a wonderful whoop-de-do that would be."

"Would be?"

"If I let him tell it. I mean, what a great defense position—No, I wasn't murdering my wife, I was in bed with a busty blonde, whose pinup photos have already been introduced as evidence in court. You think the media's having fun now? This is tame. This is nothing. All we need is Anson to change his story—Well, I was lying about the poker, I was actually getting laid.

"What a hell of a fellow that sketches him to be. The hero in detective fiction cheerfully marches into the gas chamber rather than besmirch the reputation of the woman he spent the night with. And then there's Anson, doing just the opposite."

"You mean you can't use it?"

"Right. I can't use it."

"As a matter of ethics?"

Richard looked at me. "Ethics? Are you out of your

mind? I'd use it in a flash if I thought it would do any good. The problem is, if Anson claims that, there's not one man, woman, or child in the courtroom who's gonna believe him."

"So what *can* you do?"

"I have no idea. All I know is, if that's the truth, I can't go with the truth. So I gotta find something else."

"Like what?"

"I don't know. I gotta think this out. Which is why you're here."

I'd been wondering why. Actually, I was *still* wondering.

"What do you mean?"

"I want you to ask me questions. Like you're doing now. Help me to roll with the punches. Figure this thing out."

"Okay. First off, what's Anson's story?"

"I told you. He was shacked up with the broad."

"Then he got home at two in the morning, found his wife dead?"

"So he says."

"Is that part the same—that he undressed in the dark, slipped into bed, and then felt the blood?"

"Absolutely. Which makes sense. All the more reason to be sneaking in if he's coming from the bimbo rather than the poker game."

"So what does he do then?"

Richard made a face. "This is where it gets sticky. Actually, the whole thing's sticky. But it appears our boy made some calls."

"To whom?"

"To the bimbo, for one. He calls her up and tells her, We have a small problem."

"And what does she do?"

"Freaks out. Goes into hysterics. At which point Anson decides counting on her for an alibi probably isn't the swiftest move in the world. All right, he told his wife he was playing poker. It's the story he's been telling all along, and his poker buddies are all primed to back him up. So why not let 'em? He calls the game, tells 'em what happened, asks for help."

"And they all agreed?"

Richard shrugged. "Some more readily than others. It was Sam Kestin's house, he's the one Anson talked to, he took charge, whipped the others into line."

"And the big hand?"

"They made it up, natch. Which is why I didn't hear it from Anson. He didn't know about it, 'cause they didn't have time to plan it on the phone. When he called, they broke up the game and started working the alibi out. And what they agreed on, aside from to do it in the first place, was there ought to be something specific they remembered to establish that Anson was there. So they decided on the big hand. Which wasn't nearly as difficult a concept for them as it was for me. They all play this high/low shit, so what sounded like absolute gibberish made perfect sense to them. And they all grasped it instantly—there was a big hand, Anson looked like he was going low, but went high and took it all."

I shook my head. "They all agreed to commit perjury in a murder trial?"

"Yeah, I know," Richard said. "But you gotta understand how this developed. It was a gradual thing. First off, they're not all for it, they're just going along. And to begin with, it's not to tell it, it's just not to deny it.

"In the second place, it's not perjury. No one's thinking trial. They're all thinking, Anson's in a tight spot, we tell this story to get him out of it.

"You have to understand, none of these guys think Anson killed his wife. They know where he was, banging the bimbo. That's where he's been every time they've had a poker game the last six months. It's something they laugh about. Suddenly they're not laughing. Anson calls up, While I was at the babe's, some burglar got in and killed my wife. You gotta back me up, 'cause I can't tell the cops I was there."

Richard shrugged. "No, they don't want to do it, but they do. Then he gets arrested and bound over for trial, and the way the cops and I play it, they don't tell their story right away. To anyone but you. Before they know it, they're on the hook to tell it in court. And they do. In come cases, very reluctantly."

"Right," I said. "What about the phone call?"

"What phone call?"

"You know. Phil Janson. The last redial. What does Anson have to say about that?"

"He called him. Said he had cold feet and was afraid he was going to blow it."

"Not that he couldn't go through with it?"

"No, just that he was nervous as hell."

"And what did Anson do?"

"Gave him a pep talk, told him he'd be fine."

I tried to keep the skepticism out of my voice. "And Phil Janson bought it?"

"According to my client."

"Jesus Christ."

Richard put up his hands. "I said it was a mess."

"That you did. Has Anson got an alibi for last night?"

"As a matter of fact, he does."

"Don't tell me."

"That's right. She was there."

"Great."

"Yeah. And it's just their word for it, because he lives in a town house, so who's to see him going in and out?"

"What about the other night?"

"Huh?"

"The night his wife was killed—he was at her place—so

wouldn't the doorman know what time he went in and out?"

"Sure, if he was on duty. But it's one of those buildings they lock the front door at eleven."

"With no one in the lobby?"

"There you are. And even if there was, you're talking a month ago. Who's gonna remember that well?"

"Right. What about her?"

"What *about* her?"

"Did you talk to her after you talked to him?"

"Yes, I did."

"What's your verdict?"

"What do you mean?"

"How does she come across? Is she the type to lie and give him an alibi if he really wasn't there?"

Richard grimaced, shook his head. "Close point."

"What do you mean?"

"*I* don't think she's lying. I think he was there. On the other hand, you put your finger right on it. Is she the *type* to lie like that? Absolutely. Wouldn't put it past her. It's just the sort of thing that she'd do."

"Great."

"Right. If I can see it, the jury can see it. Which makes her absolutely worthless. Not that she wouldn't be, anyway."

"But you still buy her story—about him being there?"

"Yes, I do."

"Then he didn't kill Phil Janson."

"Of course not."

"So who did?"

"Huh?"

"Who killed Phil Janson?"

"How the hell should I know?"

"Well, isn't that what we have to concentrate on now?"

"Why?"

"Why? Don't you think the same person that killed him killed her?"

"Oh, absolutely. I'd think that even if the means were different. Which they weren't. Of course, you could put that down to a copycat crime. But I don't think so. Not in this case. And I can't imagine anyone else thinking so, either. The killer strikes again, that's what we're left with here.

"Which is a bit of hard luck for Anson. If I hadn't done such a good job of getting him out on bail, this murder would have put him in the clear." Richard shook his head. "Only, if he's in jail, it doesn't happen."

"Why not?"

"Don't be silly. My client has been framed. Whoever framed him isn't going to blow it by doing something that exonerates him."

"You're saying if he was in jail, Phil Janson would be alive?"

"Not at all. If Phil Janson had to go, I'm sure he would. Only, the means would be different. The killer wouldn't cut him up with a knife. Wouldn't try to make it look like a similar crime. In that instance, the killer would go out of his *way* to make it look like something else. Preferably an accident. Getting run down by a car would fill the bill."

"Uh-huh. But with Anson out of jail, the killer tries to make it look like him?"

"Exactly."

"So who's the killer?"

"I have no idea. But it doesn't matter. As long as I can raise the inference that such a man exists.

"And that's the tack I gotta take. Tomorrow morning, this whole thing blows up. God knows how the judge is going to rule, but one thing for sure, it won't be for me."

"Rule on what?"

"My motion for a mistrial, for one thing. Well, you can

forget that. I'd have a better chance of winning the lottery. But then there's all the other stuff. What happens to the testimony? Does he strike it out? Does he let it stand? Either way, there's gonna be a brawl. My man gets killed so I lose his testimony? No way. On the other hand, the testimony goes in and Wellington doesn't get to cross-examine? I imagine he'd have something to say about that.

"Then there's the perjury counts. The charge of suborning perjury. And the prospect of me getting disbarred." Richard stopped, shook his head, looked at me. "Can you imagine the irony there? I build up a multimillion-dollar negligence business from trying civil suits and try one criminal case and lose it all."

The irony of that was not lost on me. It just didn't seem my main concern at the moment.

"What about the witnesses?"

"What about 'em? The way things stand, they're on the hook for perjury. I figure we can count on them making deals to save their ass."

"Not them. I mean the ones who haven't testified."

Richard shrugged. "Same difference. This one guy's already crossed over, you figure the others to. It doesn't matter. The thing is, it takes all of them to make the alibi. It only takes one of them to blow it."

"I mean, without the witnesses, what have you got?"

There. I had said it as tactfully as possible. It was the closest I'd come to an I-told-you-so for his sarcastic eggs-in-one-basket rejoinder to my got-another-string-to-your-bow?

It didn't faze Richard at all. "Good point," he said, as if it were a novel concept. "Without the witnesses providing an alibi, I'm left raising reasonable doubt. Which isn't as bad as it seems. The prosecution's case is full of holes. And the tiniest hole, you put your fingers in, you start pulling, before you know it there's this huge gap."

PARNELL HALL

Richard broke off. Chuckled. "Granted, we have this small gap of our own. A basic credibility gap. For providing a phony alibi. But there's a saving grace. It wasn't Anson that did it. It was his buddies tried to give him a boost. Big deal. Not his fault. My client hasn't told his story yet."

Richard raised his finger. "When he does, it's gonna be a four-hankie weeper. There's not gonna be a dry eye in the house. You are going to see a man bare his soul. He's gonna get up there and confess to being a low-life scum. A man caught in the throes of passion. A man so hopelessly head over heels in love that it blinded him to everything else. Made him forsake his wife. Betray his wedding vows. You are gonna see a man put his cards on the table, the good and the bad. You are gonna see a man bare his very soul."

I think he'd said that before. But I had to admit, on the whole, Richard was doing the sob-story routine pretty well.

"Uh-huh," I said. "That's fine, Richard. And what about me?"

"You?"

"Yeah. What do you want me to do?"

"I want you there in court, just like always."

"No, I mean now. Tonight. Whaddya want me to look into?"

"Look into?"

"Investigate. What do you want me to do?"

"Nothing. There's nothing *to* do."

"You're kidding."

"Not at all."

"But we have no idea who did this."

"And we're not gonna have," Richard said. He held up both hands, looked at me with concern. "Stanley, how often do we have to go through this? I can't solve this crime. Even if I could, that's not my job. My job is to present the case in a manner that results in the jury letting my client off. Failing that, my job is to sucker the judge into making a questionable ruling that would be grounds for a reversal or appeal."

Richard cocked his head. "I think you doubt me because I'm a negligence lawyer. You figure a criminal attorney would know better. Well, I got news for you. William Kuntsler wouldn't play it any different. You think he runs around finding out who did it? No. He listens to the police theory of the case, then he comes up with his own theory that contradicts it. You argue that, you raise reasonable doubt, your client walks and you've done your job. If I do that, I'm a good lawyer. But you, schmuck, will figure I failed for not solving the crime. Am I right?"

I said nothing.

"Come on," Richard said. "Is that how it is?"

I sighed. "No," I said. "No, it isn't."

But it was.

44

"You can't let it get to you."

Fine for Alice to say. She wasn't there. She didn't have to sit in court day after day doing nothing. And then watch all the work she'd done blow up in her face. Easy for her to talk.

"Fine," I said. "I shouldn't let it get to me. Can you suggest anything I should be doing instead?"

"Why don't you solve the crime?"

"Huh?"

Alice swiveled the desk chair around. She'd been typing at the computer when I'd come in. Turning away from it was no small concession on her part. Alice is a computer junkie. Taking her eyes off the monitor represented a major sacrifice.

"I said, why don't you solve the crime? You've got the whole evening to work this out. Why don't you go ahead and do it?"

"Richard isn't interested in solving the crime."

"So what? Who cares about Richard? You need him to think it out? Not likely. You've solved tougher things than this."

"Alice, I've been working on this for two months now."

"Sure, but now you've got a lead."

"What lead?"

"The second murder. You've got a whole fresh start now."

"No, I don't. I've got a crime just like the first crime. Nobody thinks it's anything different."

"Yeah, but who cares what *they* think? The point is what *you* think."

"I don't *know* what I think. And Richard doesn't give a damn what I think. All he cares about is creating reasonable doubt."

"What's wrong with that?"

"It doesn't solve the crime."

"Which is why you've got to solve it."

"How?"

"What about the witnesses you interviewed?"

"What about them?"

"They were lying. Now that they're telling the truth, what have they got to say?"

"Nothing. They're not involved. They were a phony alibi that didn't work. But, in point of fact, they had nothing to do with it at all."

"Then who did?"

"The bimbo. What's-her-name. Connie Maynard."

"Right. So what's her story?"

"I have no idea."

"You haven't talked to her?"

"No."

"Why not?"

I took a breath. Ticked them off. "In the first place, I wasn't asked to. In the second place, when this began, she was peripheral, she wasn't important. She was just an unfortunate circumstance we hoped the police wouldn't come up with."

"But now she isn't. Now she's the whole alibi."

"Yeah. So?"

"So, don't you want to talk to her?"

"What's to talk about? According to her, Anson was with her up till the time he went home and found his wife."

"Right. Which is what makes her so important. I would think you would want to know the details."

"The details?"

"I don't mean of their sex life. Stanley, why is this a problem?"

I wasn't really sure. I took a breath. "I think it has something to do with exceeding my authority. This whole case I've been terribly frustrated by the fact that I wasn't in charge. This is the first time I've ever been employed by a lawyer. In a murder case, I mean. And I'm not acting for me, I'm acting for him. Richard's interviewed the woman. He talked to her today. He just gave me his assessment of her testimony.

"Now you say *I* should talk to her. And it's like second-guessing him. That's like saying maybe I can do a better job than he can."

"Well, maybe you *can.*"

"Alice—"

"Don't sell yourself short. Richard's a lawyer. That doesn't make him right. In point of fact, you've had more experience with murder cases than he has."

"That's not the same as questioning witnesses. That's his job. That's what he does."

Alice threw up her hands. "Stop. Please. How did we ever get so far off the track? Never mind whose responsibility it is or who's stepping on whose toes. You say Richard talked to the woman. Fine. What was the result?"

"Huh?"

"What did he tell you? What did he find out?"

I spread my arms, palms up. Shrugged. "Just what I already said. She confirms the poker alibi was faked, he was with her and went home and found his wife."

"And Richard's opinion of her story?"

"He believes her. But that's as far as it goes. On the other hand, he says she doesn't make a good impression, and he doubts if the jury will believe her. He says she's the type of woman who gives the impression she'd be perfectly willing to lie."

"All the more reason to talk to her."

I looked at Alice. "Huh? I'm afraid I'm not following this. I just got through saying Richard thinks her story is true."

"Exactly," Alice said. "Which means Anson Carbinder didn't kill his wife."

"So?"

"So someone else did. The problem is to find out who. I would think this woman would be an excellent source of information."

"Why?"

"Don't be stupid. She was having an affair with the guy. Then his wife got killed. Assuming it's not a random crime, it's personal. The motives are going to have to do with the personalities of the people involved. I can't think of a better source of information than the mistress."

I sighed. "Alice, I hear what you're saying. But it's like I said. If I talked to her now, it would be like undercutting Richard. That's for starters. In the second place, I doubt if she'd even talk to me."

"She knows who you are?"

"Sure she does. I met her the first day, when Anson was in her apartment. And I see her every day in court. Not to speak to, but she must see me talking to Richard."

"You couldn't tell her Richard—"

"No, I couldn't!" I interrupted hotly. "I'm sorry. It's just that you're pushing me into a corner. It's like you want me to defy Richard and do something he wouldn't want me to do. Well, Richard happens to be our main source of income. Do you really think I should jeopardize that?"

"Fine, if that's the way you feel about it."

"Feel about it? How can you say *feel about it?*"

"He wouldn't fire you."

"Huh?"

"No matter what you did, he wouldn't fire you. You're his only steady investigator. You're the one he depends on. You really think he'd fire you?"

"Alice—"

She put up her hands. "I know, I know, that's not the point. It would be very unpleasant to have him really pissed off at you. Plus, you don't think she'd talk to you anyway and the whole bit. And—" She broke off at the expression on my face. "What is it?"

"It just occurred to me—what I said just now—about meeting her in her apartment."

"What about it?"

"She wasn't there."

"Huh?"

"I mean at first. It was just me and Anson." I put up my hand. "You gotta understand, this was two months ago and the story just changed, so some of this is slow clicking in. But I got beeped and sent to the address to meet Anson Carbinder. And at first I thought it was his apartment. There was no one else there. And I wasn't given any other name. Just the address, the apartment number, and him. I had no idea he didn't live there until she came walking in."

"Yeah. So?"

"So where was she? See, it wasn't important at the time because he wasn't there. He was at a poker game until two in the morning, then he was home, then he was with the cops. When they released him, he didn't want to go home because it was a crime scene, so he came there. I remember I made a big deal about the fact that, from the way they greeted each other, he hadn't seen her since the murder. At the time, all it meant to me was he must have had a key to her apartment to have let himself in. Which was going to be damaging as hell. But never mind that. The thing is, where was she?"

"What do you mean?"

"You wash out the poker game, and now Anson was with her in her apartment until two in the morning. He leaves, goes home, finds his wife, gets hauled in by the cops, bailed out by Richard, then goes to her apartment and lets himself in with a key sometime in the early-morning hours, I don't know when, but, say, six or seven. Connie isn't there, and she doesn't show up until I'm interviewing the guy around ten."

"So where was she from two in the morning till ten?" Alice said.

"Exactly."

"You see?" Alice said. "These are questions that should be answered."

"I'll talk to Richard."

"What?"

"I'll find out if he asked her, and, if not, I'll suggest that he does."

"Uh-huh," Alice said.

I looked at her. "What's the matter? That's not good enough? It doesn't count unless I do it myself?"

"Don't be silly," Alice said.

But she didn't look happy.

45

"Your Honor, I am attempting to prevent a gross miscarriage of justice."

I had to hand it to Richard. For a man without a leg to stand on, he was doing one hell of a hornpipe.

Judge Blank was not impressed. "Mr. Rosenberg, your motion for a mistrial has been denied. I am concerned with procedure now, specifically with regard to the testimony of the witness Phil Janson. What is the defense position in this matter?"

"My position is that the death of this witness abridges the defendant's constitutional right to a fair trial."

Judge Blank scowled. "Need I repeat myself? I have already ruled. The trial is proceeding. You may take that as a given. Now, with that understanding, what is your position regarding Phil Janson's testimony?"

"I have no position, Your Honor. The witness has testified. The testimony speaks for itself."

Judge Blank frowned. Turned to the ADA. "Mr. Wellington, what is the prosecution's position on that?"

Wellington put up his hands. "Fine by me, Your Honor. As far as I'm concerned, the witness's testimony may stand."

"Without cross-examination? That would be highly irregular."

"I'll waive my cross-examination, Your Honor."

Judge Blank nodded. Turned to Richard. "Is that acceptable to the defense?"

"Absolutely not, Your Honor," Richard said. "For all the points I've already made. If he waives his cross-examination, the jury will have to be told why. Which will prejudice them against the defendant."

Judge Blank turned back to the prosecutor. "What do you have to say to that?"

Wellington shrugged. "It's all the same to me, Your Honor. If the defense would prefer, I'm willing to have Phil Janson's testimony expunged from the record, just as if he had never testified."

"And how would you expunge it from the minds of the jury, would you mind telling me that?" Richard said irritably. "You see what I'm up against, Your Honor? Here's the assistant district attorney, oozing cooperation, making one suggestion after another, all of which would be extremely detrimental to the defense."

"That's hardly fair, Your Honor," Wellington said. "The witness lied—that's what's detrimental to the defense. The witness committed perjury. The fact that he committed perjury is now obvious. Any way you slice it, it's going to be somewhat detrimental."

"You see, Your Honor," Richard said. "I try to address these points and all I get is sarcasm and derision."

"*What* points?" Wellington said. "The witness *lied*. All the points in the world can't get away from that."

"Gentlemen, gentlemen," Judge Blank said. "Could we avoid personalities and stick to the issue at hand?"

"The issue at hand, Your Honor," Richard said, "is that circumstances have conspired to deprive my client of a fair trial. The jury hasn't been in this courtroom in days. Assuming they haven't read the paper—and that's a big if, what with the story on the front page—then they have no idea what is going on. All they know is that they are being excluded from the court. The longer that happens, the more curious they become. And the less capable of rendering an impartial verdict."

"And just who is dragging the proceedings out?" Wellington said. "I've offered to stipulate that the testimony go in or out, either way. The prosecution will stipulate to just about anything to expedite the matter and proceed with the trial. It's the defense that's dragging its heels."

"Oh, Your Honor," Richard said, and they were off again. As they had been all morning long. Finally, Judge Blank couldn't take it anymore and broke for lunch.

Formerly, that had been the signal for Anson Carbinder to get up from the defense table and slip out of the courtroom with the comely Connie Maynard. Not anymore. The moment he stood up, there were two court officers there, ready, willing, and able to escort him back to his cell.

Poor, lovesick man. As they led him out the door, I could see him looking back over his shoulder, his eyes seeking out hers in the crowd.

And there she was, second row, side aisle, right behind the defense table, right where she'd sat every day since the beginning of the trial. It occurred to me, with Anson out of the way, there was nothing to stop me from walking up to the young woman, introducing myself, and offering to take her to lunch.

Except that Richard would have a shit fit.

But so what? As Alice had said, what was he going to do? So maybe I should.

Providing she'd even talk to me.

As I watched, vacillating, Connie Maynard gathered up her coat and made her way up the aisle.

Should I follow her out in the hall? Try to strike up a conversation when she was safely out the door, where

Richard couldn't see? No, don't be silly. Use the lunch break to talk to Richard. Find out what he knows, and make the suggestion. Hell, maybe he already asked her. Maybe he knows the answer. Maybe this is a big fuss over nothing, and—

My mouth dropped open.

Alice, with her glad rags on and looking like a million bucks, had just glided up to Connie Maynard and flashed her a dazzling smile. Connie smiled back, and, chatting amiably, the two of them sailed on out the door.

I bolted up the aisle. At least, I tried to. There were a lot of spectators in court, and they were intent on leaving too. I clawed my way through them, fought my way out into the hall.

Just in time to see an elevator door close.

And no sign of Alice.

Damn.

Was another elevator coming? If so, could I afford to wait for it?

Damn.

I turned, sprinted down the stairs.

Bad move. By the time I reached the lobby, the elevator was already on its way back up.

I ran to the front door, jerked it open, plunged outside.

I stopped on the sidewalk, looked up and down the street.

Half a block away, Connie Maynard was heading down the street in the direction of the restaurant. It was cold, and she was bundled up in her scarf and overcoat, but it was her, all right.

No problem there.

But Alice was gone.

46

I found MacAullif hanging out in the upstairs hallway.

"Let's take a walk."

He must have seen the agitation in my eyes—he didn't even argue, just grabbed his coat off the bench and headed for the elevator. We rode down in silence, went out the front door.

Snow had begun to fall. I don't know if it was that or the wind chill, but somehow it seemed colder than it had before.

MacAullif shivered, turned up the collar of his coat. "Great," he said. "Where you wanna walk?"

"How about I buy you a cup of coffee?"

"I've heard worse ideas."

We found a little shop on Lafayette Street, ordered coffee, and got a booth in the back.

"All right, look," MacAullif said. "I don't know how many ADA's frequent this place, but bein' seen with you right now would not be a smooth move. The reason I'm here is you look like you've seen a ghost. So start talking, but you better make it good."

"Okay," I said. "How did you get a line on the witness?"

"Huh?"

"Phil Janson. Way back when. You called on him. You left your card. How did you get a line on him?"

MacAullif cocked his head. Frowned. "I'm afraid you're not doing very well. Let's try it again. You look like walking death. You wanna tell me why?"

I took a breath. "Okay, I'll tell you why. I'm talking to my wife last night about the case—naturally, what with the alibi blowing up—and I'm talking about, what should I do now?"

"I can see where you might," MacAullif said. "Suborning perjury's just fine until you get caught."

"I wasn't suborning perjury."

"Of course not. I know that. You have a TV mentality. If you had the faintest idea those guys were lying, you'd have kissed off the case. Which is one reason I'm talking to you now. Whereas, to everybody else from the prosecutor on down, you are living poison, you are the kiss of death, and so is anyone else connected to this stinking, odoriferous defense."

"I know."

MacAullif looked at me. "You must be *really* down. You're not even going to point out stinking and odoriferous are redundant? You really *must* be fucked up. Let me make it easy for you. You found out your client's guilty, didn't you. You know he did it, and it's eating you up."

I looked at him in surprise. "Not at all."

"Then what the hell's going on?"

I told him about Alice showing up at the courtroom and talking to Connie Maynard.

MacAullif listened without interrupting, his brow furrowed, his eyes squinting. When I finished, he said, "But they didn't leave together?"

"No. She went to lunch. Alice disappeared."

"You call home?"

"I live way uptown. She wouldn't be there yet."

"Oh. Right."

"Assuming she *went* home. If she did, fine. If she didn't . . ."

"You think she's on to something?"

"I have no idea. But she comes to court all dolled up and talks to the woman. What am I to think?"

"You didn't ask her?"

"I told you. I couldn't catch her."

"Not her. The woman. You said she went to lunch. You happen to know where?"

"If it's the same place she went with Anson, I do."

"So why don't you ask her?"

"What?"

"What your wife said. You're going crazy not knowing. Why don't you find out?"

"Yeah, I know."

"So why don't you?"

"In the first place, I don't know if she'd tell me. In the second place . . ."

"Yeah?"

I grimaced. "What if I made it worse."

"How's that?"

"I'm scared to death she's doing something dangerous. Why it would be dangerous, I don't know. But this Connie Maynard—she doesn't know who Alice is. She's got no reason to think twice about her talking to her. Depending on what she said, granted, but say she doesn't. Then I come in wanting to know and queer the deal. By asking, I blow my wife's cover. Then she really *is* in danger. You see?"

"Yeah, I see." MacAullif looked thoughtful. "Then this broad—the girlfriend—what's her name?—Connie Maynard, right?—why is she suddenly so important? Is she the new alibi?"

"Oh, shit."

"What's the matter?"

"Don't do this to me. Ever since this goddamn case

started, all I get is beat up for giving you information. Now Richard's gonna think I gave you this."

"That's practically a confirmation."

"Damn it, MacAullif."

"Hey, don't obsess. I'm a cop, and I think like a cop. I hear a story, I make deductions. You can tell Rosenberg anything you want. As for this girlfriend bit—it's not such a novel idea. If he wasn't playing cards, where was he? Either killing his wife or bangin' the broad. The defense position would naturally be he was bangin' the broad. It doesn't take a genius to figure that out."

"Yeah, I know."

"So stop kicking yourself in the head and get on with it. I don't know about you, but I gotta get back to court."

"Me too."

"Okay. So what's this got to do with the dead witness—this Phil Janson?"

"I don't know, but I gotta find out. Alice is out there somewhere, and I don't know if what she's doing is dangerous. So I'm desperate for anything that will give me a clue. It occurs to me, a big one is Phil Janson. He was killed, yeah, but he was also the only witness you got a lead to. I'm wondering if there's a connection, so I'm wondering how you got the lead."

"You don't think I was following you?"

"No, I don't. Frankly, if that was the answer, right now it would be a huge relief."

"I see."

"You're not going to help me out?"

"This is somewhat below the belt. You dangle your wife in front of me, say, I'm scared, tell me what you wouldn't tell me before?"

"Aw, fuck." I pushed back my coffee, stood up.

"Oh, sit the hell down," MacAullif said. "Did I say I

wouldn't tell you? The lead to Phil Janson was an anonymous tip."

"No shit?"

"None. Telephone tip. Male voice. Saying Janson was a
witness in the Carbinder case."

"Alibi witness?"

"No. Just witness. The alibi idea came from you."

"Thanks. Anything else?"

"What do you mean?"

"About the phone call. Anything useful?"

"Not really. Male voice, most likely Caucasian, educated."

"Educated?"

"Well, at least literate. In other words, there was nothing
to indicate the caller was *il*literate. You gotta understand,
this is not rock solid. This is just the impression of the officer who took the call."

I frowned. "Uh-huh."

"Yeah. So what does that give you?" MacAullif said.
"The call could be any one of these poker players. Though
why they'd call is beyond me."

"Me too. What about? . . ."

"What?"

"Could it have been Phil Janson himself?"

"It could. But why he'd do that . . ."

"I can't imagine why *anyone* would do that."

"Yeah, but him in particular. He tips me off to come,
then clams up when I get there?"

"He could have had a reason."

"What reason?"

"One that got him killed."

MacAullif waved it away. "Yeah, he gets killed, so he's
important. That's the thing. It doesn't make everything he
ever did important." He took a sip of coffee, set the cup
down. "All right, look. Now that I've violated department

policy by giving you this information, what does it do for you? How does it help you find your wife?"

"I didn't expect to find her."

"Or feel better about what she's doing?"

"That's closer to the truth. Look, we got a case here, I haven't the faintest idea what happened. That's because the defense position is ass-backwards, all it cares about is who *didn't* commit the crime. So every time I try to make sense of it, I feel like I'm starting from scratch. Right now, I'm saying, if that woman gave Alice a lead, what could it be to?"

"You want me to ask her?"

"Huh?"

"You say *you* don't want to talk to her—you want me to bull in there and shake her down?"

"You'd do that?"

"I'd probably catch hell if I did. I haven't thought it out—whether I could come up with a plausible excuse."

"Thanks, but I don't want you to do that. For the same reason I wouldn't talk to her myself."

"That's what I thought you'd say. I just make the offer. So what about the Janson thing—do you think that's it?"

"I don't know. It's just one thing."

"What's another?"

"This private detective—the one Barbara Carbinder hired."

"What about him?"

"Exactly. She hired the guy, got the dope on her husband, and then what?"

MacAullif shrugged. "Presumably, she planned to divorce him. Whether she told him or not is something only he would know."

"Right, so who was he spying on?"

"Anson Carbinder."

"And?"

"The broad. Oh, I see. You come back to the broad, your wife talked to the broad, is there any connection?"

"Is there?"

"How the hell should I know?"

I took a breath. Exhaled. "Maybe it *has* been long enough."

"Huh."

"I'm calling home."

There was a pay phone in the front by the cash register. A woman was on it, planning her life. I thought about telling her it was an emergency. I didn't. Instead, I told myself it wasn't. And tried to make me believe it.

Finally, she got off the phone. I dropped in a quarter, punched the number in.

And got our answering machine.

I waited for the beep, said, "Alice, it's me. I saw you in court, I don't know where you are. As soon as you get this, page me on my beeper. I know it's been a while, but the number's in our address book under *Beeper*. If you can't find it, call the office and tell Wendy/Janet to beep me and have me call you. Do it now, please. I'm worried."

I went back to the table.

"No luck?" MacAullif said.

"No."

"Think she had time to get home?"

"Assuming she *went* home."

"The subway's erratic."

"Assuming she took the subway."

"It's an expensive cab ride."

"Yeah, I know."

"What else can I do for you?" MacAullif said.

I ran my hand over my forehead. "I don't know. You close to solving this crime?"

"I made an arrest," MacAullif said pointedly.

"That doesn't mean he's guilty."

"It doesn't mean he isn't. That's your TV mentality again. In real life, occasionally a guy gets arrested because he really did it."

"You don't have to sell me."

"Oh, no? Look, if you want to put it that way, you don't know who did it and I don't know who did it. But if we had to handicap the thing, the odds-on favorite would be Anson Carbinder." MacAullif ticked them off on his fingers. "He took out insurance on her just last summer. He's playing around with the broad. His wife had the goods on him and was probably planning divorce. Plus, he faked an alibi which blew up in his face."

MacAullif shrugged, looked at me. "Now, you're worried your wife's playing around with a killer. Well, this is the best I can give you. Right now, the best bet for the killer is Anson Carbinder. And he's in jail."

47

Alice sailed in at six-thirty that evening.

I jumped on her the minute she got in the door. "Where the hell have you been?"

"Getting my hair done."

I blinked.

And noticed her hair was curly. Very curly. I must have been really upset not to have noticed right away.

I stared at her. "You were at the hairdresser?"

Alice smiled. "I was at *her* hairdresser. Connie Maynard." She shook her head. "I don't think you wanna know how much it cost."

I blinked again. "You went to Connie Maynard's hairdresser?"

"Sure. I went up to her after court, said, Wow, you look great, who does your hair?"

"And she told you?"

"Sure. Why not? I called up, asked for an appointment, and damned if they didn't slip me in."

"Good lord."

"What's the matter?"

"What's the matter? I've been worried sick."

"Why?"

"I was there. In court. I saw you talk to her."

"So?"

"What do you mean, so? I had no idea what was going on. You didn't tell me you were going to do this."

"I didn't know. I just thought of it. I'm at home working on the computer, thinking how can I get a line on this woman." Alice smiled. "Well, for a while it was hard because I kept thinking of her as *this woman.* You know, this mythical figure involved in the case. Then I started thinking, never mind that she's special, how could I get a line on *any* woman. Then it was easy. Of course. Her hairdresser."

I shook my head. "Yeah, but—"

"And I actually got something."

"Huh?"

"Believe it or not, I got something you can use."

"What?"

"That's right. I got a lead and traced it down."

"You're kidding."

"Well, why not?"

"Why not? Alice, this is not a game. This is someone who kills people."

"Yes, of course."

"What do you mean, yes, of course? You could have been killed."

Alice had hung up her hat and coat and taken off her boots. Now she turned, patted me on the shoulder. "Stanley, you sound like a Jewish grandmother. Nothing happened. Everything's fine. I mean, look, here I am."

Yes, she was. And I have a confession to make. When my wife gets a new hair style, it turns me on. In this instance, that reaction was late kicking in, due to the anxiety factor. But, as she said, nothing had happened. And with her hair curly and in her Sunday-go-to-meeting clothes, she sure looked good.

I suppressed the thought. "Yeah, fine," I said. "As it happened, you didn't get hurt. The point is, you could have. Because we don't know what we're dealing with."

"We know more now."

"Huh?"

"You wanna hear what I got, or you wanna keep carrying on? And stop looking at me like that."

"Like what?"

"You know like what. Like you like my new hair." Alice smiled. "Look, I know you. You're overprotective and you're horny. Fine. I know that. You know that. So why don't you just calm down, sit on those impulses, and let me tell you what I got."

48

Ricky Pomerantz looked like a peevish bullfrog. A hunched little man with a bald head and no neck, he sat in a wing chair as if on a lily pad, and regarded me with cranky eyes. "I was wondering when you'd get around to me."

"I almost didn't," I told him. "You willing to talk?"

"Of course I'm willing to talk."

"How come you didn't come forward?"

"I wasn't coming forward, but I wasn't hanging back, either. Tell me, how'd you find me?"

"You were the only Ricky Pomerantz in the book."

"I mean, how'd you know?"

"Phil Janson told me. Way back when. First time I questioned him. I asked him to name the players in the game. He named you, then looked like a golfer just shanked an iron. At the time, I put it down to nerves."

"It *was* nerves."

"I know. I mean, rather than a lie."

"And you didn't suspect?"

"You gotta understand, this was two months ago, when we all thought Anson was in the game."

"Right. And what a great idea that was."

"I take it you didn't approve?"

"No kidding. I told them not to do it."

"But they didn't listen?"

"Obviously. And Phil told you I was in the game?"

"Right."

"And then said he was mistaken?"

"That's right."

"And you didn't get to me till now?"

"At the time, there was no reason to doubt him. When it turned out Anson wasn't in the game, I finally asked myself who *was*."

"Too little, too late," Ricky Pomerantz said. "A month ago I could have saved you some trouble. But you don't need me anymore. The alibi's blown."

"I still want to hear your story."

"Why? My story's the same as theirs. At least, the one they're telling now. Anson Carbinder wasn't at the game."

"I know. I'd still like to ask some questions."

"Go ahead, for all the good it's gonna do."

"Were you there when he called?"

"Huh?"

"When Anson Carbinder called to say his wife was dead and to ask you guys for an alibi—were you there then?"

"Yes, of course."

"What time was that?"

"Two in the morning."

"That's when the game broke up?"

"You think we played after that?"

"No, I don't imagine you did."

"Good thinking. Anson called, dropped the bombshell, broke up the game."

"And what happened then?"

Pomerantz eyed me suspiciously. "You setting me up for something?"

"What do you mean?"

"These other guys are making deals, getting immunity.

I'm not. I suppose there's some statute I violated, not re-
porting what I knew."

"I'm not a cop."

"You say you work for Anson?"

"For his attorney."

"What's the difference?"

"No real difference. The attorney is his agent. I work for
his agent, therefore I work for him."

"Uh-huh."

"Anyway, I'm not about to get you in trouble. Talking to
me obligates you to nothing. Consider we're just chatting
here."

"Oh, sure. Tell me another one."

"Anytime you don't like my questions, you don't have to
answer. Let's see how far we can go. The point is, you were
there at two o'clock when the call came through?"

"That's right."

"Which is when the other guys concocted the alibi?"

"Yeah. So?"

"Whose idea was it?"

"What do you mean?"

"Who came up with the idea of you saying Anson was
there?"

"Anson, of course. He called and asked us to do it."

"Who answered the phone?"

"Sam. It was his house."

"Did you hear the call?"

"Huh?"

"When Anson called—did you hear the call? Were you
there when Sam answered the phone? Did you hear what he
said?"

"Not at first."

"What do you mean?"

"We were playing in the dining room. The phone was in
the kitchen. Sam went in the kitchen to answer the phone.

He answers the phone, he talks a bit, then he says, Oh, my god! He comes walking into the dining room with the phone. It's a wall phone on a long cord. He comes walking up to the table, tells us Anson just got home and his wife got killed."

"What happens then?"

"Well, we're all stunned, we can't believe it. We all start talking at once. Sammy shuts us up and tells Anson what to do. He tells him to call his lawyer, call the cops, and clam up on 'em till his lawyer gets there. He says don't tell the cops a thing, but tell his lawyer he was playing cards."

"He told him you guys would give him an alibi?"

"He sure did," Pomerantz said. "Without even asking us. He tells him that and hangs up."

"How'd you feel about that?"

"I told him how I felt about that. I gave him a good piece of my mind."

"And what happened?"

"You know what happened. Sammy's a good talker. Very persuasive. He lays this whole trip on us about Anson needing our support, and damned if he doesn't sell it."

"Even to you?"

Pomerantz looked at me. "You gotta understand something. I still don't think the guy killed his wife."

"Okay. So what happened then?"

"We all agreed to tell the story. Anson was there at the poker game. Okay, fine. Except for one thing. You don't have a poker game with eight people. There's not enough cards. Very few games you can play. So if Anson was there, one of us wasn't." He shrugged. "They picked me."

That was not surprising. Ricky Pomerantz was an obstinate, opinionated son of a bitch. Even if he'd been willing to go along, he'd have driven the rest of them nuts.

"Uh-huh," I said. "So you went home?"

"Not right away. I wasn't going to leave until I knew exactly what was going on."

"So you were there when this was planned out?"

"You sure you're not trying to implicate me in something?"

"Word of honor."

"Yeah. I was there. I know what was agreed to."

"And what was that?"

"You know. To tell the story. That Anson was there."

"And were there any other specifics?"

"What do you mean?"

Under Ricky Pomerantz's gaze, I began to feel like a fly. I shuddered involuntarily. Put up my hands. "Okay," I said. "This was two in the morning. So Tim Hendricks had gone home, right? So there were only six of you there."

"Yeah, so?"

"No one else had left, had they? Just him?"

"Yeah. Just Timmy. The rest of us were there."

"Right. Excluding you, that left five others. Sam Kestin. Marvin Wainwright. Phil Janson. Ollie Pruett and Barry Brown. Is that right?"

"Yeah. What about it?"

"And the five of them agreed to tell that story—that Anson Carbinder had been there all night, that he never left until two o'clock, and that he was there instead of you?"

"Yeah. So?"

"They also agreed that Tim Hendricks went home at twelve o'clock, but, aside from him, everybody else was there all night. Is that right?"

"Yeah. That's right. So?"

I took a breath. The phrase, an elephant never forgets, came to mind.

I couldn't recall anything about frogs.

I shrugged.

"Is it true?"

"Bring in the jury."

Thank god. We were finally getting on with it. But it had been a long haul and taken half the morning.

First off, the matter of Phil Janson's testimony had to be resolved. The ruling Judge Blank finally came up with— that the testimony be stricken from the record as if the man had never testified—wasn't really satisfactory, but, then again, what could be? At any rate, at least it was done.

Then there was the matter of the other witnesses. It was Richard's contention that, in the light of what had happened, there was no longer any reason to keep them under the rule and they should be allowed to sit in court. The readiness with which ADA Wellington agreed told the story—obviously, Richard's witnesses were in Wellington's pocket, and it didn't matter what they heard. At any rate, the request was granted, the ban lifted, and the witnesses allowed in.

From my usual spot behind the press, I had watched as Sam Kestin, Marvin Wainwright, Ollie Pruett, Barry Brown, and Tim Hendricks filed in and sat down.

Sergeant MacAullif, also no longer banned, had clomped in and joined them.

And now, at long last, the jury was returning. They filed

in and took their seats. They looked curious, yes, but also somewhat miffed. After all, it had been two days. What the hell was going on?

When the jury was seated, Judge Blank said, "Ladies and gentlemen, I must apologize for the delay, but we've been dealing with certain matters of procedure. I regret that this has taken some time, but we are ready to proceed now. Before we do, I should explain that the testimony of the last witness that you heard, the witness Phil Janson, has been stricken from the record. You will recall, you heard only his direct examination. His cross-examination was yet to come. That will not happen. Instead, his direct examination has been stricken. You are to put it from your minds, give it no weight. For all intents and purposes, it is as if the man had never testified. As far as you are concerned, that witness did not appear.

"If we are all clear on that point, we may proceed. Mr. Rosenberg. Call your next witness."

As Richard stood up, the attention of the courtroom shifted. No, not to him. To her. Because, aside from the jury, everyone in the courtroom knew what had happened here. Anson Carbinder's alibi had blown up. The poker players were no longer witnesses. Richard had to call someone else.

And there was only one other person.

The mistress.

The model.

The pinup.

The mystery woman.

As I watched, every head in the press row in front of me turned to where Connie Maynard sat in the second row behind the defense table, knowing that she was the witness he was going to call.

He didn't.

He rose to his feet and said, "Call Stanley Hastings."

As I walked to the witness stand, ADA Wellington lunged to his feet. "Objection!" he roared. "This is outrageous! He can't do that! He—"

The gavel cut him off.

"That will do," Judge Blank said. He glowered at both attorneys, then pointed. "Bailiff. Show the jury out."

The jurors couldn't believe it. Having waited that long to get into court, they were going to be sent out without hearing a single question? Not possible. There was considerable grumbling as they stomped out.

As the door closed behind them, Judge Blank said, "Now, Mr. Wellington, what is your objection?"

ADA Wellington's face was bright red. "Your Honor, Your Honor," he said. He wheeled around, pointed to where I stood next to the witness stand. "This man is a detective in the defense's employ. He's the one who was present when the body was found. Phil Janson, I mean."

"Yes?" Judge Blank said. "And what is your objection?"

"Your Honor," Wellington said. "We just got through striking Phil Janson's testimony from the record. It was agreed that this be done without explanation and without alluding to his death. And I must say that I, for one, consider that a considerable concession to the defense."

Wellington turned, hunched his shoulders, spread his arms. "And now he's going to present the whole thing from the point of view of his own investigator. And put whatever slant he wants on it. I consider it sharp practice, bordering on misconduct."

Judge Blank pursed his lips. "What do you have to say to that, Mr. Rosenberg?"

"It's a moot point, Your Honor. I have no intention of asking the witness anything of the kind."

"You're not going to have him testify to finding the body of Phil Janson?"

"Absolutely not, Your Honor. What purpose would that

serve? We're trying the murder of Barbara Carbinder, not the murder of Phil Janson."

"That's not the point," Wellington said. "The point is the way in which a clever attorney can prejudice the jury by the method in which these other matters are presented."

"But counsel says he isn't going into these matters," Judge Blank said.

"And you believe him?"

"That will do," Judge Blank snapped. "Mr. Wellington, I understand you are somewhat upset. But try to control your tongue. That remark was not only rude but bordered on contempt. Have I made myself clear?"

"Yes, Your Honor," Wellington said. "I take it you're denying my motion?"

"What's to deny?" Judge Blank said dryly. "You're objecting to questions that have not yet been asked and which defense counsel states he has no *intention* of asking. The point is, indeed, moot."

"I further object on the grounds of prior notice. This man is not on any witness list, and never has been. I was given no notice as to his appearance, and I am therefore not prepared. Indeed, I had no idea this man was even a witness.

"Your Honor," Richard said. "As the prosecutor himself stated, Mr. Hastings is a detective in my employ. He has been with me since the onset of the trial. His job, of course, was to investigate any matters that came up. I'm calling him, not as a witness to what he saw, but merely to report on what he's found."

"Same objection," Wellington said. "No prior notice."

Judge Blank exhaled noisily. "This case is rapidly assuming a trend I do not like. Mr. Rosenberg, you have called this witness to testify to matters he investigated during the trial?"

"That's right, Your Honor."

"Might I ask if the things you intend to have him testify to were known to you at the conclusion of court yesterday?"

"They were not, Your Honor."

"You had no knowledge of these matters when court adjourned?"

Richard smiled. "That's a little broad, Your Honor. I would not wish to profess to be utterly ignorant. But the *majority* of Mr. Hastings's testimony will cover matters unknown to me and only discovered after court adjourned."

Judge Blank nodded. "On that assurance, I'll allow it. The objection is overruled. Bring in the jury and let the witness be sworn."

There was actually a considerable delay before the jury came clomping in again. Doubtless, one of the jurors was merely in the bathroom, or some other such simple explanation. Still, I couldn't help envisioning the court officer telling the jurors the judge was ready for them, and them digging in their heels and telling him huffily he could damn well wait.

When the jurors had been seated, and I had sworn to tell the truth, the whole truth, and nothing else but the truth, I was finally allowed to sit down, for which I was grateful. I had been standing there for some time.

Richard rose, approached the witness stand.

"Your name is Stanley Hastings?"

"That's right."

"Mr. Hastings, what is your occupation?"

That question always throws me. I still think of myself as an actor and a writer, and the detective work is just what I do between gigs. And I've never thought of myself as a *real* private detective, in any case. But I wasn't going to get into that now.

"I'm a private detective," I said.

"By whom are you employed?"

"Actually, I'm self-employed. But my agency is employed by you."

"And you personally have been assisting the defense throughout the trial?"

"That's correct."

"Might I ask if you made any investigations yesterday after court had adjourned?"

"Yes, I did."

"What were you attempting to find?"

"Evidence that would prove the defendant, Anson Carbinder, was not guilty."

"And did you find it?"

"Objection, Your Honor. That's a conclusion on his part. Let him testify to what he found, not what he thinks it proves."

"Sustained. Rephrase the question."

"Yes, Your Honor. Mr. Hastings, what did you find?"

"I found evidence that Anson Carbinder is innocent of the crime."

"Objection. Not responsive to the question. Move to strike."

"Granted," Judge Blank said. "It will go out. Ladies and gentlemen of the jury, you should consider that last question and answer stricken from the record. Put it from your minds and give it no weight." He turned to Richard. "Mr. Rosenberg. The vice in a leading question lies in asking it. This is a friendly witness, in your employ. One would expect his testimony to be favorable. Without being led."

"Yes, Your Honor. Mr. Hastings, let me put it this way. Did you find anything which in your opinion tended to indicate that the defendant, Anson Carbinder, might be innocent of this crime?"

"Yes, I did. I found evidence which, in my own opinion, would indicate that Anson Carbinder did not in fact kill his wife."

"You did?"

"Yes, I did. And with all due apologies to the court, as a result of my findings, in my own mind there is no doubt whatsoever that he simply couldn't have done it."

"Oh?" Richard said. "And why is that?"

"Because Sam Kestin did."

50

In the silence that followed, ADA Wellington lunged to his feet. If his face had been red before, it was purple now. "Objection, Your Honor!" he roared. "Your Honor, that is the most outlandish—"

Judge Blank nearly broke the gavel. Wellington's shout had triggered an outburst, and the courtroom was in an uproar. Judge Blank pounded it quiet, then sat rigid at his bench, his chin set, his eyes smoldering. I swear his lips never moved. "Attorneys," he said. "In my chambers."

With that, he stood up and stalked from the courtroom. After a brief pause, Richard and ADA Wellington followed.

So there we were, once again, in suspended animation, just as we were the time before, when Sam Kestin was on the stand. Only that had been a ploy, a stunt, a clever trick, the banker claiming his constitutional right not to incriminate himself, when all he'd been doing was playing poker.

This was something else.

From my position on the witness stand, I looked out over the courtroom. In the back row, Sam Kestin sat with his buddies, Marvin Wainwright, Ollie Pruett, Tim Hendricks, and Barry Brown. It seemed to me they were regarding him somewhat oddly—not the same hail-fellow-well-met there had been when they'd sat down. Of course, it isn't every day a friend of yours is accused of murder in open court.

And it isn't every day you hear yourself accused.

I had wondered how Sam Kestin was going to take it. On the whole, I'd have to say he did pretty well. After all, he had become the center of attention. The jurors, who at first couldn't place the name, it having been so long since he'd testified, finally worked it out and were now whispering, nudging, and pointing. And the spectators, taking their cue from them, were turning around to look. The press were on their feet, and once their quarry was spotted, several reporters made their way up the aisle. I was too far away to hear what was said, but I could see them asking questions and Kestin refusing to comment.

That should have been enough to break him—it would have been enough to break me—but the banker sat there smiling, shrugging, declining to comment with a shake of the head, until the reporters finally gave it up as a lost cause and made their way back down the aisle, talking among themselves.

I'm sure they would have loved to have questioned me, had there been a chance, but they all knew better—no court officer would let them inside the rail. So there I sat, all alone, in my lofty perch on the witness stand, way up there in the front of the courtroom, like some cosmic director overseeing the whole scene.

Waiting for Kestin to crack.

Which I was sure he would. Because, for all his cool exterior, for all his apparent poise, there was one thing he couldn't seem to do.

Look at me.

Since I had made that statement, Sam Kestin had been unwilling to meet my eyes. I suppose he could have considered me beneath contempt, but I didn't think so.

I don't know how long he might have sat there, surrounded by his friends, not looking in my direction, but at that moment the door in the back of the courtroom opened and Ricky Pomerantz came in. He didn't look quite so much like a frog with his hat and coat on and standing up, but it was him, all right. He looked around, spotted his buddies, went over, squeezed in, and sat down.

And Sam Kestin got up.

He slid out of the row and went out the back door.

He could have just been going to the bathroom, and he might have come right back, but I was not to know it, for at that moment a voice said, "Mr. Hastings," and when I looked around, there was a court officer standing next to the witness stand.

"Come with me."

51

It was the first time I'd ever been in a judge's chambers. For the most part it looked like in the movies and on TV. A little starker, perhaps. A little less plush. But still, the elements were there—the desk, the chairs, the shelves of law books.

Judge Blank was seated behind his desk. Richard and Wellington were seated off to either side.

There was one chair smack in front of the desk, and this was where I was invited to sit. I did so, feeling very much like a schoolboy who had just been summoned to the principal's office.

The look on Judge Blank's face did nothing to dispel that impression. "Mr. Hastings," he said. "You've just made a statement in open court which, at best, could be considered irresponsible and, at worst, contempt of court. In the event of the latter, it is entirely possible that Mr. Rosenberg here, in conspiring to allow you to make such a statement, could find himself guilty of misconduct. I am telling you this up front, so that you are aware of the gravity of the matter."

He exhaled. "And all this, I might add, is *on top* of being responsible for making an unfounded accusation of murder. I have been attempting to ascertain from Mr. Rosenberg what grounds you have for making such a statement. He feels you should be allowed to speak for yourself. From which I gather that some of your opinions may be exclusively your own." With a glance at Richard, Judge Blank added, "Which would not excuse him from the responsibility of having presented them."

He turned back to me. "At any rate, I would like this matter cleared up. You will pardon me if my patience is somewhat short. You have just testified in court. I am concerned with whether that testimony is true. If so, you will be the *only* defense witness *not* to have committed perjury."

"It's true."

Judge Blank glared at me. "I don't recall asking you a question."

"Sorry, Your Honor."

"Not as sorry as you're going to be."

My god, he even *sounded* like a principal. I held my tongue.

"All right, let's get on with it," Judge Blank said. "You say Sam Kestin is guilty of the murder?"

"Yes, I do."

"On what do you base that statement?"

"On the investigation that I made."

"Yes, yes, I understand," Judge Blank said impatiently. "I am asking for the specifics."

"Yes, Your Honor. You understand a good deal of what I am about to say is based on hearsay."

"Yes, of course. You question the witnesses, that goes without saying."

"Actually, Your Honor, my wife questioned some of them."

"I beg your pardon?"

"I'm sorry, but that happens to be the case. A good deal of the facts I am about to present were actually gathered by her."

Judge Blank turned to Richard. "You didn't mention this."

"It's one reason I thought the witness should speak for himself."

"You just accused a man of murder on your wife's say-so?" ADA Wellington said incredulously.

Judge Blank raised his hand. "Please. Let's not have a brawl. The circumstances are unusual. They seem to get more unusual by the minute, but let us take it *for granted* that they are unusual and push on. You say your wife made some of these investigations for you. Would you please tell us what the two of you found?"

"Yesterday, during the noon recess, my wife approached the young woman Connie Maynard and asked her who cut her hair. My wife then made an appointment with this person to have her hair done. During the course of which, she pumped the hairdresser for information. One of the first things she learned was that, prior to her attachment to Mr. Carbinder, Connie Maynard had been dating Sam Kestin. It was actually through him that they met."

"Are you saying that's a motive for murder?" Wellington said.

"Not in and of itself. But there were other things."

"Such as?" Judge Blank said.

"My wife next ascertained where Anson Carbinder went to school. It turns out he lived in Great Neck and attended public high school.

"So did Sam Kestin.

"So did Barbara Carbinder.

"An interview with one of the teachers proved useful. He remembered Anson Carbinder and Sam Kestin quite well because they were the top two students in his class. Indeed, they were the top two students in the school.

"Anson Carbinder, he recalls, was the valedictorian, beating out Sam Kestin by a percentage of a grade point.

"He recalls it as a great rivalry. Neither of the two were particularly athletic but competed fiercely in the chess club. Anson, again, holding a slight edge.

"Unfortunately, the man knew nothing of the students' social life. Fortunately, there was another teacher there who did. A classmate of theirs who had subsequently returned to teach. She remembered them quite well, not for the academic prowess, but because they had been rivals for the affection of the same girl.

"That girl was Barbara Branstein.

"Who became Barbara Carbinder."

"And that's your motive?" ADA Wellington said sarcastically.

I looked at him. "What's your beef, Wellington?"

He didn't catch it, but out of the corner of my eye I could see Richard having a hard time controlling his face. It's tough not to break up yourself, under those circumstances, when you know someone else is on the verge of going, but I knew a smile would be fatal. I squared my jaw, tried not to look at Richard.

Fortunately, Judge Blank stepped in. "All right," he said. "I can see how this might breed contempt. But to kill Barbara Carbinder? Why her?"

"It fits the psychological profile, Your Honor."

"Psychological profile," Wellington said. "Give me a break."

"I will thank you to hold your tongue," Judge Blank said. "At the moment I am interested in the man's thought process, not your opinion of it. Now, why do you say it fits?"

"If the motive is jealousy and revenge—as I believe it to be—then what we are dealing with here is a very sick individual and a very angry individual. The question is, who is he angry with? Aside from the psychological analysis that the man is angry with himself, you have two obvious choices: Barbara and Anson Carbinder. The woman who betrayed him, and the hated rival who stole her away. You have a subconscious resentment, repressed and lying dormant for years and years and years. And what triggers it? Same thing. Exact same thing. The guy does it again. Anson Carbinder sees Sam Kestin with an attractive woman and once again steals her away.

"It's the last straw.

"Kestin cracks."

"Bullshit!" Wellington exploded.

Judge Blank turned on him. "I warned you to hold your tongue."

"I'm sorry, Your Honor, but this is too much. This is all theory and speculation. He hasn't a single fact."

Judge Blank took a breath. "You will agree, Mr. Hastings, that your story is a little thin."

"There's more, Your Honor."

"Well, let's have it."

"All right, let's look at the evidence. What are the main things the prosecution has against Anson Carbinder, aside from the alibi that exploded in his face? Well, you got the insurance policy he took out on his wife, and the private detective she hired to get the goods on him. Pretty damning on the one hand, and pat on the other. One wonders how these things transpired. With a little bit of research in each instance, I think it can be shown the ideas originated with Sam Kestin."

Judge Blank's eyes showed the first flicker of interest. "Do you have any proof of this?"

I wished I did. "Only indirect, Your Honor. Anson Carbinder, when pressed, recalls that the idea to insure his wife actually came from Connie Maynard."

"You're kidding."

"Not at all. The reason was somewhat convoluted. If his wife found out about the affair, she'd cut him out of the will. So he should insure her life in his name, so in the event that happened, he wouldn't lose out when she died."

Judge Blank blinked. *"Miss Maynard* came up with that?"

"Of course not. That's the whole point. Sam Kestin did."

Judge Blank put up his hands. "Wait a minute. Now you're saying Sam Kestin and Connie Maynard conspired in this crime?"

"No, I'm not. Not necessarily. Most likely, she was an unwitting accomplice. But, you gotta understand, this was a young woman who knew where the gravy was. She'd been intimate with Kestin, she was still friendly with Kestin. He was a banker who knew about money matters, and she was all too willing to take his advice."

"This is pure speculation," Wellington said. "All you have is a self-serving declaration from the defendant himself. There's no offer of proof."

"Try the private detective."

"I beg your pardon?" Judge Blank said.

"Robert Tessler, the private detective Barbara Carbinder hired. If you check it out, you'll find that suggestion also originated with Sam Kestin."

"Check it out how? Kestin won't talk, and Barbara Carbinder is dead."

"True. But the detective agency is still open for business. I called them this morning under the guise of running a credit check. They were no help in the case of Sam Kestin, but they gave a glowing credit reference for Timmy Hendricks. They'd obviously done some work for him at some time, which is where Sam Kestin had heard of them, and why he recommended them to Barbara Carbinder."

"Very thin," Wellington said.

"Perhaps a bit," I said. "The problem is, we don't have the resources of the police. And the other problem is, it's not our job."

"I beg your pardon?" Judge Blank said.

"Solving the crime. It's not our job to prove who did it, only who didn't. Which is how we got so far behind in this case."

"Just a minute," Judge Blank said. "You're not off the hook here. And I'm damned if I'm going to listen to a lecture on the workings of the judicial system. Let's understand the situation here. You made a statement on the witness stand that could lay you open to prosecution. You are attempting to justify yourself. So far, I haven't seen conclusive proof that you have."

"As I was saying, Your Honor, I'm ill equipped to get such proof. I'd say the proof probably exists in the records of the telephone company."

"The telephone company?"

"Yes, Your Honor. The police did an excellent job of tracing the telephone calls from Phil Janson's apartment on the night he was killed. In particular, his call to Anson Carbinder. I'd think a little effort applied to Sam Kestin's bill would probably be illuminating."

"What do you mean?"

"Why do you think Phil Janson made the call? Because Sam Kestin told him to. Kestin called him up, told him he looked shaky on the stand, gave him a pep talk, and told him to call Anson Carbinder and assure him he wasn't going to crack. Why? So there'd be a record of that call. So when Kestin bumped him off, Carbinder'd be on the hook."

"You call that proof?" Wellington said. "First off, you don't even know if such a call exists. But say the police check and find Sam Kestin made that call—it doesn't prove what you say it proves. In fact, it couldn't. How could he tell him he looked shaky on the stand? He's under the rule. He didn't *see* him on the stand."

"Let's not go off on a tangent," Judge Blank said. "The point is well taken. Even if it turns out Kestin made the call, it doesn't prove anything. They both testified in court. It's only natural they'd want to compare notes."

"Exactly," Wellington said. "It doesn't prove anything at all."

"Do you have anything else?" Judge Blank said.

"Okay. Go back to the private detective."

"What about him?"

"He finished his job. He got the goods on Carbinder and reported to the wife."

"So?"

"So, what did she do? Did she confront him with the evidence? She got it a whole week before she was killed. So, did she use it? From everything we know, she did not. And the question is, why? We don't know why, but the fact is, she changed her mind. Either that or she was waffling, not sure she should go through with it.

"And for Sam Kestin, it's the last straw. He's shown her her husband's a louse. He got her the private detective, the private detective's got the goods. She has everything she needs to divorce him, and she and dear sweet Sam Kestin can live happily ever after.

"Only, she won't do it. She dumps him again in favor of her two-timing schmuck of a husband with a mistress she knows about. Which is what drives the guy over the edge."

"Filibuster!" ADA Wellington said.

Judge Blank looked at him. "Huh?"

Wellington pointed at me. "That's what's going on here. Filibuster. The guy's on the hook. He knows as soon as he stops talking he's going to be charged, so he won't stop talking. But the fact is, he's got nothing. Everything he's giving you is sheer speculation. A relationship between Barbara Carbinder and Sam Kestin? I mean, a present-day relationship. Does he have one shred of evidence to support that? Not at all. He's throwing up a smoke screen to try to keep us from seeing what he's doing. And what he's doing is stalling."

"Is that true, Mr. Hastings?" Judge Blank said. "Are you stalling?"

I most certainly was. And how damnably astute it was of ADA Wellington to have figured that out.

But it didn't seem prudent to say so.

"Certainly not, Your Honor," I said. "I am testifying to facts based on my investigation. If I have to fill in the gaps between them with theories, that is of course true of any set of facts."

"Mr. Hastings," Judge Blank said. "We are waiting to *hear* a fact. If you have any evidence at all to present, it had better be now."

"Yes, Your Honor. The fact is this. I have uncovered a witness by the name of Ricky Pomerantz. Mr. Pomerantz is the poker player who actually played in the game that night instead of Anson Carbinder."

"You're admitting the perjury?" Wellington said. "You're conceding Anson Carbinder was not at the game?"

Judge Blank held up his hand. "Please. This is the first concrete fact, and I for one would like to hear it. You say this man was actually at the game?"

"That's right. And he was there at two in the morning when the phone call came through."

"Phone call?"

"From Anson Carbinder. Saying he just found his wife dead and asking them to back up his alibi."

Judge Blank looked at Wellington. "Were you aware of this?"

"Absolutely, Your Honor. This is not news. The witnesses have conceded the alibi was faked. I fail to see the importance of this witness, except in confirming what we already know. And," Wellington said, "he certainly doesn't help the defense."

"He does in one respect. Since he was the only one who wasn't programmed to back up the alibi, his recollection hasn't been colored by the story he was coached to tell."

Judge Blank frowned. "What do you mean?"

"I'm sorry. I'm getting ahead of myself," I said. "You've got to understand who this guy is. Ricky Pomerantz is a sour, cranky, opinionated cuss. It was no accident he was the one chosen to be left out. He wouldn't go along with telling the story, and it was all they could do to get him to butt out and not deny it."

"He's stalling again," Wellington said. "How about some facts?"

"Okay, here's the facts. Ricky Pomerantz was there at two in the morning when the call came through. According to him, the idea to give Anson an alibi was all Sam Kestin's. Anson called, hysterical, his wife had been killed, and Sam Kestin took over and told him what to do."

"Oh, yes?"

"Yes. Moreover, he steamrolled it. Told Anson that without consulting anyone. Then hung up the phone and whipped the other poker players into line. Told them exactly what to say. That Anson had been there all evening, never left till two. That everyone else had been there all evening, never left till two, except Tim Hendricks, who went home at twelve.

"And then he made up the bit about Anson winning the big hand." I raised my finger. "There's another thing the cops can check. Phil Janson on the witness stand said he had a straight to the jack. Well, you know what? When I first questioned him, he said he couldn't remember what he had in the hand. I told him that was fine, it was better to say you don't remember than to say something that's wrong.

"So what happens? He comes into court, says he had a straight to the jack. Why? Because Sam Kestin called him

the night before and told him to say that. If you trace Sam
Kestin's phone records you'll find that call too."

Judge Blank frowned. "Why would he do that?"

"Same reason he tipped MacAullif off to him to begin
with."

"I beg your pardon?"

I looked at Wellington. "You remember way back, when
Sergeant MacAullif got a line on the witness? He called on
him, left him his card? You know how he got a line on
him? From an anonymous tip. You know who gave him
that tip? Sam Kestin. Why? Because Phil Janson was the
weak link that was supposed to destroy the alibi."

I put up my hands. "Because that was the whole point.
The alibi was designed to explode. Sam Kestin set it up
that way. It was the perfect frame. Give the guy an alibi
that blows up in his face. It was diabolical. Anson
Carbinder claims he was playing cards, everyone supports
him, two days later the weak link crumbles. The weak link
was Phil Janson or Ollie Pruett.

"But the way the defense plays it, Anson doesn't pull his
alibi right away. So the cops never get on to these guys. So
Kestin tips them off to Janson. Only, instead of cracking,
Phil Janson bites the bullet and calls his lawyer. So the alibi
holds and we wind up in court."

"He's off again," Wellington said.

"Yes, but in more promising ground," Judge Blank said.
"What were you saying about the phone call?"

"Oh. Sam Kestin wants to make sure the testimony
won't stand up in court. So he calls Phil Janson the night
before they testify and tells him to say he had a straight to
the jack."

"What does that do?"

"It makes his story false."

"How so?"

"Sam Kestin testified that in that hand he had three

eights. Barry Brown said he had a straight to the queen. Well, if Phil Janson had a straight to the jack, both of those straights have an eight in 'em, and that's five eights."

Wellinton frowned. "Is that right?"

I looked at him. "You mean you never noticed? After the story blew up it didn't matter anymore, but that's what tipped me off to it. Phil Janson changed his story, creating five eights. If you'd cross-examined him that afternoon, he probably would have cracked. But when cross-examination was delayed, and when the fifth eight went into the record and no one batted an eye, Sam Kestin decided to push the deal. So he got him to make the phone call to Anson Carbinder, and then he bumped him off."

"We're back to sheer speculation," Wellington said. "Aside from the name of this witness, I haven't heard anything new."

"Okay," I said. "Here it is. According to Ricky Pomerantz, Tim Hendricks left at midnight."

"So? Everyone agrees to that."

"Sam Kestin saw him out. This was his habit. Walking Timmy down—Deal me out, I'm walkin' Timmy down. It was something he did at midnight when Timmy left. He'd be gone a half hour, forty-five minutes, come back from the deli with chips and Coke."

"So?"

"*Walkin' Timmy down*. It was a joke with them. They knew he was with a woman. They just didn't know it was her."

"Oh, come on."

I held up one finger. "Same thing that night. Only, Ricky Pomerantz has a feeling he was gone a little longer."

"A feeling?" Wellington said.

I held up my hand. "Let's not quibble. The point is, he was gone. And what makes Pomerantz special is that he's the only witness who will say so. Because he's the only one who wasn't indoctrinated to give the party line. Which is, Anson was there till two in the morning, Tim Hendricks left at midnight, aside from him everyone else was there till two. Which is why no one mentioned Sam Kestin went out. No, we were all here, we were all witnesses for Anson. That's the solidarity part. That's what they were sold on.

"The fact they were actually giving *Sam Kestin* an alibi never occurred to them.

"But Ricky Pomerantz never told that story. He wasn't programmed to lie. Just to keep quiet. Once he talked, he told it the way it was. And the way it was, was Sam Kestin went out. At the very time Barbara Carbinder was killed."

Judge Blank frowned. "Is that all you've got? Aside from the theories and speculation you've already advanced—is your only hard evidence the fact that this man will testify that Sam Kestin was not at the poker game for a certain time after midnight on the night of the crime?"

"No, there's more," I said. "The morning after the murder, I interviewed Anson Carbinder. In Connie Maynard's apartment. I didn't know it at the time. That it was her apartment, I mean. I thought it was his. I'd been sent there without being told anything, I'm talking to him, I'm finding out about the murder, and suddenly the door opens and she comes in and falls into his arms. At the time I'm thinking she obviously wasn't there when he got there, so he must have a key to her apartment, and wait'll *that* comes out. So that's all that concerned me at the time.

"But once the alibi blows up, once he wasn't playing poker, the question is, where was she?"

Judge Blank frowned. "What do you mean?"

"Say he's with her in her apartment till two in the morning. He goes home, finds his wife dead. He arranges the alibi, calls his lawyer, calls the cops. Gets picked up, taken in for questioning. His attorney gets him out. He doesn't go home, because it's a crime scene. He goes to Connie

Maynard's apartment and lets himself in with a key. She isn't there and doesn't show up until ten in the morning. The question is, where is she?"

"What's the answer?"

"At Sam Kestin's."

"Why would she go there?"

"She's upset, she doesn't want to be alone. That's for starters. In the second place, Kestin calls her up and asks her. He tells her she's upset and she shouldn't be alone, but the real reason he wants her over there is to make sure he's got *her* story sewed up just the way he wants it. The woman is not the swiftest thing ever lived. He's gotta sell her on the idea, make sure she doesn't blow the alibi too soon."

"What do you mean?"

"The main thing implicating Anson Carbinder is his alibi blowing up. After that happens, no one's going to listen to the idea that he was actually with her. But if she comes forward first, way back when, says, No, no, he was with me—particularly since he hasn't sprung his poker alibi yet—well, Anson Carbinder may be a bit gullible, but, even so, Sam Kestin would have a hard time convincing him he should claim he was playing cards when his mistress has already come forward and said he was with her. So shutting her up is a top priority."

"So what?" Wellington said. "He's talking just to hear himself talk. He's still stalling. What the hell is he waiting for?"

As if on cue, there was a knock on the door.

Movie moment.

Deus ex machina.

A court officer came in. "Excuse me, Your Honor," he said. "I have a message for Mr. Wellington. There's a Sergeant MacAullif on the phone. He's at La Guardia Airport. He says the witness Sam Kestin appears to be about to leave the jurisdiction of the court. He wants to know how far you'd like to let him run before he reels him in."

I exhaled noisily, wiped my brow.

Talk about cutting it close.

I'd just about run out of bullshit.

Be careful what you wish for, you might just get it.

I have no idea who said it, but that's the line that came to me as I walked out of the Criminal Court Building. And that's the line that ran through my head as I sat sipping coffee in a small coffee shop near the courthouse.

Guess who I was having coffee with.

No, not Anson Carbinder. That would be too much to hope for, finally sitting down with the gentleman after missing him for so long. But, no, just because you're innocent doesn't mean they let you go. Ironically, before the case was dismissed, Anson Carbinder was free on bail and could come and go as he pleased. Now that the case was dismissed, there were innumerable technical details that had to be tied up.

And I didn't have coffee with Richard. He was the one doing the tying.

Nor with MacAullif, who was at La Guardia, riding herd over our new chief suspect.

Or with Alice. She'd gotten a job programming someone's computer and hadn't even shown up in court.

Connie Maynard? I like the way you think. You have a dirty mind.

You also happen to be wrong.

ADA Wellington?

Judge Blank?

Not likely.

I'm sorry. It was a trick question.

I had coffee with Sergeant Clark.

Yeah, I know. That isn't fair. Dragging him in out of left field. I mean, he had nothing to do with the case, and I hadn't even mentioned him before.

But the problem is, real life isn't like a book. All neat and tidy. With the hero tying things up in the last chapter with one of the principals in the case, preferably his chief rival. But, no, the guy I ran into didn't have a goddamn thing to do with it.

And while that might not have done much in terms of art, it suited my disposition just fine.

Sergeant Clark was a straightlaced homicide sergeant that I'd run into twice in my dealings with the New York City Police Department. He was not exactly a friend—in fact, the first case I worked on I couldn't stand him. The second time was only slightly better. So buying him a cup of coffee was not the sort of thing I'd normally do.

Which made it seem just perfect for this case.

I sat him down, told him what had just transpired.

He didn't seem that surprised.

"Bit of a shame for MacAullif," he said.

"Oh?"

"A perfectly simple, straightforward case has to blow up like that."

"Carbinder was innocent," I pointed out.

Clark nodded. "Sure, but who would know? That's the problem with a case like that. It used to be if a man was charged with murder, he'd tell his story and you'd work it out from there. Now you have a lawyer who makes him clam up, and you have a pitched battle on your hands. Maybe the man's innocent, but who's to know?"

"I don't think it's as bad as all that," I said.

"Well, it isn't good," Clark said. "MacAullif's a good officer. If he makes an arrest, there has to be grounds. Here it turns out the man was framed, well, that's unlucky for him. I know it happens in books a lot, but in real life, ninety percent of the time the guy who looks guilty, is."

"Yeah, I know."

"Well, it looks like you were very lucky."

"Yeah."

"So, what's the problem?"

"I feel bad about MacAullif."

"Why? Just because he lost the case?"

"No. Because of what Richard did."

"On the witness stand? Yes, I heard about that. He brought up the movie and the whole bit?"

"That's right."

"Well, how is that your fault?"

"I didn't say it was."

"I know. But that's how you're thinking, right? That's why you're so glum?"

"I don't feel good about it."

"You think MacAullif's sore?"

"Don't you?"

Clark shook his head. "Not at all."

"Why do you say that?"

"Didn't you tell me you were in the judge's chambers and the ADA got a call and it was MacAullif at the airport, wanting to know if he should pull the suspect in?"

"Yeah. So?"

"How long has MacAullif been on the job? How many suspects do you think he's tailed? You think he needs some ADA's advice? No. He was in court when you made the accusation. He knows you're in the soup. He called the judge's chambers to get you off the hook."

My eyes widened. "Are you kidding me?"

"Not at all. And consider this. This is the only murder case you've been working on for some time, right? Do you think that's true of MacAullif? Well, guess what. He's got a dozen cases he's working on. You think it kills him if one blows up? We don't arrest people just for the hell of it. We arrest them because we think they're guilty. If this guy Carbinder isn't guilty, well, that's all right. We're not really that upset. You see what I mean?"

"Yeah," I said.

"What's the matter?" Clark said.

"I don't know," I said. "Who said, Be careful what you wish for, you just might get it?"

Clark frowned. "Rudy Giuliani?"

I nodded. "That's as good a guess as any."

Half an hour later I was on the subway, heading home.

Thinking about the case.

And what Clark had said.

The guy was right. When you came right down to it, it was just another case. Chalk it up, and move on.

Yeah, I suppose. But not without a certain loss of innocence. I'd certainly never look at Richard Rosenberg the same way again. Which was a little sad. I guess I'd paid the price for my two hundred bucks a day.

Just as Anson Carbinder had paid the price for his little fling.

I wondered if he regretted it.

I wondered if Sam Kestin did.

Or Connie Maynard, for that matter.

I guess that was the problem with criminal law. You didn't get to like your clients much.

Not that he was *my* client.

Not that that mattered.

Yeah.

Chalk it up and move on.

A woman with a handbag the size of a steamer truck el-

bowed me away from the pole I was hanging on. I didn't re-
sist, just moved on down the car.

I smiled slightly.

Be careful what you wish for, you just might get it.

Yeah, life goes on.

At twenty bucks an hour and seventy-five cents a mile.

Next morning I'd call Wendy/Janet.

Tell her to put me back on the clock.